PLAY TO WIN

WYNN HOCKEY

KELLY JAMIESON

Electronic book ISBN 978-1-0690706-1-6

Print book ISBN 978-1-998717-13-2

Book Cover design: Dar Albert, Wicked Smart Designs

Formatting: Weaver Way Author Services

CONTENT NOTES

Content notes for this book and all my books are available on my website at
https://www.kellyjamieson.com/content-notes

THE WYNN DYNASTY

Bob Wynn, owner of the California Condors. Originally married to Grace Rogers (deceased), parents to Mark and Matthew with Grace. Parents to Everly, Asher, Harrison, and Noah with Chelsea Wynn. Grandfather to Jean Paul (JP), Théo, Jackson, and Riley.

Chelsea Wynn (formerly Clark), married to Bob Wynn, mother of Everly, Asher, Harrison, and Noah.

Matthew Wynn, owner of the Long Beach Golden Eagles. Son of Bob Wynn. Married to Aline Gagnon. Father of Théo and Jean Paul (JP).

Mark Wynn, coach of the Long Beach Golden Eagles. Son of Bob Wynn. Divorced from Victoria (Tori) Kendall. Father of Jackson and Riley.

Théo Wynn, general manager of the California Condors. Son of Matthew Wynn and Aline Gagnon. Grandson of Bob Wynn (with Grace).

Jean Paul (JP) Wynn, son of Matthew Wynn and Aline Gagnon. Grandson of Bob Wynn (with Grace). Plays for the Long Beach Golden Eagles.

Jackson Wynn, son of Mark Wynn and Victoria (Tori)

Kendall. Grandson of Bob Wynn (with Grace). Plays for the Chicago Aces.

Riley Wynn, daughter of Mark Wynn and Victoria (Tori) Kendall. Granddaughter of Bob Wynn (with Grace). Goalie coach for the San Diego Hawks, affiliate team of the Long Beach Golden Eagles.

Everly Wynn, daughter of Bob and Chelsea Wynn. Executive director of the Condors Foundation.

Asher Wynn, son of Bob and Chelsea Wynn. Sports reporter for *Playmaker* (hockey blog).

Harrison Wynn, son of Bob and Chelsea Wynn. Plays for the Pasadena Condors, affiliate team of the California Condors.

Noah Wynn, son of Bob and Chelsea Wynn. Plays for the San Diego Hawks.

1

THÉO

This is the weirdest fucking job interview I've ever had.

I rise from the chair in my Las Vegas apartment and carry my glass of whiskey—Crown Royal XO—over to the window. Outside, the pool shimmers turquoise in the dusk, palm trees silhouetted against the cobalt sky.

"Come on, Théo." My grandfather speaks from my big brown leather couch where he's still sitting. "I can't believe you're not jumping at this opportunity."

I turn to face him. At seventy-two, he's still a fit-looking man. I don't think he's lost an inch of his six feet two height. His physique isn't as muscled as it was back in the days when he played hockey, but he's still imposing. His mostly gray hair has receded at the temples, but he *has* hair. After living in California for nearly forty years, the legendary scar across his right eyebrow isn't as prominent now that his face is tanned and his forehead and eyes are more creased.

He fixes his blue eyes on me—eyes that were once piercing but now look a little cloudy.

I walk back over and sit on the chair across from him. I lean forward, elbows on my knees. "Grandpa. You know I can't take this job. My dad would crap hockey pucks and go ape shit on my ass if I came to work for you."

Grandpa smiles. "Yeah."

I narrow my eyes at him. "Is that why you're doing this? Because I don't want your fucking job if you're just doing it to piss off Dad."

"No." His smirk morphs into a scowl. "That's just a happy side benefit."

I roll my eyes. Christ. This feud between my dad, my uncle, and their father—now sitting here in front of me—is bringing back my stomach ulcer. I ignore the gnawing feeling in my upper abdomen.

Yeah, my dad would flip shit if I took a job working for his father, but there's more to my refusal than that. I'm not afraid to admit that I want my dad to be proud of me and what I do, but I could live with pissing him off. What I couldn't live with? Taking this job and failing miserably. I've had enough experience letting down the family to know that this would be the ultimate disgrace. And it wouldn't just be my dad . . . it would disgrace the entire Wynn family, the hockey dynasty known worldwide. No pressure at all.

"I told you why I want you for this job," Grandpa continues in his rough voice. "You're a smart guy."

I almost snort. Yeah, I'm smart. So smart everyone thought I was a total dork growing up.

"You know hockey," Grandpa says. "More important,

you know the hockey *business*. Look what you've done here in Vegas."

"I haven't done it all myself."

I'm the assistant general manager of the expansion NHL team here. They hired me three years ago even though I was only twenty-five years old and had no experience managing a hockey team. But I'd built my hockey analytics business Coast 2 Coast into something people were taking notice of. Yeah, we've had some success here, and despite my protest, I know I've contributed a hell of a lot to that success.

"Don't you want to, though? Don't you want to manage a team?" He eyes me shrewdly.

Dammit. I do.

The idea of being the general manager, of being in charge of everything—responsible for acquiring the rights to player personnel, negotiating contracts, moving out players who no longer fit on the team, the challenges of constructing a team under the salary cap, along with managing the scouts, the trainers, the coaches—it's what I've wanted . . . well, not my whole life. What I'd wanted my whole life was to play in the NHL, and I'd achieved that . . . for six short months before it had been slew-footed (hockey talk for when some asshole kicks your feet out from under you).

But since then . . . hell yeah. I want it.

But taking a job working for my grandfather, owner of the California Condors hockey team in Santa Monica, with all the shit that exists in my big, crazy, fucked-up family . . . if I think my ulcer is bad now, holy shit, I'd be not only eating proton pump inhibitors, I'd be downing beta-blockers for my blood pressure and probably Xanax too.

Not that I'm stressed or anything.

Not only is there bad blood between my dad and my grandpa, for a whole lotta reasons, I'm not on speaking terms with my brother, JP. That jackhole fuckstick. JP plays for the Golden Eagles, which my dad owns, coached by my uncle Mark, who my grandpa recently fired. (That whole shit show is a long story.) The Eagles play out of Long Beach, only a short freeway drive away from Santa Monica, meaning it would be tough to avoid seeing JP.

Ah fuck. The Condors haven't made the playoffs in years. The challenge of it yanks at something inside me, making my skin prickle everywhere. The palms of my hands tingle as I toss back the rest of the whiskey. "This is nuts, Grandpa."

"You're the one I want. You've got the brains, the logic, the common sense . . . but you also have the passion for the game. You work your ass off all the time."

Another uncomfortable truth. I may have been called a workaholic a time or ten.

Then Grandpa says the magic words. "You'll have complete autonomy to rebuild the Condors as you see fit."

I sit back in my chair and study Grandpa. While this is enticing, I'm skeptical that he's going to turn everything over to me.

"There's something special about you. Lots of people in the league are seeing it. We can do great things together."

I can't help but smile as I slowly shake my head. "You're good."

"I'm not blowing smoke up your ass."

Grandpa is known for his colorful language.

"This is serious business," he adds, his voice gravelly. "You know this team is important to me."

I nod. "Yeah."

Hockey's been Grandpa's whole life. He grew up in rural Saskatchewan, Canada, playing hockey on a pond. He had a long, successful career with the Toronto Maple Leafs, was traded to the Condors, where he played three seasons before retiring, and two years after that he bought the team he'd played for. The Condors had a lot of good years, but sure as shit not lately.

Grandpa has four Stanley Cup rings from his time with the Leafs, but that was five decades ago. The Cup has eluded him ever since, and I know he wants it one more time. I get it. I'll never get to hoist the Cup as a player . . . but I want it too. So fucking much.

"I don't make rash decisions." I meet Grandpa's eyes.

"I know. You'll think about it." He stands. "I'm flying home tonight. Thanks for listening to me."

I walk him to the door and we shake hands, pulling each other in and giving each other a smack on the back. "Good to see you, Grandpa."

"You have until Friday to make a decision."

I snort out a laugh. "Good to know."

Alone in my apartment, I stand for a moment and draw in a breath. Shaking my head, I let it out and head to my computer. Where else would I go? If I'm going to make a life-changing decision, I need data. I need all the facts.

We're building something great here in Vegas, and I'm a part of that. I could stay here and continue that trajectory. Even though I don't always agree with everything my boss does. Even though I can clearly see different paths to where we want to go.

Or I could take a risk on trying to build a losing team into a winning one.

I try to ignore the push and pull of excitement and fear, the tug between desire for change and maintaining the status quo. I make decisions based on sound rationale, not emotion. That's me. Logical. Analytical. Sensible. I gather information, weigh the alternatives, and consider the pros and cons. Emotion shouldn't come into it. Just feasibility, acceptability, and desirability.

First, I need some extra-strength Tums. And another shot of Crown Royal.

2

LACEY

"OH, FOR THE LOVE OF A MILK COW." I SQUEEZE MY EYES shut, unable to believe what I'm seeing on the computer screen.

My bank balance is negative four hundred and forty-two dollars.

When I open my eyes, that's not what I will see. That was a hallucination. Blurred vision. Or something.

I'm not even drunk or high, though.

I crack one eye open and peer at the laptop again. Shit.

"How can this be?" My stomach clenches painfully. I click to look at the transactions in the account. "Jesus." My gaze fastens on the large withdrawal four days ago. All my savings . . . gone.

It's not like I had millions or anything, but damn, I'd just gotten out of the debt I'd accumulated when Mom had gotten sick. I was just starting to get ahead of the game.

I swallow and press my fingers to my mouth. My insides start trembling.

I'd bought groceries and paid the electric bill not knowing my bank balance was zero, which had put me into overdraft. "Chris. What the fuck have you done?"

I slump back in the couch, the laptop on the table in front of me.

I haven't seen my brother in two days. How did he do that? Steal my bank card? Guess my PIN? Where the hell is he?

I want to cry. I want to scream and punch things. Possibly my brother, who, while being the same age as me since we're twins, feels more like my child.

This wasn't always true. But Chris got himself into trouble and I've been yanking my hair out trying to get him to change his life.

I give up.

I hate to think those words. I'm not a quitter. I take pride in my ability to bounce back. To land on my feet. But I'm tired. So tired.

I need a plan. But I'm too exhausted to figure it out right now. I have to get to work—my shift at Silk Lounge starts in an hour. What's the point of even going, though? What's the point of anything?

No, no, I can't think like that.

I rub my aching forehead and haul my weary ass up out of the chair to get ready for work. I have to go, since it's the only job I have right now, other than my freelance work. It'll be worth going in just for the tips. I can do pretty well in an evening. Silk is a high-end cocktail lounge located on the top floor of the Wellborne Resort on the Vegas Strip, with panoramic views of the city, chill-out tunes, and pricey artisan cocktails.

I wriggle into my black dress—short, tight, with narrow straps—do my hair and makeup, and toss my heels into my backpack. With my black Chucks on my feet, I head out to take the bus to the Strip. I lean my head against the bus window, staring sightlessly through it as the bus bumps its way across town from our little apartment on South Decatur to the glitzy Vegas everyone knows.

I've lived here my whole life. I both love it and hate it. Las Vegas, the entertainment capital of the world. For most people who live here, it's just like everywhere else; and yet it's also like nowhere else. This town is alive and awake twenty-four/seven. Money, sex, and gambling are everywhere. And yet there are people who work ordinary jobs, like teachers and doctors, who go to work and go home and never interact with the tourists who flood the city. Then there are people like me and Chris—who grew up a part of the entertainment industry because of our mother. And people like Chris, who fall prey to the gambler's self-centered interest in winning and the parts of the city I hate —addiction and despair.

In the staff room at the Silk Lounge, I add some shiny gloss to my lips and slide into black high heels. My feet will be dying in an hour, but it's part of the job.

I used to love the vibe at Silk, and there's no denying the beauty of the glittering view of the city outside the windows, but now it's like wallpaper—always there. Inside, the lounge glitters too, with lots of metallics and crystals and little white lights everywhere, the furniture upholstered in purple, blue, and gray velvets. Silk draperies in similar shades hang from the ceilings to separate table groupings.

I swing into the rhythm of my work, keeping my smile

fixed in place, flirting mildly with customers. Inside, I'm a mess of frustration and anger and hopelessness, but nobody cares about that. My co-workers know me as perpetually cheerful and dependable no matter what's going on in my life, and customers don't want doom and gloom from their server.

Around nine o'clock, a group of men come into the lounge. I don't know who they are, and they're not dressed in suits and ties, but Enrico, the shift manager, springs into action to arrange some of the curved couches, chairs, and brushed metal tables into a grouping for them. In my section.

I sigh. Probably a bachelor party. Guys from Omaha or something, out for a wild time. Yay.

This is a tradition I have come to despise. The guys all expect the groom to act like a complete jack wagon because it's his last night of "freedom." For fuck's sake. I've seen fights break out. Saw a groom fall over the railing and break both his ankles. I've dealt with the drunks hitting on me in all kinds of ways—groping me, cornering me, trying to kiss me . . . including the groom.

I can only hope they have money and will tip well.

There are about ten of them, and wow, they're all big guys. Nicely dressed and clean cut. A few middle-aged guys, some younger, like, in their twenties. I smile at them all. "Hello, gentlemen. I'm Lacey. I'll be taking care of you tonight."

I wait for the lewd comments about how I could "take care of" them.

Instead they all chorus, "Hi, Lacey," making me smile.

In a glance I can see they've already been drinking, but none of them seem hammered. Yet.

"You guys celebrating something tonight?"

"Yeah." The man nearest me nods and gestures to another guy. "Théo here got a new job."

I smile at the man he gestured to. "Congratulations." Okay, not a bachelor party. Whee.

"He's moving to California," another guy says. "Tomorrow. Fucker."

Théo grins.

My guess is . . . accountant. Théo's a good-looking dude, with dark-rimmed glasses that give him a sort of sexy scholar look. His brown hair is cut short, but longer on top. Compared to the other guys, who are all dressed in casual clothes—although I notice expensive watches and more than one pair of red-soled shoes—he's wearing a neat, button-down shirt over black dress pants. My gaze lingers on wide shoulders and flat abs. If he's an accountant, he must work out. "What you are all drinking tonight?"

I wait with a smile. They order bottle service—bottles of expensive vodka, scotch, and tequila.

Back behind the bar, Crystal, one of my co-workers, says, "Lucky you, waiting on those guys!"

"Mmm. Why?"

"Don't you know who they are?"

"Well, one of them is Théo Somebody, and he just got a new job in California."

"They're all hockey players! From the Nevada Mustangs!"

"Ah." We've had a hockey team in town for a few years now; they made quite an entertainment splash in Sin City.

"Well, they're not *all* players." Crystal eyes the group. "I think the big older guy is the coach. I forget his name. And I don't know who Théo is."

"You're not much of a fan." I flash her a teasing smile.

"I've only been to a few games," she admits. "But it was fun."

I pick up my tray loaded with glasses. I don't know anything about hockey, and I don't usually have time to watch much of it, between this and the two other jobs I was working until recently.

The guys are all laughing uproariously about something when I arrive with their drinks, and I smile as I set things on the tables. No one grabs my ass as I bend over, so I count that as a win. Not only that, they all say thank you when I'm done. I'm impressed. Hopefully they're good tippers.

"Should I bring food menus by?" I ask, making eye contact with a couple of the men.

"Yeah, yeah," the first man who spoke says. "We should order some food."

"Absolutely."

After I've taken orders and served a variety of small plates for them to share, I take stock of the table to see if they're getting low on anything. "Is your new job a promotion?" I ask the man named Théo.

I'm not really flirting with him. I like to be friendly and make conversation with the customers I'm taking care of.

"Yeah." His grin is a little loose, like he's well lubricated. "Sort of." He runs a hand through his hair, messing it, which is very attractive. My gaze drops to his legs; he has one foot crossed over the opposite knee, wearing expensive-looking loafers, his feet and ankles bare—no socks. For some reason, this strikes me as insanely sexy, and I have a hard time looking away. "Whole new job."

"I'm sure you'll do well at it." I smile as I say it, even though I have no idea if that's true. "Good luck."

The man sitting beside him snorts. "You're gonna need a fuckton of luck."

This sparks my curiosity.

"I sure as hell am," Théo agrees. "That's why I'm getting shitfaced tonight."

The other man's forehead creases. "You sure you made the right decision, man?"

I sense his genuine concern and surmise they must be pretty good friends.

"I'm sure." Théo nods, still smiling indolently. "You know me. Every decision carefully thought out."

"True."

"And I'm just joking about the luck. I got this, dude." He lifts a hand, slaps it onto his friend's thigh just above the knee, and squeezes.

"Yow!" The guy flinches.

Apparently Théo has strong hands.

"Get your mitts off me, asshole." The man shoves Théo, but they're both laughing.

I'm standing here watching them instead of working, and I give myself a mental shake. "Anything else I can get for you right now?" I keep my smile pleasant.

This time Théo meets my eyes, and I feel a little zap through to my core, a sizzling connection. He's more attractive than I first thought. Maybe it was the glasses, or maybe I just wasn't paying attention, but there's something about him that pulls at me. The corners of his mouth are tipped up and his eyes gleam, as if he wants to ask me for something inappropriate.

And I kind of want him to do it.

3

LACEY

"WE'RE GOOD FOR NOW," ONE OF THE OTHER GUYS SAYS. Without taking my eyes off Théo, I smile and turn away.

There are two other men now seated in my section I need to serve. I head their way with my smile in place. Immediately I feel creeped out by the way they look at me. I swallow a sigh, contrasting this with the group of hockey players.

"Hi, Lacey," one man says with a gross smirk. "I'm Ed. This here's Lincoln."

Neither of these guys is attractive, although they're both wearing suits and ties and are clean cut. "Hi, Ed. Hi, Lincoln." I take their drink orders, ignoring the way their gazes roam over me even though a shiver crawls up my spine.

Ugh.

I get flagged down by another table on my way by, and I'm glad things are busy tonight. When Enrico sends me off for a break, I reluctantly head to the staff room. I grab my

15

phone and take the elevator to the main floor so I can step outside for a few minutes and get some air.

The night is balmy, the heat of the day easing now. Surrounded by the glitter of the Strip with the noise that goes along with it, I make my way across the stone terrace and sit on a low wall with flowers and greenery behind me. I unlock my phone and check to see if Chris has answered any of my texts or voice messages.

Nothing.

Damn.

Blowing out a breath, I tip my head back and stare up at the night sky. No stars are visible with the light pollution of the city, just a blank dark canvas, the sky beam of the Luxor slicing through it.

"Everything okay?"

My head jerks around at the question, and I see Théo the hockey player standing near me. The evening breeze ruffles his thick hair as he tilts his head.

"Oh. Yeah." I press the button to darken my phone screen. "Fine."

"Boyfriend troubles?" He takes a seat on the wall near me.

"No. Phht." I shake my head. "No boyfriend."

"No?"

"Nope." I stretch my lips into a casual smile. This guy is apparently leaving for California tomorrow, so I don't feel intimidated by his question. Or his presence, even though he's a little drunk. "No time."

"Well, I'd say that's sad except"—he gives me a rueful smile—"I know the feeling."

"So you're not uprooting a girlfriend to move to California with you?"

"Nope." His mouth tightens briefly.

"Did you get traded?" When they'd first talked about his new job, I assumed he was an accountant, but now knowing he plays hockey, I wonder if he didn't have a choice about this move.

He laughs. "No. I don't play hockey."

"Oh. Sorry. Someone said you were all hockey players."

"Not me." He meets my eyes. "Not anymore, anyway. I was the assistant GM of the team. General manager," he clarifies for me. "My new job is manager of a team."

"Ah. I see. What are you doing out here? Are you leaving?" I pause. "You better not be stiffing me on the bill."

He chokes out a laugh. "Ah, no. Just wanted some air. And don't worry, the guys are good for the tab. I'm not paying."

"Nice of them."

He lifts one broad shoulder. "Yeah, I guess it is. They insisted on taking me out before I go. Ended up being my last night in town."

"Are you going to miss Vegas?"

He purses his lips attractively, looking around at the people milling about the entrance, some coming, some leaving, others like us just hanging out. Laughter bursts from a group of people over near the fountain. "In some ways I will."

"How long have you lived here?"

"Three years. It's a crazy place, but it grows on you. How about you?"

"Born and raised here."

"No shit." He slides me a look. "Are there actually people who were born and raised here?"

I hold my arms out to my sides. "Yep."

"I guess you like it then, since you're still here."

"Not so much right now." I bend my head to look at my phone again. "Sometimes this place sucks."

"Uh-oh. Something *is* wrong."

I shake my head, rising. "Nope, it's all good. I need to get back to work."

He stands too. "I better get back before they think I passed out somewhere."

"Wouldn't be the first time someone's done that."

He laughs and rubs his face. "I'm drunk, but not that drunk."

We cross the luxurious lobby, past slot machines ringing and dinging, and step into the elevator that goes to the top floor. "Everything is over the top in Vegas," Théo comments.

"Yep."

He eyes me with what appears to be concern. Apparently I'm not doing a very good job of hiding my feelings. I need to do better.

Except my evening isn't going to get any easier.

At Ed and Lincoln's table, Ed gives me a smile that makes my skin crawl. "So, lovely Lacey. Sit and have a drink with us."

I smile politely. "I'm sorry, I can't do that. It's against the rules."

"How can that be? Tsk." He looks around. "Who's in charge here?"

My smile slips, but I try to keep my expression pleasant. "Enrico is the manager on duty tonight."

"Send him over."

My stomach tenses. The last thing I need is to get into trouble here.

Normally, I'd ask what the problem is and try to fix it, but I already know what the problem is. Swallowing a sigh, I say, "Of course." And I go to hunt down Enrico.

Enrico's one of the better managers here, so when I tell him that they want me to have a drink with them and I refused, he rolls his eyes. "Do they think they're at the Pink Pussy Club?" he mutters. "I'll talk to them."

"Thanks."

I'm busy for a few minutes with the hockey gang, making eye contact with Théo as I pick up empties and see if they need anything else, but out of the corner of my eye I see Enrico talk to the men. My jaw drops to my chest when Enrico approaches me and says quietly, "Just sit with them for a few minutes. I told them you can't drink on the job, but you can chat for a few minutes."

I level him with a hard stare. "What?"

He shrugs.

"Oh for . . ." I tip my head back briefly. I don't know how they got him to agree to that. Probably a wad of cash.

"I didn't realize this was that kind of place," Théo says to me. No one else hears, and Enrico has already gone.

"It's not," I snap.

He holds up his hands. "Kidding."

I sigh. "Sorry." I force another smile. Despite our little conversation out front, he's still a customer. "Other duties as assigned! I'll be back shortly."

I take my time strolling to the bar with my tray, leaving it there, and slowly walking to the table with the two creepy dudes.

"So glad your boss is a reasonable man," Ed says.

I sit and give him a tight smile. He *is* a customer, so I'll be polite for a few minutes, but if he tries to touch me, I will punch him in the dick.

"Your brother owes us a lot of money."

Shit. Fuck. Fucking fuckity fuck.

"Where is he, lovely Lacey?" Ed reaches out to finger my hair and I jerk back.

"Do not touch me," I utter through closed teeth. "I don't know where he is. I've been trying to get hold of him for days."

"Hmmm." He eyes me as if trying to decide whether he believes me or not.

"It's true."

"You could be protecting him."

"I'm done protecting him." Honestly, I'm not sure if that's true or not. Chris is my brother, the only family I have left. I've been trying to help him and bailing him out for years. But it should be true. Because this is too much.

"Really? Not sure I believe that."

"Chris said you might be able to help us out," he continued. "So as not to end up with both his legs broken. Or maybe he takes a long drive out into the desert and . . . never comes back."

Jesus Christ. My throat constricts to the size of a cocktail straw. My insides tremble. "I don't have any money," I answer as coolly as I can. "Wish I could help, but Chris stole my money too."

"Yeah." Ed leans in and shrugs. "Not surprising. Addicts get desperate. Especially when their lives are on the line."

I stare back at his vile brown eyes, his full lips curved into a nasty smile. Thoughts tumble around in my head but the only thing I can think is that I have to maintain my composure and not let on how scared and pissed I am.

This isn't my first encounter with bookies Chris has stiffed. But this time it feels scarier. These guys are scarier. And I know it's because Chris owes them a lot more money this time.

"There's a way you can help Chris out."

"I'm not a call girl."

His smile makes my blood chill. "There's good money in that. And you need money, don't you, lovely Lacey?"

"I'm not working for you."

He tilts his head. "You haven't even heard us out." He lays a pudgy hand on my forearm. I jerk it back and shove my chair away from the table. "We have an offer you won't be able to refuse."

"Ha. Funny." I'm about to stand when a body appears next to the table. A tall, broad, very fit body. I look up at Théo.

The frown on his face has his eyebrows drawn down beneath the frame of his glasses. His eyes radiate wrath, and his mouth is a thin line. "Everything okay here?"

"Yeah, yeah." Ed scowls at him and waves a hand. "Bugger off, man."

I meet Théo's eyes. Things are not okay, but I sure don't need to drag him into this. "It's all good." I wave a hand casually. "I'm done chatting with these gentlemen anyway."

I stand and bestow a smile on them. "Another whiskey sour?"

Ed glowers, but it seems he doesn't want to make a scene. "Yeah."

I nod and keep my expression pleasant as I turn away. "I'm fine," I tell Théo. "Go back to your friends."

Eyebrows still knit together, he gives a slow nod and walks to their table, but he shoots a glance back at Ed and Lincoln as he does so.

I'm shaking both with fear and anger as I stride to the bar. My teeth are clenched so hard it's a wonder my molars aren't cracking. I need to get a grip on my emotions and do my job.

What the fuck, Chris?

Did he really send these guys to me? I'm going to break both his legs myself the next time I see him, which better be fucking soon.

4

THÉO

DON'T ASK ME WHY I CARE ABOUT THE WAITRESS.

Lacey.

She's pretty, sure. Big eyes, full lips, killer cheekbones shown off by her hair pulled back into a bun. And that little black dress shows off some sweet curves and long, sleek legs.

I appreciate a gorgeous woman as much as the next guy, but I don't usually hit on waitresses, and I sure as hell don't get up and defend them from other customers. Well, in fairness, I've never actually seen something like that happen before. But still, what the fuck made me do that?

Leaning back into the comfortable couch, I sip my whiskey and let my gaze fall on those two asswipes across the room. They annoy the hell out of me, for another mysterious reason.

"What's up, man?" Andy elbows me.

Andy's the director of hockey operations for the Mustangs. He's my closest friend here in Vegas. Okay, pretty much my only friend. It's not a good idea for me to hang out with the guys on the team who play hockey, or the other guys who technically work for me, and I've never had time to socialize much with people outside the hockey club, but I've known Andy since we played together for the Penguins. He's a few years older than me, and he's a good guy.

"Nothing."

"Why were you talking to those guys?"

"Looked like they were giving Lacey a hard time."

"Lacey?" He cocks an eyebrow.

I elbow him back.

"Never knew you were such a knight in shining armor."

I snort. "I'm not."

Lacey is back at their table and my muscles all tense, but she's giving them their check. Good. That must mean they're leaving.

"They gotta fix that rule, man." Brent shakes his head, continuing their conversation about video replay. "There's gonna be a bad call, and it's going to impact the outcome of a game."

"A whole playoff series, potentially," Jeff says.

"True."

"That's happened in the past, though," Andy says. "Calls got missed on the ice. Goalie gets steamrollered, it never gets called, goal stands even though it was clearly interference."

"That's true too."

Now I see the manager dude is back talking to the guys again. This gives me a nasty feeling in my gut. This is the guy who told Lacey she had to go sit with them. I frown as I watch them talk. Is she in trouble?

Fuck, what kind of place is this? I mean, I get that there are working girls here in Vegas. Sex is everywhere. But Lacey doesn't strike me as someone who's into that. She was trying to hide how pissed off she was, but I could see it.

I straighten, my senses on alert as the manager appears to be apologizing profusely for something, placating the customers. I narrow my eyes and take another gulp of spirits, which burn their way down my chest.

"Right, Théo?"

I blink and turn to Jeff, my boss. Former boss. "What?"

He laughs. "Time to cut you off?"

I shake my head. "Nah, I'm good, sorry."

"Should they do away with reviewing goaltender interference?" Jeff asks again.

"No. We have the technology, let's use it."

"But they're not using it right," Andy objects. "Nobody knew they were going to challenge every fucking call."

"The problem is, goaltender interference isn't black and white. The puck crosses the line or doesn't—black and white. But whether the contact was incidental or intentional, that's a lot harder to decide." I rub my chin. "Hard to figure out someone's intention on a video. And the rule is so subjective that two similar plays will have different results on different nights, hell, even in the same game. Even worse, some of this year's calls were really hard to understand." I'm usually cautious about airing my opinions on league governance in public, but I'm comfortable with these guys.

"No shit."

We get into a discussion about possible changes to the rule, but then I'm distracted again when I see Lacey across the bar. She has a backpack slung over her shoulder, and as she walks down a hallway, the lighting glints on her face. Her face is wet. Is she fucking crying?

I shoot up out of my seat.

Then I pause. I have no idea what's going on here, and it's none of my business. It's not like me to spontaneously jump into a situation without carefully considering all the consequences.

Fuck it.

I stride after her.

"What the . . . ?" I hear the guys muttering behind me.

"Lacey." I call to her as she reaches the elevator. The lobby area on this floor is empty, dimly lit, with music pumping through speakers, the hostess stand around the corner.

She starts and turns to me, those big eyes glossy but also flashing sparks. "What?"

I stop a couple of feet from her. "What's going on? Why are you crying?"

She closes her eyes briefly then shakes her head. "This is not your business. Don't worry."

"There's something weird going on." I set my chin determinedly.

"Okay, fine. I just got fired." She lifts both hands.

"Whaaat?" I stare at her. "Just like that?"

She hitches a shoulder and swipes a hand across one cheek. "Yeah. Just like that."

"Was it because you wouldn't sit with those guys?"

Her lips pucker up as she considers my question, then her gaze shifts past me, over my shoulder. I turn and see the aforementioned guys in their crappy suits, apparently also coming after Lacey. Oh no. Fuck no.

I slide my hand around her upper arm and gently pull her away from the elevator door. "You're coming with me."

She inhales a shaky breath, her eyes darting back and forth between me and the other dudes.

"She's coming with us," the taller guy says. "Right, Lacey?" His smile is menacing.

I feel Lacey shaking and I pull her closer. What the fuck is happening here? "Your choice," I murmur in her ear.

Her trembling intensifies and she sinks her teeth into that plush bottom lip. Her eyes flicker back and forth. What the fuck? Is she actually considering whether to go with them? I squint at her.

"I'm with him," she finally says, lifting her chin and speaking to Douche One and Douche Two.

I give them a slitty-eyed look and lead her away.

"This isn't over, lovely Lacey," Douche One calls as we walk away, his voice hard. "We know where to find you."

That sounded like a threat.

I glance down to see Lacey's beautiful face scrunched up. She inhales unevenly.

"You okay?"

She nods, her small chin coming up again.

I take her to our table and all heads snap around when I settle her on the couch next to me, nudging Jimmy to shift over. We're both big guys, but Lacey's little ass doesn't take up much room. We're pressed body to body, though.

"Lacey here just got fired," I say cheerfully to everyone. "Before she got the big tip we were going to leave her. Right?" I meet some eyes, hoisting an eyebrow.

"Uh, yeah," the guys all mumble.

"So I brought her back. I think she needs a drink, though. Who's looking after us now?" I search the room.

"Probably Crystal," Lacey murmurs beside me, her fingers twisted together, maybe to hide the fact that they're shaking. She shifts on the couch.

"That her?" I gesture.

"Um, yeah."

I wave a hand and catch Crystal's attention. A stunning tall blonde in a short black dress that almost looks as good as Lacey's, she starts toward us. Then she spots Lacey and her eyes pop open.

Lacey gives her former co-worker a weak smile. "Hey."

"Lacey here would like a drink," I say. I look down at Lacey. "What would you like?"

"Um." She swallows. "This is awkward."

One corner of my mouth lifts. "Who cares? You don't work here anymore. You're a paying customer."

"I'll have a Jack Daniel's on the rocks. Please."

I nod approvingly. I'd been ready to order her a tequila shot if she asked for some kind of fruity cocktail, because clearly she needs something strong.

"Okay, why did you get fired?"

Her bottom lip quivers.

Shit. I don't want her to cry again. "Never mind."

She waves a hand. "Those assholes told my boss that I changed the amount of the tip they left me on the credit card slip. They showed him how the numbers were changed to increase the tip, but I didn't do it."

"Assholes is right," I snarl.

"Enrico believed them."

"He's an asshole too."

She sighs. "He really isn't. I don't know why he was acting so weird tonight. Unless . . ." She pauses.

"What?"

"Never mind."

"Why'd they do that? Just to get back at you? That's beyond assholery."

"It's a long story." She glances around at the other guys.

I get it. It's none of our business. Call me crazy though, I'm concerned about her. And about the comment Douche One made as they left, which was definitely threatening. She's in trouble of some kind.

I'm leaving tomorrow, so there's nothing I can do about it, but at least I helped her out tonight.

Crystal arrives with Lacey's drink, and I watch Lacey tip it to her lips and take a big swallow.

"Man." She shakes her head, her lips gleaming with the spirits. "What a day. Cheers." She holds up the glass, then takes another swig.

"Attagirl."

Some of the guys disappear to go play a few rounds of blackjack, including Jimmy, so I shift away from Lacey to give her space. Not that I mind having her pressed up against me. But that's sure as hell not what this is about. Now that we're almost alone, Brent and Jeff sitting across from us arguing about whether players should be suspended for licking (it happened, no shit), I ask again, "Wanna tell me now what's going on?"

She's making short work of her drink, and it's apparently loosening her tongue. "My brother owes them money." She tosses down the last of the Jack.

I lift a hand and catch Crystal's eye. I hold up my own empty glass and point at Lacey's empty one as well. Crystal nods.

"I don't know where Chris is," Lacey continues. "He disappeared days ago. After cleaning out my bank account." Bitterness laces her words.

"Jesus."

She meets my eyes. "This isn't the first time this has happened." The curve of her lips is glum. "He's a gambling addict."

"Well, shit."

"I know." She heaves a huge sigh. "It's been going on for years. Since before our mom died. As if we didn't have enough financial problems because of that. She was sick for a couple of years, and I . . . well, we didn't always have the money for the treatment she needed. I got into debt myself and Chris got this crazy idea that he could make enough money gambling to help pay for her medical care."

My gut cramps up hearing all this.

"Sometimes it worked," she admits, accepting the next drink from Crystal. I take mine as well. "And he felt like a hero, contributing. But then it wouldn't work, and he'd lose money, and . . . he started going into debt too. Only not just with Visa and Mastercard." She lets out a short laugh. "Who are bad enough to owe money to, believe me."

One problem I've never had in my life is financial troubles. But I'm not an idiot. I know not everyone's been as lucky that way as me. "Yeah."

"I know he's been dealing with some bad actors. They've showed up at the apartment looking for him. But none of them have ever threatened me before."

"How did they threaten you?"

"Apparently my brother is trying to pimp me out." She takes another gulp of booze, blinking rapidly, and I can see the pain in her shiny eyes.

I slap a hand down on the couch between us. "Fuck that!"

"Preferably not." She gives a watery smile. "I mean, I've worked a lot of bizarre jobs to try to get ahead financially, but I've always hoped I wouldn't have to resort to prostitution."

"Hell no!"

She slumps against the back of the couch. "I don't know what I'm going to do now. I get the feeling those dudes aren't going to give up. Chris must owe them a whack of money. Oh my God." She rubs her forehead. "I've bailed him out before, but now I have no money either."

"Maybe it's better *not* to bail him out," I offer.

A puff of air escapes her lips. "Yeah. I know. It's just . . . hard." She turns big brown eyes on me. "He's my brother."

Given my strained relationship with my own brother and the fact that her asshole brother tried to pimp her out to some mobbed-up bookies he was stupid enough to do business with, I have a hard time mustering a lot of sympathy. But the look in her eyes—sad, forlorn, hopeless— tugs at something inside me.

Hold the fuck up. Is she after something? I can't get suckered by a hard-luck story from a Vegas cocktail waitress I don't even know. This could be a total con job.

I'm smart, but I'm not always the best judge of people, which I've learned the hard way.

Her smile seems sweet and sincere . . . she genuinely

seemed terrified of those dudes. She can't be pulling a con on me. Can she?

"You care about him." I manage to sound empathetic rather than suspicious.

"Yeah." Her lips droop and she drops her gaze to the amber liquid in her glass. "He's the only family I have."

"Christ. I *wish* my brother was the only family I had."

She turns shocked eyes on me.

"In fact, I wish I didn't have a brother."

Her mouth drops open. "You don't mean that!"

"Okay, maybe not all the time." The truth is, I actually miss my brother like hell, even though I'm pissed at him. "But sometimes . . . yeah. My family's, uh . . . well, basically we're one tent short of a full-blown circus." She has no idea who my family is, so I feel okay saying this. If anyone else criticizes my family though, they'll wear their dick as a necklace.

She laughs. "Well, at least you *have* a family." Then her expression shifts as if she too is realizing the extent of her brother's betrayal. And I feel in my gut that she's not making all this shit up. "On the other hand, maybe you're right. Life without family would be a lot easier. If I only had myself to worry about . . . I'd be golden!" Her face clears and she tosses back more Jack Daniel's.

"There you go." I clink my glass against hers. "Seriously though, when you're dealing with addiction, bailing them out isn't really helping them. They need to hit rock bottom and figure things out themselves. The only one who can save him . . . is him."

She scrunches up her face adorably, then huffs. "I know.

I know. I went to a few Gam-Anon meetings. It's just easier to say than to do when . . . well."

"I get it." Probably if my brother was on fire, and I had a glass of water . . . I'd drink it. No. I'd save him. Maybe. "Well, we have something in common. My brother fucked me over too."

Her eyes round. She sips her drink. "Really? How?"

"He stole my girlfriend."

"Oh no."

I make it sound casual, like we were fourteen or something, but it was anything but casual. It basically ripped my guts out. I shrug. "She cheated on me with him, I caught them together, kicked her out, and they ended up together."

She blinks, drawing my attention to long, thick eyelashes. "Oh wow. That really sucks. How could a brother do that?"

I give her a look.

"Oh. Yeah." She drops her gaze again and sighs. "People really suck, don't they?"

"Sometimes, yeah." I study the curve of her cheek, the arc of her lips, the strands of hair around her face—I'm not sure of the color . . . blond? Light brown? Her skin is perfect, smooth and glowy, all the way down from her cheeks to the opening of her dress that reveals more curves . . . enticing and lush. My gaze wanders farther, to the hem of the dress riding up on smooth thighs. My groin tightens.

Ah hell.

Yeah, yeah, I'm attracted to her. But it's my last night in town and even though the guys joked about it, I'm not out to get laid.

I wouldn't do that to Lacey anyway, since she's had a rough day. Rough . . . years, even, it sounds like.

"I should go, I guess." She doesn't move.

"What are you going to do? About those bookies your brother owes money to? About your brother?"

"I don't know. But I always figure things out." She smiles and it's thin but genuine. "Really."

"I believe you." She shouldn't have to figure shit like this out. It's not fair. "Where are you going to go? It sounds like they know where you live." I frown. "You can't go home."

Her eyes shadow and she catches her bottom lip between her teeth. "Yeah. Shit. I guess I can go crash at my friend Karine's place tonight. Although I'd hate to have those guys show up there. Karine and her husband just had a baby."

What's she going to do, though? She can't stay away from her home forever, trying to avoid those guys. Worry gnaws at my gut. "Well, have one more drink."

"I shouldn't. I have to take the bus to Karine's place."

"I'll get you to Karine's place."

Her smile is sardonic. "I don't even know you."

"Hey." I lay my hand on my chest. "I helped you out."

"True. I'm sorry. You can understand why I'm a little . . . wary, though." To my surprise, she reaches out to pat my arm, and when her hand lingers, my blood heats up. Our eyes meet.

Heat pulses between us. She feels it too.

"Yeah," I manage to grate out. "I get it."

"Okay." Her voice is husky. "One more drink."

The guys come back from the blackjack tables then, and they're whooping and throwing their arms around one another. Danny holds up a huge wad of cash. "I won!" he shouts.

Holy crap.

"Here's your tip," Danny declares, handing a bunch of bills to Lacey. They're fucking hundred dollar bills.

She slowly takes the money, glancing at me, then the bills. I have no idea how much is in there, but I know it's a good tip. "No." She shakes her head. "I can't take all this."

"Sure, you can." Danny grins. "I have lots more." He waves the money.

"Shit, man." Jeff grabs his arm to keep him from flaunting his cash. "You want someone to roll you on the way out of here?"

"Best way to avoid that is to spend this." He waves over Crystal and orders bottles of Piper-Heidsieck.

Jesus. He's even more hammered than *I* am now.

Lacey's laughing at him, but still holding the money. I nudge her backpack, sitting on the floor next to the couch, toward her so she can put it away. "We were going to tip you," I say in a low voice.

She nods and pulls a small purse out of the bag to tuck the money into, clearly still uncomfortable with this. "I appreciate it."

I know it's not anywhere near what she needs to get her brother out of trouble, but I hope she doesn't even try to do that. She needs to use that money for herself. She needs to cut him loose and let him face the consequences of his actions. I also know from family experience that's easy to say but not so easy to do.

5

LACEY

THIS IS TURNING INTO A PARTY, WHICH I'VE ALWAYS LOVED, but I wish it was anywhere else but here. The servers are giving me weird looks, and it's only a matter of time until Enrico discovers I'm sitting here drinking champagne after being fired.

But like Théo said, I'm a paying customer now. Well, except I'm not paying. Someone is, though.

Hmmm, I knocked back those glasses of Jack pretty quick.

Fuck it. Right now, I don't give a shit about anything. I lost my job and don't have enough money in the bank to pay the rent. Chris has disappeared and sicced the mob on me. I could go home and lock my doors and cry in my bed, but that won't change anything, and staying here and having a few drinks with some . . . well, strangers, but they seem decent, isn't going to change anything either.

I'm on my own in the world. I have been for a while, I have to admit, since Chris sure as hell isn't there for me.

He's doing the opposite in fact. I might as well do what I want.

I knock back my first glass of champagne all at once. Hey, those flutes are small.

"Easy there, lush puppy," Théo says. "I know you had a bad day, but you don't want to get ham sandwiched."

This strikes me as hilarious. I start to laugh, but then the laugh turns into a sob. This man doesn't even know me, but he knows I've had a shit day—no, a shit life—and my own brother doesn't care, and . . . and Théo's looking out for me. I could bawl my eyes out.

No. I am not going to feel sorry for myself. "I'm fine." I meet his eyes, determined to be cheerful. "But if I want to get ham sandwiched, I will."

His lips quirk. "Okay, sure."

"Let's go down to the pool bar," Brent suggests.

This sounds like a fun idea.

"But we just ordered all this champagne," Théo points out.

"That's not a problem," I tell him. "We can get to-go cups."

Crystal brings us the giant plastic wineglasses we give customers to take their leftover wine with them, which hold about half a bottle, and we fill them up and head to the elevator. She's giving me bug-eyed looks that clearly say, *What the hell is going on?*

We're all drinking champagne as Danny gets us into the pool party by giving the doorman some folded bills. I feel the thumping music inside me, dazzled by colored lights everywhere—the pool glows turquoise, the walls around the pool area shimmer with multicolored lights, and there's a big video screen above the stage at one end with spotlights that swing around. The beat of the music the DJ is playing surrounds us along with half naked, wet dancing bodies. The air is still warm and lots of people are in the pool, dancing in the water with their drinks in the air. It's a crazy party vibe, and we stroll around the pool taking it in. We're pretty much the only ones not wearing swimsuits, but oh well.

The song is "Make It Bounce" by Martin Vide, and everyone's bouncing all right. I can't help but move my shoulders to the music as we wander. A bunch of girls in bikinis eye the group of guys and smile at them, and next thing I know we've joined them. I don't know if these guys are all single or married, but I guess it's not my business if they want to party.

"Okay, not my scene," Jeff says to the guys. "I'm out. You young pups have fun."

"Same," says Ivan, who is apparently the coach of the team. They both give Théo bro hugs, exchanging final goodbyes and good lucks and backslaps while I stand and groove to the music, drinking champagne and wondering what the hell is happening.

The girls have a big high-top table, so I drop my backpack beneath it. And what the hell . . . I toe off my high heels and plant my bare feet onto the cement pool deck. Aw fuck, that feels good. I wiggle my toes and rock back and forth on my angry soles.

The music changes to "In My Mind" by Dynoro, a slower song but with a catchy, sexy beat. I'm still moving, and Théo notices and grins. He grabs my hips and pulls me up to him, moving our bodies together now to the sultry beat.

I smile at him as I drape my arms over his shoulders. "Are you married?"

"Fuck no." He frowns. "Why?"

"Just wondering." I jerk my head toward the other guys, now dancing with the girls they just met. "Are they?"

"No."

"Okay. Not that it matters to me. I mean, I don't even know you guys, and you're leaving tomorrow."

"Right."

Our bodies grind together in a way that's a bit dirty and a lot sexy, our eye contact holding and drawing out. The electronic beat of the music fills me up. I've still got my champagne and I take a sip.

"This is wild," Théo says.

"You don't party like this every weekend?"

"God no. I work way too much for stuff like this."

"Ah. Too bad." I pat his chest. Which is firm and muscular. I'm feeling a little warm between my thighs at our sexy dancing and the feel of his hands and his body and . . . his smile. The way it heats his eyes and reaches way inside me . . . My hand lingers on his chest, absorbing the heat from his body through his shirt. "Everyone deserves to have fun once in a while."

"Even you?" His gaze fastens on to my face. "Why do I have a feeling you don't get much fun either?"

I huff out a sigh. "Okay, not lately, true."

"I know you've got some big problems. But tonight . . . can just be for fun."

I slowly smile and move with his body. His eyes darken and his fingers tighten on my hips.

My skin buzzes, my heart picks up speed, and our eyes lock together in a trancelike connection of heat and desire.

When the song ends we move apart and turn back to the table.

"You guys are way overdressed for a pool party." One of the girls points at all of us.

"Yeah, you need to get wet!" another says.

Danny and Brent look at each other, shrug, and then they toss their cellphones onto the table, take two big steps, and jump in to the pool with a big splash.

I laugh and cringe a little as water drops splash me. I glance at Théo. His sculpted lips are curved into a smile and he's shaking his head. "Idiots."

"Come on, Wynn! Get in! The water's nice."

"I'm not the type of guy who jumps into a pool with his clothes on," he calls back to them.

I shoot him a curious, smiling glance. "No? No spontaneity?"

"I like to plan my spontaneity well ahead of time."

Another laugh bubbles up inside me, and as our eyes meet again we share the joke.

"Well, *I'm* the type." I walk to the edge of the pool, take a step, and drop straight down into the water. It's not deep here, only up to my chest.

The guys cheer me, and Théo is once again shaking his head, arms crossed.

"Come on!" I splash some water his way. "What did you just tell me?"

Sighing, he toes off his shoes, adds his cellphone to the

others on the table, and takes a running leap, sending up a geyser of water around us.

I'm laughing so hard. He finds me in the pool and clasps my waist. He's grinning too, water dripping from his hair. "This is nuts."

"This is Vegas, baby. Your last chance to let loose in Sin City before you leave."

The girls have jumped in too, now flirting with the other guys. There appears to be an unspoken understanding that Théo and I are together.

We dance and party in the pool as the DJ spins some great music. When we all get out, the guys take off their shirts and then their pants. They're all wearing boxers, which aren't much different than the swim shorts most guys are wearing. I'm jealous, because I'm stuck in a wet dress, not about to strip down to bra and panties.

I'm also having a hard time keeping my eyes off Théo's ripped torso and muscled shoulders. I mean, I can't even.

"You're wet," Théo says with a gleam in his eye.

"I am." I look down at myself, at the already tight dress clinging even more. "But this fabric will dry fast." There's no sun, but the air is still warm. I reach up to pull out the pins that hold my hair back for work, which kept it mostly dry in the pool, and let my long hair fall around me. I run my hands through it and shake it back. When I look up, Théo is regarding me with a hot, hungry expression.

"You have gorgeous hair," he says hoarsely.

"Thanks."

I don't know how much time passes or how many drinks are consumed as we party and dance, until the other guys are putting their clothes back on, apparently leaving with the girls. There are a few low-voiced comments between the men, and then they say goodbye to Théo as well with more hand clasps and bro hugs.

And Théo and I are alone.

We both still have drinks to finish. We lean on the table, music and lights pulsing around us.

"So, what are you going to do about those assholes who came after you tonight?"

I blow out a breath. "I don't know."

"Here's an idea." He sips his drink. "Come to California with me."

6

—

LACEY

"I wish I could do that," I say wistfully, gazing at people partying in the pool.

"Why not? You just got fired. You can't go home. You know you can't fix your brother. You don't have control over him."

"I know." I give a soft snort and shift to face him. "I can't even *find* him."

"He's going to show up. He's going to be looking for money."

"You're probably right. But I can go back to working as a budtender."

"A what? Bartender?"

"Budtender. At one of the cannabis dispensaries. I did that for a while."

"Seriously? Selling marijuana?"

"Yeah. I also worked as a camp counselor at a doggie daycare, and I've done face painting for kids. I actually loved that job." I pause. "Also, I do freelance makeup for some showgirls here, when I can."

"Uh . . . okay. I mean, I'm sure you'll have no trouble getting another job, but that's not the point. You need to cut him loose. You can't keep enabling him."

My bottom lip quivers. "I *know*."

"So come with me."

My chin drops nearly to my chest. "Are you serious?" I'd been sure he was making a drunken joke.

"Yeah. You might think this is spontaneous, but—"

"You can't tell me you've been planning all night to ask me to come with you."

"Well, no, but I have thought through the pros and cons. Listen, this could be a win-win situation for both of us. You can't go home. You don't have a job. Your brother needs to deal with his problems himself. You can stay with me as long as you want. His bookies won't find you there. *He* won't find you there."

"All true," I say slowly. "But what's in it for *you*?"

"I told you about my brother and Emma."

"Your girlfriend."

"Ex."

"Right."

"If I go home with a gorgeous new girlfriend, I won't feel like such a pathetic loser."

Gorgeous. My belly heats. "But I'm not your girlfriend."

"We'll tell them you are."

I throw back my head and laugh. "Oh my God! Are we acting out a romance novel? Nobody does that in real life."

"Why not?"

"Because it's crazy, that's why."

"You seem like you don't mind a bit of adventure."

I purse my lips and regard him. He's right. And I'm just drunk enough to think that disappearing for a while with this man is a *fantastic* idea.

The responsibility I've had to learn over the years, looking after my mom, looking after Chris, finding jobs and paying bills and cooking meals, is instilled in me enough that I hesitate. I don't even know this man. This could be the stupidest thing I've ever done, and I've done some dumb things.

The allure of it is irresistible, though. A chance to chuck my problems, leave them behind me and escape. Even if it's just for a while.

"Okay, if you don't want to be a pretend girlfriend, here's something even better . . . you can be my real wife."

My mouth falls open again, my eyes bugging out wide. "Wife?"

"We're in Vegas. A quickie marriage totally makes sense. Right?"

I laugh. "Absolutely." Now I know he's not serious.

"How do we do that?" He pulls out his phone and starts swiping at the screen.

"Stop. We don't have to get married."

"Sure, we do. I have to make an honest woman of you."

Laughter bubbles up inside me again. "You'd only have to do that if we'd slept together first."

"If you insist." He's still looking at his phone, but his lips quirk. "Damn. We need to get a marriage license."

"Oh well."

"No, we have time. They're open until midnight. Let's go."

I'm laughing and protesting as he grabs my backpack. I nearly trip as I try to slide my feet into my pumps, one hand in his as he tugs me out of the pool party. This is not happening.

Out in front of the hotel, I try to reason with him, even though my blood is racing with excitement. I haven't done something this wild in a long, long time. There hasn't been a lot of time for fun in my life for a long, long time.

"Look," I say. "If you're not the kind of guy to jump into a pool with your clothes on, you're not the type of guy for a quickie Vegas marriage."

"I *did* jump into the pool with my clothes on."

"Um . . . okay, you got me there. I'm just worried you're going to regret this."

"It's just temporary. You need to get out of town. I need a girlfriend. Er, wife. Right?"

I shove a hand into my hair, rub the back of my head and then down through my hair. Then I grin. "Right."

He grins back. A taxi pulls up and we jump in. He gives the driver the address on Clark Avenue. "And hurry," he says. "We have to make it there by midnight."

"You got it."

It takes us about ten minutes to get there. As we drive, Théo is on his phone again. "Okay, I found a chapel that's still open." He makes the call and books us in.

We arrive at the courthouse. Théo asks the taxi driver to wait for us, which seems extravagant to me since we have no idea how long this will take. Actually, it can't take that long, because they close in ten minutes. As we run up the steps, I take in the sign above the door: MARRIAGE LICENSE BUREAU.

I know it's crazy. I just don't care.

It's not busy at all there; in fact on this Tuesday night, we're the only ones there, so it doesn't take long to get the license. Then we're back in the taxi, on our way to Las Vegas Boulevard.

I've been to one of these weddings before; my friend Karine and her husband did this. Only they planned it a little more than we did. She at least had a white dress and flowers and me there as her maid of honor. I have nobody. I'm wearing a dress I just wore in a pool, smelling of chlorine, and I bet my mascara is smudged under my eyes.

I don't care.

The neon sign above the door of the wedding chapel glows hot pink and blue. I laugh out loud at the flashing bulbs around the sign. Ridiculous.

We cross the terra-cotta tiles past some potted palms and bright flowers, and enter the building. Again, at this hour, we're the only ones here.

The woman who greets us starts to talk, then says, "Lacey!"

Oh my God. "Janaya! Hi!"

Théo watches, bemused, as we hug.

"How are you?" I ask her. "I haven't seen you in ages."

"I'm good! I have three babies. They're awesome!"

"Oh wow, that's amazing!"

I turn to Théo. "Théo, this is Janaya. We went to high school together. Janaya, this is Théo."

"You're getting married!" She claps her hands together. "Exciting!"

I'm not about to tell her the whole story. "*So* exciting!"

"Okay, let's do this. Come this way."

Janaya is obviously experienced at her job, running through the different packages. "The traditional wedding is $79.99. It includes the officiant signing the marriage certificate, a witness—which I assume you need since you're here alone; that would be me." She flashes a white smile. "And one complimentary photograph. Then there's the signature wedding, which is $149.99, and includes music, fifteen digital photos, a wedding bouquet and boutonniere, witness if necessary—again, me." She beams. "We also have—"

"We'll take that," Théo says. "The signature wedding."

"Of course!"

"We don't need to spend that much," I say to Théo in a low aside.

He laughs. "You need a bouquet."

I roll my eyes.

Janaya bustles away to do her stuff, and when she returns she's carrying not only a bouquet and boutonniere, but a veil. "It's not included," she whispers. "But who cares."

She helps me fasten the veil to my head in front of a mirror. "I like it." I turn my head and the tiara glitters in the lights. "I've always loved tiaras." I've always loved anything sparkly.

Moments later, it's all over and we are pronounced man and wife. "You may kiss your bride," the officiant tells Théo.

Our eyes meet. I suddenly feel shy. Not that I don't want to kiss him—I do. I have pretty much since I met him, when was that . . . four hours ago?

But kissing is for real.

He smiles at me, bends his head, and brushes his mouth over mine.

My belly flutters and flips even at that brief touch, my skin electrifying. We stare into each other's eyes again, and then Théo wraps one arm around my waist and pulls me up against him, like when we were dancing earlier, except this is different. Then he crushes his mouth to mine.

I melt into him, clutching the bouquet of pink silk roses in one hand, the other going to his neck. My mouth opens to his hungry kiss, and, oh my God, he tastes good, he feels good, and wow, can he ever *kiss*.

We draw apart, breathing a little fast, blinking a lot. I swallow. "Wow," I whisper.

"Yeah." He smiles.

We pose for photos, which I don't take seriously at all given our rumpled, drunken state, making faces at the camera while Théo dips me in his arms and I clutch my tiara, then me pretending to throw my bouquet.

Amazingly, our taxi is still waiting for us. I have no idea how much the fare will be, but apparently Théo doesn't care. He directs the driver to take us back to the Wellborne.

Standing out front, the lights in the hotel lobby glowing, we face each other. Our eyes meet in another one of those showers of sparks that keeps happening, sparks I feel way down low in my belly.

What happens now?

I think about that kiss at the chapel, and how I want more. And yet, I'm nervous.

"What do you want to do?" Théo asks in a husky voice. "Celebrate?"

"Absolutely!" I jump on this suggestion. "It's only one-thirty in the morning. Early by Vegas standards."

"Are you hungry? I'm hungry."

"Yeah."

The Strip is still glittering and flashing, still lots people walking, cars swishing up and down Las Vegas Boulevard.

He takes my hand. "Let's wander a bit."

"Wait. I want to change my shoes." I sit on the stone wall and pull my Chucks out of my backpack.

Théo grins.

We stop at a place that has tables and chairs outside on a patio, and he buys us burgers and fries.

"Thank you," I say, picking up a French fry. "If only they had chocolate sauce."

"Say what now?"

I laugh. "I love chocolate sauce on my fries."

He tilts his head and gives me a narrow-eyed look. "You can't be serious."

"Sure. Why not? It's good. Salty and sweet. You must have some kind of weird food combo you like."

"Uh . . . okay, but you can't tell anyone else." He leans closer.

I mime zipping my lips shut.

"I put salt and pepper on apples."

My eyes pop wide. "No way!"

"Hey. I accepted your weird food fetish."

"It's not a fetish," I object, picking up another fry. "A fetish is a sexual desire. Although I'll admit chocolate on fries is nearly orgasmic." I eat my fry, then ask, "Do you have food fetishes?"

"No. Not food."

"Oh . . . what then?" I too lean forward.

"I don't think we know each other well enough to share our sexual fetishes."

"We're married!"

"Hmm. True. Okay, I'll share mine. I love long hair."

I smile and fluff my hair. "Oh really?"

He eyes my hair with such a heated look I feel it down between my legs again. "Yeah."

After we finish eating, we stroll along the Strip. As we walk, we approach a couple of women dressed in what I guess are supposed to be cop uniforms, although the short shorts and tight jackets over silver-sequin bras are probably not regulation.

"Hey, guys! You wanna get spanked?" One woman holds up a crop, the other a pair of cuffs.

"Speaking of fetishes," Théo mutters.

We keep going, laughing.

"Is it the uniform that turns you on?" I tease. "Or the spanking?"

"I'm not into *being* spanked."

"Ah." This is interesting.

We next encounter a man in a Batman costume who jumps out at us with his wings spread, then a couple of women dressed like showgirls with big feathered wings and headpieces, except they're both clearly drunk. One has a drooping wing and a broken heel on her shoe, making her limp, the other holding on to her, her headpiece sagging over her eyes.

We go into a couple of casinos, and Théo spends twenty dollars on a few slot machines. I refuse to touch the things because I'm terrified that I'll be like Chris, and the slot machines will be like crack and once I push those buttons I'll be addicted and descend into gambling hell.

When we leave there, we pass a place that sells tequila slushies. "As if we need more booze," he mutters, but then he buys us each one to go, and we carry them as we stroll down the street. I suck some back and, whoa—not only are these huge, they're strong.

Eventually we stop and sit on the edge of the fountain outside the Cipriani, drinking our slushies. I toe off my shoes and swivel to put my feet into the cool water. "Aaaaah."

"Is that allowed?" Théo asks.

"I have no idea. I don't care. It's not like there are a lot of people around."

He takes off his shoes, rolls his pants up, and dunks his feet.

"You don't wear socks."

"Nope. Never. Socks are the devil."

I laughed. "Even with a suit?"

"Even with a suit."

I stir my slushie with the straw. "Okay, tell me more about where we're going."

"Marina del Rey. A guy who used to play for the Condors owns the condo. Apparently there are three units, and his was sitting empty, so I'm renting it from him."

"The Condors are . . . ?"

"The team I'll be working for. The California Condors."

"Ah."

"My mom's helping get things set up for me."

"Your parents live there too?"

"Oh. Yeah. Well, not Santa Monica. My dad actually owns a different team."

"What? Are you serious?" I gape at him. "Your family owns *two* hockey teams?"

He smiles. "It does sound kind of crazy, doesn't it? My grandpa owns the Condors, and my dad owns the Golden Eagles in Long Beach. Well, my dad and some other investors. That's a pretty recent thing." He sighs. "I think my dad just bought the team to piss off my grandpa."

"That's quite a gesture." I can't even imagine how much a hockey team costs, but I'm sure it's more than I'll ever see in my lifetime. "He must have been *really* pissed."

"It's a long story. Long and ugly."

"Ugh. Families." I hold out my slushie cup.

He taps his against it. "Right?"

"So you're going to work for your grandpa . . . and your dad's team will be one of your opponents."

"Yep."

"What does your dad think of that?"

"Now he's pissed at me too. Fraternizing with the enemy."

I study the way his jaw has tensed. "That must have been a tough decision."

He rubs the back of his neck. "Yeah. It was."

"Your dad will get over it."

He shakes his head. "You don't know how my dad holds a grudge."

"But you're his son." I bump his shoulder with mine.

"Eh. Who knows. Meanwhile, I have a job to do."

"How old are you?"

"Twenty-eight."

"Isn't that young to be running a team? How old is Jeff?"

Théo's lips curve. "Jeff's forty-five. There's only been one other GM in the league who was under thirty."

"That's impressive. Or did your grandpa just hire you to piss off your dad?"

His entire body tenses, and I slap my hand to my mouth. "I'm kidding! Of course he didn't do that."

"Not so sure," he mutters, dropping his head. "Although he did talk a good game when he came to recruit me. I either have the most amazing opportunity ever or I've been completely suckered."

"You don't strike me as a sucker."

"Kinda felt that way when my girlfriend was cheating on me with my brother behind my back."

Right. He'd mentioned that earlier. "That doesn't make you a sucker," I say firmly. "That makes them jerks."

His smile warms me and he leans into me. "Thanks."

I eye Théo. He rescued me from those thugs earlier. Twice, sort of. He seems like a good guy, maybe a little nerdy, but that's not a bad thing. His body is anything but nerdy, though, and I'm finding him more and more attractive.

And he feels like a pathetic loser because of what his skanky ex-girlfriend did. I run my tongue over my teeth. I can't wait to meet that bish and make her realize what she lost out on.

"Oh my God!" I throw my hand out toward the lightening sky. "The sun is coming up!"

"Happens every morning," he agrees.

"We've been up all night!"

"Yep."

"When are you leaving?"

"I plan to leave at noon. It's about a four-and-a-half-hour drive."

"Oh my God. You must want to get some sleep before we go."

"That would probably be a good idea."

I shake my head. "This is so nuts."

"Yep." He swivels, stands, and holds out a hand. "Come on."

We walk back to the Wellborne, not the only ones staggering down the Strip at dawn. In the lobby, I pause at seeing some of the shops which stay open twenty-four/seven. "I'm going to need a few things."

"I can take you to your place to pack some stuff before we leave tomorrow."

"Today."

"Oh yeah. Right."

"Okay. I'll just grab a couple of things for now."

I pick up a toothbrush, toothpaste, and antiperspirant. A pair of panties and a sundress to wear later. I have other basics in my backpack—a makeup kit, hairbrush—which will get me through til I can get home. I also grab a phone charger. I pay for these items with the tip I was given earlier, for which I am now grateful.

We go up to Théo's room. Walking in, quiet coolness envelops us. A suitcase sits open on the luggage rack, the contents packed with precise neatness. Unlike how I pack. Not that I've traveled a lot.

I yawn.

"Tired?"

"I think I'm crashing. Can you be hungover before you even go to sleep?"

He chuckles. "Possibly. Want a shower before we go to bed?"

The air in the room instantly goes hot. Electricity sizzles over my nerve endings as we eye each other. I know what we're both thinking.

7

LACEY

"Probably a good idea," I say in a husky voice.

He gestures to the bathroom. "Go ahead. I'll shower after."

I can't help the flicker of disappointment. I nod and trudge into the bathroom, suddenly exhausted. There, I wash my hair, face, and body, which still smell a little like the chlorine in the pool, and after, rub hotel-provided body lotion into my skin.

I only half-dry my hair because it takes for-freaking-ever, it's so long and thick. I just want to get most of the water out of it. It'll look terrible later, but I'll deal with it.

Théo's sprawled in a chair looking at his phone when I come out, a towel wrapped around me. He's already shed his pants and shirt, and is in his boxers, his long legs stretched out in front of him, ankles crossed.

"Your turn!" I say brightly, clutching my towel.

He looks at me and his eyes sweep down from my face

to my toes and back up, lingering on my bare legs and then my shoulders. My skin heats and my belly does a little flip.

He drops his phone on the dresser and rises. He moves toward me, and in the narrow space there's barely room for him to pass me without touching. He deliberately sets his hands on my waist to shift me out of the way and shivery sensation slides down inside me.

But he keeps going and strides into the bathroom.

A sigh escapes me.

I open the curtains and gaze out at the early morning view of Vegas, mountains hazy in the distance. Then I dig in my purse for my phone and send Karine a text message.

I deliberate over what exactly to tell her. No matter what I say, she's going to freak out, so I settle for telling her I'm going to Los Angeles for a while. I don't want to alarm her, but . . . I bite my lip.

Théo left his wallet on the dresser, so I flip it open. The water's still running in the bathroom. Feeling a bit guilty, I finger through it and find his driver's license. He's already changed it to a California license with his new address, so that's a win. I take a picture of it with my phone and send it to Karine.

I am with this man. If you don't hear from me in a week

I pause. Delete, delete, delete.

I am with this man. If you don't hear from me in three days, call the police and tell th

Delete, delete, delete.

I am with this man. Just FYI. We're going to Marina del Rey for a while.

I slide the license back into his wallet as I hear the water stop. Still no contact from Chris. Damn.

I eye the lone king-size bed in the room. I should be in bed when Théo comes out, but . . . dammit. I smack my forehead. I didn't buy anything to sleep in.

I did buy panties though, and I quickly pull a pair out of the bag, remove the tags, and slip them on under the towel.

Théo emerges with a towel around his waist, and once again, it's hard to tear my eyes away. Jesus on a pita, he's in good shape. Droplets of water cling to his golden skin—he must not spend *all* his time in an office, because he's got a tan—and I want to lick them off, starting at the one just above his navel . . . or maybe that one tracing down over a very fit oblique . . .

I lift my gaze to see him watching me. I hope I'm not literally drooling. I wipe my mouth, heat spreading from my chest up to my face, turning my cheeks what must be crimson. "I, uh, was going to get into bed, but I don't have anything to sleep in."

His lips quirk. "Fine with me."

I tilt my head and give him a reproving look.

He strides over to his suitcase and pulls out a neatly folded T-shirt. "Here you go."

"Thanks." It's super soft, well-worn gray cotton. Swallowing, I give him my back, drop the towel, and lower the shirt over my head. I hear a faint noise almost like a groan as I do so, and I know he's watching me, naked other than white panties that don't cover much.

I turn to face him, lifting my hair free of the shirt. He's still standing in the exact same spot, his eyes glittering behind his glasses, his lips parted.

My body vibrates with tension and arousal as heat flares between us.

I break the eye contact and move over to the bed, tugging the puffy duvet back to slide beneath it.

Heaven.

I worked at this hotel, but I've sure as hell never slept here. This bed is amazing. The mattress molds to my body, the pillow is like a cloud, and the duvet sinks slowly down over me in a light hug.

Théo turns to his suitcase and yep, I watch as he drops the towel and steps into another pair of boxers. My chest tightens and my belly heats seeing his amazing body completely naked—from behind, mind you. It's an athlete's body, with strong thighs, a firm ass I want to bite, and rippling muscles all up his back.

When I assumed the guys he was with were all hockey players, he said he didn't play hockey. *Not anymore, anyway.*

Which means he must have played hockey at some point. That would explain the muscles. I need to know more.

Except . . . I'm so very sleepy . . . I'm not so drunk that the room is spinning, but I'm definitely buzzed. My eyes drift closed.

I vaguely feel the bed move as Théo joins me, the duvet lifting then settling again. He hesitates, then wraps an arm around my middle and pulls my back against his front. I wriggle in to get comfy, reveling in the feel of hot, hair-roughened male skin, big bones and muscles curved around me, which elicits another faint groan. Laying my hand over his arm, I plunge into sleep.

THÉO

I'm dreaming about birds. No, cats. No . . . it's a baby. Crying.

But right here beside me, in bed.

Not a baby. It's Lacey.

I jerk out of sleep and into wakefulness. "Lacey." I set a hand on her shoulder. She's rolled away from me and onto her stomach, her shoulders shaking, her face buried in the pillow, which muffles her sobs. I massage her gently. "Hey. What's wrong?"

She shakes her head violently and takes a shuddery breath.

"Baby. Shhh. It's okay." I stroke my hand up and down her back over my T-shirt. Crying usually freaks me out, but right now I only have a strong urge to comfort her and protect her. "It's okay."

I have no idea what she's crying about. Clearly, it's not okay, but I don't know what else to say.

"Tell me," I urge softly. "What's wrong?"

"M-my brother." She shifts onto her side and swipes at her face. "I can't believe he d-did that to me."

"Ah."

I guess it just sunk in, after our night of drunken revelry. What he did was definitely a douche move.

"He sent those guys after me!" She sobs again. "His own sister! How could he do that?"

I have no answer for that, because I want to punch Chris's face. Repeatedly.

"He's my only family."

Her doleful words yank at my heartstrings.

"I thought we'd be there for each other after Mom died. All we had was each other. I didn't expect him to look after me, but I at least thought we'd have each other's backs. And then he does *that*! It's the w-worst thing he could do," she cries. "Selling me to pay his debts! He had to know what those guys wanted to do with me. Oh my God!" Then she flips and turns into me, burying her face in my chest. "What if you hadn't been there? What would I have done?"

I wrap my arms around her, one hand cupping the back of her head and holding her close. I don't want to think about what she would have done if I hadn't been there. Except . . . "I don't know you very well, but I have faith that you would have been okay, baby." I stroke her hair gently. "And you know what? I bet Chris had faith in you too. That somehow you'd come through."

She sniffs and pulls in a juddering breath. "He shouldn't have done that. He shouldn't have put me in that position. And I don't know if I would have been okay. Those guys were serious. Seriously bad."

"Can't argue with that. But you're strong. I know it. Shhh. It's okay. It's done." I keep petting her, trying to comfort her, but damn, her sweet, soft body pressed up against mine like this is distracting me. Arousing me. "You're safe. You're here with me. And I'm going to make sure you stay safe."

"Thank you." She hiccups. "I'm sorry I woke you."

"No, it's fine. You're okay."

She nods and her breathing settles down, with the odd sniffle and sigh. And she falls back asleep.

That fucking asshole.

I set the alarm on my phone for noon. I'd planned to

leave at noon, but I hadn't planned to stay up all night, so I grudgingly move back my departure time. I want to get on the road before it gets too late. When I hear the tones of the alarm though, I sure as hell don't want to get out of bed.

My head is pounding, my mouth is dry and tastes like I licked the bottom of a trash can. It hurts when I crack my eyes open, even though the drapes are drawn. And . . . there's a warm, soft woman snuggled up in my arms.

Lacey.

My wife.

I was pretty hammered last night but I remember everything. We went and got fucking married. Total Vegas cliché, just as I'm on my way out of town.

A groan climbs up my throat. Lacey stirs next to me and rolls her head around. "You okay?"

"I'm not sure." I reach out a hand and slap it down on the night table to find my phone and shut off the eardrum-rupturing noise. "You?"

She moans and my morning wood takes notice of the sexy sound. "I need some Advil."

"Me too."

"I have some." She rolls out of bed, shoves both her hands into her hair and pushes it off her face, then marches to her backpack sitting on the floor by the desk. She returns with a small bottle and a glass of water from the bathroom. "Here."

"Thank you, Jesus." I toss the pills into my mouth and swallow them down, then fall back onto the pillow. "Okay. Give me a few minutes and we'll know if I'm going to live."

She laughs softly and climbs back on the bed, sitting cross-legged. Her tits jiggle enticingly beneath my T-shirt and her legs are gorgeous—long, smooth, and tanned. I'd love those legs wrapped around me while I— "You'll live. Wow." She shakes her hair back again. "I haven't gotten that drunk in a long time."

"Me neither."

She nibbles her bottom lip. "You, ah, remember . . ."

"I remember." I blow out a gusty breath. "I must have lost my mind last night. I do *not* do shit like that."

I fucking jumped in a pool with my clothes on, drinking champagne out of a to-go cup. And then I got married. Jesus Christ.

"Neither do I. Well. Not for a long time anyway."

My eyes laser on to her face. "You've been married before?"

"No! I just meant I haven't partied like that for a long time. I used to be a bit of a wild child. Then my mom got sick and I had to grow up fast."

I frown. "Right. You mentioned she'd passed away."

"Yeah. She had ovarian cancer. She died a couple of years ago."

"I'm sorry."

"I miss her. We had a sort of strange life, but she was a good mom."

I want to know more, but we need to hit the road. "You want to shower?"

"I'm good. I just need to fix my hair." She rolls her eyes and ruffles it. "The bane of my existence."

"I love your hair." Shit. The words popped right out of my mouth.

"It's that hair fetish, right?" She smirks at me and slides off the bed.

True enough. I could fantasize a whole lotta dirty things about her and her hair.

She disappears into the bathroom. I just showered a few hours ago too, so I drag my hungover ass out of bed and get dressed, finding a pair of khaki shorts and a T-shirt. I pack what I was wearing yesterday neatly into my suitcase. I just need my toiletry bag from the bathroom and I'll be good to go.

I sit on the edge of the bed and rub the stubble on my face, then roll my head to ease the stiffness in my neck. I'm afraid to think too much about what happened last night. Except thinking and analyzing is what I do best.

Am I really taking this woman to California with me? I don't even know her. The doubts from last night prod me again. Do I really believe her? About her brother, about getting fired from her job? Am I once again the biggest sucker in the world? Have I learned nothing?

I can't trust people—I've learned that the hard way. I thought Emma loved me. I thought my brother loved me. They both screwed me over. My dad is pissed because I took this job. Everything good in my life gets yanked away from me. I need to be more careful.

But then I think about the way she was terrified and trembling. Her sobs last night when she was so devastated by what her brother did. She can't be pulling a con on me. Can she?

Welp. We're married. I committed to taking her to California. But it's not forever, and I'm not going to get sucked into anything more than that. She's not getting half my money, that's for damn sure, and I'll start looking into how we get a divorce or annulment ASAP. But just in case she's really in danger from those assholes—and although my memories from last night are a tad fuzzy, I do remember being pretty convinced they're scum of the earth—she's coming with me.

Also, I had a reason for getting married. It may have been a quick decision, but there was a rationale behind it. It'll be so satisfying to show up with a woman when I have to face JP and Emma.

Lacey comes out of the bathroom wearing the dress she bought last night, her hair back up in a loose bun. She looks fresh and pretty, which is unfair because I feel haggard and old. She also does not look like a con woman. Even so, I need to stay woke.

She eyes my shirt. "Nice shirt."

I look down it. It reads, I'M RIGHT 97% OF THE TIME. I look back up with a grin. "Truth."

I forgo shaving, just brushing my teeth, splashing cold water on my face, and rubbing antiperspirant onto my pits. The pounding in my head is starting to ease.

"We need food," I announce as I leave the bathroom. I set my toiletry kit into the space reserved for it in my suitcase and zip it up.

"Sure. Want to eat here or grab something on the road?"

"Let's eat here."

We have a quick breakfast in the coffee shop, getting our coffees in paper cups that we can take with us.

The valet brings my car around to the front of the Wellborne. It seems like it should be early morning, but it's early afternoon. I've experienced this kind of disorientation before in Vegas . . . in the casinos and bars, you never know what time it is.

"Nice car," Lacey says as we load our things into the back.

I just bought this Audi Q8, a sort of SUV-coupe crossover. Audis are nice, but also practical. "Thanks. I've already filled up with gas, and I have some bottles of water and snacks for the road."

"You're prepared." She slants me an amused glance as she fastens her seatbelt.

"I do like to plan ahead." I pause. "Usually."

She laughs softly.

"Also, I've mapped out the route, so I know where gas stations are. We don't want to run out of gas in the middle of the desert."

"Certainly not," she agrees.

I switch out my regular glasses for my prescription sunglasses because the sun is burning my eyes up, and we're off.

Lacey gives me directions to her place. As I drive, she pulls out her phone and busies herself with reading and sending some text messages. "My friend Karine," she explains. "In case you're thinking about killing me and throwing my body into the Pacific Ocean, she knows I'm with you."

I choke. "Good God."

She grins.

A short time later, I park in front of a nondescript but well-kept apartment building.

"I'll be right back." She flicks off her seatbelt.

"Oh no. I'm coming with you." I have visions of Ed and

Lincoln skulking in her hallway. Or maybe even having broken into her apartment to wait for her.

She hesitates. "Okay."

Her apartment is on the second floor, so we take the stairs. I'm on alert, and when she stops at her door I try the knob before she can insert her key. Still locked. That's good.

I don't let my guard down though, motioning her to wait as I open the door and step inside. I sense the emptiness of the apartment—still, flat air scented faintly with the same fragrance I smelled on Lacey's skin last night when she snuggled into me . . . apples and flowers.

I poke my head into each room.

"What are you doing?" Lacey frowns at me.

"Just checking the place out."

"I know it's not the greatest." Her frown slips into a crooked smile.

"I'm just making sure Ed and Lincoln aren't here."

Her eyes widen. "Shit. You think they'd break in?"

"Seems like they'd do pretty much anything if they're threatening your brother's life."

She glances nervously over her shoulder, closes the door, and locks it. "I'll pack."

I tag behind her into her bedroom. The scent is stronger here, and the room is prettier—the walls pale pink, the comforter on the bed a sort of watercolor floral pattern in shades of bright pink, blue, and green, with about five hundred pillows stacked against the headboard. A pink shag rug sits atop worn linoleum.

Lacey hauls a suitcase out of the closet and sets it on the bed. Then my eyes bug out and horror grips me as she opens a drawer, grabs a handful of what appear to be panties and tosses them in the suitcase. This is followed by bras, T-shirts, shorts, and some things she seizes from the closet. She makes a halfhearted attempt to fold a couple of dresses, then smashes them in with the other clothing.

I press a hand to the pain in my chest. "What are you doing?"

"Packing. There are some things in the bathroom I need." She disappears and returns a moment later with a bright pink sequined bag apparently stuffed with . . . I don't even know. She flings it into the suitcase too. Next she grabs a bag with knitting needles sticking out the top—knitting needles!—and tosses it in.

Sucking her bottom lip between her teeth, she stands and looks around. She takes a few steps over to a tall dresser, shoots me a self-conscious glance, then picks up a stuffed toy. She quickly buries it beneath the crumpled clothing in the luggage.

I smile. "What is that?"

"Pete. Pete the Penguin. My mom gave him to me. I was always fascinated by penguins as a kid."

The pain in my chest from watching her chaotic packing eases and shifts into warmth. I nod.

"Okay, I'm ready!" She attempts to close the case, wrestling with the zipper.

I sigh. "If you packed things neatly, you'd have more room."

"No, I wouldn't. It's the same amount of clothes. It won't make a difference in how much room they take up if they're arranged differently."

"Yes. It will." I nudge her aside and zip up the suitcase, then lift it off the bed. "Anything else you need to do?"

She walks out to the living room, stands in the middle, and looks around. "I have no idea how long I'll be gone. I don't have any plants to water. I don't get much mail. I guess it's all good here for a while."

"Okay. Let's hit the road, Jack."

She smiles and starts singing the song. "No more, no more, no more," she sings as she locks the door behind us and we start down the hall.

We're just entering the stairwell when the elevator dings at the other end of the hall. I glance over my shoulder and —*fuck!*—Ed and Lincoln step out of the elevator.

"Shit!" My heart lurches. "Lacey—go!" I whisper, giving her a shove.

"Jeez, slow your roll," she mutters.

"They're here," I say in her ear. "Get your cute ass down the stairs right fucking now."

I hear a shout at the end of the hall.

"Fuck, they saw us. Go!"

She scampers down the stairs and I follow. I can't move fast enough with this goddamn suitcase, so I abandon it and leap down the stairs close behind Lacey. Blasting into the building's foyer, I hear steps clattering behind us.

"Run to the vehicle!" I grab my key fob and fumble to unlock the doors as we run. Lacey yanks open the passenger door and throws herself in. I sprint to my own door, start the car before my door's even closed, pitch it into gear, and peel out.

Lacey's crumpled on the seat, but she leans over to peer out the back window. "Oh my God! I can't believe this!"

"Put your seatbelt on." I fasten my own with one hand.

"Thugs are chasing us, probably with guns, and you're worried about our *seatbelts*?"

"Habit." I rub my chest. "I think I'm having a heart attack."

"Me too." She lets out a long breath. "Holy shit."

"Yeah." I keep glancing in the rearview mirror to see if they try to follow us. I make a fast right turn, then a left, then a right, zigzagging through the residential neighborhood.

"My suitcase . . . ?"

"I'm sorry. I had to leave it."

She's silent, and when I glance at her a moment later, she swipes at a tear on her cheek. Shit.

"We'll get you new stuff in L.A."

She nods, her chin quivering.

"What's wrong?"

"Pete. I lost Pete."

Ah, fuck. I forgot about the penguin. "I'm sorry."

She nods. "I know. We didn't have much choice if we wanted to get away from them." She emits a long sigh. "And I was going to knit on the way there."

She gives me directions to get onto the freeway. Even if they followed us, there is no way they'll find us in this traffic. "I don't know if they even tried to follow us, but I think we're okay."

"I'm sorry." Her voice is small.

"For what?"

"For dragging you into this mess."

"I think I kind of dragged myself into it," I say ruefully. "It's all good. We're fine and you're leaving that mess behind."

"Yeah." She gazes out the side window. Then she says, "Now I'm really worried about Chris. Those guys mean business." She pulls out her phone and taps away at the screen.

"Trying one more time?"

"Yeah. I just told him I got married and I'm moving to California to get away from him and his thugs. Let's see if *that* gets a response."

I hope so, because much as I think the guy's a loser, he's Lacey's brother and doesn't deserve to die in the desert.

"This isn't the most scenic drive," I offer once we've left the city and are in the desert.

"I like the desert."

It's flat, monochromatic golden-brown except for a bit of scrub here and there, even the mountains carved out of golden-brown earth, the highway stretching out smooth in front of us. The sky extends wide open clear blue above us. I set the cruise control so I'm not tempted to hit the pedal to the metal and speed past the other traffic, which would be easy to do on this road.

"Okay," I say. "I think we lost them."

"Whew."

I have so many questions for this woman. I'm still hesitant to believe everything she says, but she makes me curious. "Tell me about your mom."

Her head whips around. "What?"

"You mentioned earlier that your childhood was a bit crazy. Why's that?"

"Oh." She draws in a breath and lets it out. "My mom was a dancer. A showgirl."

"Whoa."

She smiles. "Yeah. She danced in a lot of different shows. And yes, she was topless sometimes. Other times, she'd wear pasties. She was gorgeous—tall, long legs, perfect figure." She sighs. "And a beautiful face. She loved dancing. She was talented. She'd done well in her younger days, and she had an amazing run, really. She was forty-two when she got cancer, and well, it was getting tougher for her to find jobs. She'd actually been unemployed for a while before that."

"She must have had you when she was young. Although I don't know how old you are." I'm guessing early twenties.

"I'm twenty-four. And yes, she was young. Accidental pregnancy." She flashes a crooked smile. "I never knew my dad. Some dude in town for a business convention that she hooked up with, and despite protection, my brother and I were born."

"You're twins?"

"Yeah. I'm older. I like to remind him of that. Anyway, she never planned to be a single mom, but there she was. We got to hang out backstage at a lot of the resorts. I was fascinated by the costumes and the makeup, which inspired me to take some courses in stage makeup after high school. I would have liked to get a college diploma or something, but then Mom got sick, so that didn't happen."

"Right. You mentioned you do freelance work."

"Yes." She nods. "I met lots of people in the business through my mom, and they knew I was good at doing makeup, so they hired me. It's not bad money, except it would be better if it was a steady paycheck and not just here and there. I've done some fashion shows too, and once

I helped out with a movie being filmed in Vegas. That was cool. I learned a lot."

"I'm impressed."

"It's just makeup."

I'm getting the feeling that life hasn't been easy for Lacey, despite her air of cheery optimism. "A job is never 'just' anything," I say. "Especially if you love it."

"True enough. Even being a budtender. I know you think I'm a stoner now."

I choke on a laugh. "No, I don't!"

She laughs too. "Kidding. Okay, you better tell me about your family. First your brother. What's his name? Or should I just call him Ben?"

"Ben?"

"Short for Benedict Arnold."

"Ha. Good one. His name is Jean Paul, but we call him JP." I sense her staring at me, and I glance sideways at her. "What?"

"Are you French?"

"Yeah. I mean, my mom's French."

"Like French Canadian?"

"Yes." A smile lifts my lips.

"Oh my God! You speak French?"

"Oui."

"That is so hot!"

I laugh again. "Okay."

"So, JP and . . . Emma? They're still together?"

"As far as I know. I haven't been in touch with them much since that all went down."

"Ugh. Don't blame you. What does JP do?"

Bitterness squeezed my throat. "He plays for the Golden Eagles."

"The team your dad owns?" Her voice rises.

"Yep." My hands tighten on the steering wheel.

"Wow."

"JP played for them before Dad bought the team."

"So . . . let me get this straight. Your dad bought the team to piss off your grandpa because he owns a rival team. Your brother plays for your dad's team and you . . . 'play' for your grandpa's team."

"That's it in a nutshell." There was actually more to it than that—a lot more—but that was enough family feuding for now.

"Plus you and your brother are on the outs because of a woman."

"Right."

"I just have one question."

"What?"

"Can you turn the car around and take me back to Vegas?"

8

THÉO

My head whips around, my jaw going slack. "What?"

"Kidding! Hey, eyes on the road!"

I snap my gaze back in front. "Jesus."

She laughs. "Sorry. I was just joking. Believe me, your family feud sounds less scary than Ed and Lincoln."

"Which dude was Lincoln?"

"The short one who didn't talk."

"Huh."

"Okay, tell me more about your family. What are your mom's and dad's names?"

"My dad is Matthew; my mom's Aline."

"Aline." She pronounces it carefully, imitating me, so that it sounds like Ah-lynn. "Okay. No other siblings?"

"Nope. I have a couple of cousins, and I have an aunt and three uncles who are younger than me."

"Wait, what?"

"I know, I know, it's weird. My grandpa—"

"Your boss."

"Yes. He's on his second marriage. My grandma died before I was born, and Grandpa remarried. They have four kids who are technically my aunt and uncles, but they feel more like cousins."

"Wow."

"Just wait till you meet them all."

She grimaces. "Can't wait." She slouches a little into the seat, then lifts her bare feet up onto the dash of my car. The loose skirt of her sundress falls down on her thighs and my body tightens in response to seeing those long, bare legs.

"Hey. Feet off the dash."

"My feet are clean."

"Well, sure, but . . ."

"But what?"

"This vehicle is brand new."

"I'm not doing any damage with my bare feet. I just had a pedicure the other day."

Her purple-painted toenails gleam in the sun. And yeah, her feet look soft. Pretty.

Jesus.

"Fine," I mutter. "Want some music?"

"Sure."

I start one of my favorite playlists, the Beatles.

She shakes her head. "Beatles? Really?"

"I like them."

"Their songs are really dirty."

"They are not."

"Yes, they are. There are all kinds of hidden dirty messages in them. And the titles . . . what's this song?"

"'Come Together.'" As soon as I say the words, I'm laughing. "Oh shit."

She chuckles too. "See? Then there's 'Please Please Me.' And 'Why Don't We Do It In the Road?'"

"'Ticket to Ride.'"

"Now you're getting it."

"'All You Need Is Love.'"

"Uh-huh." She starts singing along with "Come Together." Her voice is pretty good. Unable to resist, I start singing too. I know all the words and there we are, belting out a song together as we cruise along the highway.

We sing the next one too, "Do You Want to Know a Secret," hamming it up and laughing through parts of it.

After that playlist is done, she turns off the speakers. "Okay, let's play a game."

"A game?"

"Yeah. We have to pass the time somehow. Would you rather . . . ?"

"Oh no."

"Would you rather not be able to feel any sexual pleasure or never eat your favorite food again?"

I snort. "Easy one. Never eat my favorite food again. There are lots of good things to eat in the world. No way I'd give up sexual pleasure."

"I agree. What is your favorite food, by the way?"

"Prime rib."

She wrinkles her nose.

"What's yours?"

"Hmm. I guess pizza. But that's a bit unfair, because there are so many kinds of pizza—thick crust, thin crust, all different toppings . . ."

"Pizza's a close second for me. Pepp and mush."

"Good to know."

"Yours?"

"I like pepp and mush too. Also ham and pineapple."

"Fuck no. Pineapple does not belong on pizza."

"How about chicken?"

"Nah. No chicken on pizza."

She laughs. "That, I agree with. Okay, your turn."

I grunt. I have no clue what to ask. After a moment, I say, "Would you rather have sex in a hot tub or on the beach?"

Her peal of laughter delights my ears. "Ha! You surprise me. I'm impressed. Okay, hmmm." She taps her chin. "I think in a hot tub. I've heard sand in, uh, intimate places can be kind of unpleasant."

"No doubt."

"My turn. Would you rather"—she pauses—"have an animal best friend—it could be any animal you choose and it would be intelligent and speak to you. And you could ride on it, if it's big enough, like a bear or a . . . a buffalo. Or would you rather be married to someone with a hot body?"

"Jesus Christ." I rub my chin.

She laughs.

"That's fucking crazy."

"It's just a game. Come on. Lighten up. It's not like world peace depends on your answers."

I replay the question as I change lanes to pass a truck. "All right then, an animal best friend I could talk to would be cool."

"What kind of animal?"

I run through choices in my head. I've heard elephants are smart. And dolphins. Dolphins are cool. But they live in the water.

Jesus. I'm actually analyzing this like it matters.

"A chimpanzee," I blurt out.

"Oh, good answer! I'd love to have a chimpanzee friend!"

I can't stop the smile that pulls at my lips, shaking my head.

We continue on with the game until Lacey gets bored. Her feet go back up on the dashboard. "Climax in ten miles."

My head snaps around to look at her. "What?" My mind immediately goes into the gutter, imagining what this could mean . . .

"The sign. We just passed it. There's a town called Climax and it's coming up." She pulls out her phone and starts swiping and tapping. "Oh! We have to stop there. It's a ghost town."

"We're not stopping."

"What? Why not? We need a break."

"We'll be stopping for gas in a while. We can't throw off my plans."

"You have got to be kidding me."

"I am most definitely not kidding."

"But it will be fun! Come on! A ghost town! And there's a trading post."

"A trading post?"

"That's what it says." She taps her phone. "How can you not want to go to a town named Climax? I mean, really."

I give her a long glance and let out a sigh. "Fine."

"Yay!"

We watch for the sign, I signal and turn off the

interstate. This road is narrower, not as smooth, heading into the desert away from the highway. After five minutes, I ask, "How far off the interstate is this town?"

"Oh, I don't know. Hang on." She studies her phone again. "Ten miles."

"Jesus. Well, we're halfway there. But if we run out of gas because of this little detour, you're going to be walking to the nearest gas station."

"Phht."

We arrive at Climax and I slow down to cruise the main street. The only street. A few cacti and scrub have encroached on the town. Rickety wood buildings line the dusty street, most of them clearly empty and abandoned . . . except for one.

"This is creepy," Lacey says in a hushed tone, gazing around.

"Should we check out the trading post?" I nod at the neon sign.

She grins. "Of course!"

I'm almost nervous about entering this dilapidated store. We push open the creaky wooden door. Inside it's dim and only a few degrees cooler than the broiling heat outside. Wood shelves hold a few products . . . bags of potato chips, candy bars . . . condoms. Behind a counter sits an old man with a weathered brown face.

"Howdy. Welcome to Climax."

"Thanks."

"Cold drinks here." He spits chewing tobacco into something behind the counter.

"Uh, great." We approach the counter. Lacey eyes the stuffed gopher sitting on the worn wood. Nice.

We both order a Pepsi.

"How long have you lived here?" Lacey asks the man as we pay.

"I came here in the seventies. Looking for gold."

"Ah." She nods as if this makes perfect sense. "How'd you do?"

"Well enough to retire." He grins, revealing brown teeth. "And I got a pool out back."

"Oh! Awesome."

"What do you do for fun here?" I ask warily, taking my cold can of Pepsi.

"All kinds of things. Never a dull moment. The desert is mystical and awe-inspiring. Beautiful and harsh. 'You, God, are my God, earnestly I seek you; I thirst for you, my whole being longs for you, in a dry and parched land where there is no water. I have seen you in the sanctuary and beheld your power and your glory.'"

Lacey and I exchange uneasy glances.

"Psalm 63," he adds. "A psalm of David. When he was in the Desert of Judah."

"Ah." Lacey rolls her lips inward.

"And once a year we have Climax Days. People from all over come for a long weekend and party. Anything goes."

Lacey and I exchange another glance.

"Uh, wow," she says. "That sounds like fun."

"You just missed this year's party. Maybe next spring."

"We'll keep an eye out for it."

He nods. "I'm Charles." He reaches out a tobacco-stained hand and I shake it.

"Théo," I say. "This is Lacey."

"What brings you to Climax?" he asks.

"Well. Oral sex works for me," Lacey says.

There's a beat of silence, then Charles guffaws.

I'm standing with my mouth hanging open. Did she just say that?

Her eyes twinkle. She did that on purpose. Jesus.

"You're good." Charles points at her. "I use that line on everyone. Not many people have a good comeback."

She gives me a chiding look, seeing my unsmiling face. "Come on. That was funny."

It actually was. I was just too stunned she'd said it to laugh. "We better get back on the road."

"Where you heading?" Charles asks.

"L.A."

"Safe travels." He spits his tobacco again.

"Thanks, man."

We head out into the bright, scorching heat. We walk past buildings that used to be a post office, a hotel, a saloon, and one with a sign that reads, CLIMAX EMPORIUM.

"That's the brothel." Lacey points.

"Get out."

"No really. I read it when I was looking up the town. I mean, a town named Climax had to have a brothel, right?"

I laugh helplessly. "Right. Absolutely."

"I think I want to come back for Climax Days. It sounds . . . satisfying."

I choke on a laugh as I open the door of my Audi for her to climb in.

When I'm in my own seat, she says, "You need to lighten up and have some fun."

"I have fun."

"I bet last night's the only time you've let loose in a long time. Am I right?"

I frown. "Maybe."

She grins. Her bare feet go up on the dash again. "Can I find some music to play?"

"Sure." I hand her my phone, which connects to the Bluetooth speakers. When I hear country music twang, I groan. "Oh hell no."

"It's Carrie Underwood!"

"I hate country music."

"Oh my God. I'm starting to think our marriage is in trouble. We're not compatible in a lot of ways."

My lips twitch. "Okay, we'll compromise. We'll listen to country for half an hour, then I get to choose."

"You already got to choose the Beatles music earlier."

"But you liked that too."

"So you're going to pick something that I don't like, just to get your turn?"

"No!" I frown.

"I'm just kidding," she says. "Again." A soft sigh escapes her. "Just yanking your chain. Deal."

This woman's a handful. I'm now thinking she may have been able to hold her own with Ed and Lincoln and the entire Vegas mob.

After an hour of music, my choice being a mixed playlist of indie tunes, we arrive at a gas station. I'm still good for gas, but I want to fill up just to be sure. We both get out to stretch our legs, Lacey thrusting her arms over her head and twisting her spine.

Christ, she's sexy.

Her hair is falling out of the bun, all wavy pieces

shining gold in the sun. Last night at the pool when she let her hair down, I almost went to my knees. She's beautiful without all the hair, but I have to admit I have a thing for long hair on women (okay, maybe it's a fetish). Lacey's hair is long and wavy, parted in the middle, gorgeous shades of light brown and dark gold and pale blond. Masses of it. Stunning.

I want to pull it all down and run my hands through it. My fingers tighten on the gas pump.

My gaze lowers to her slender, toned calves, remembering her skirt falling down her thighs with her feet propped up on the dashboard . . .

I better think about something else, or the rest of this drive is going to be very uncomfortable.

"Should I grab anything inside?" she asks. "Drinks? Snacks?"

"I have bottles of water in a cooler. And granola bars."

"Sensible," she murmurs. "I was hoping for some Cheetos."

I shake my head. "Go find some Cheetos if you want."

"Okay." She lopes into the small store with her purse and I find her there moments later chatting with the woman behind the counter when I come in to pay for the gas.

"Yes, she was in Folies Orleans!" Lacey spots me. "This lady remembers seeing my mom!"

"Wow. Small world."

"Yes."

"You didn't want to be a dancer like her?" The woman rings up my gas purchase.

Lacey sighs. "I thought of it. I like to sing and dance, but I'm not good enough. And there aren't many shows for that type of dancing these days. To make good money, you have to dance wearing nothing but a smile."

I cough.

"Plus we couldn't afford dance lessons."

I hand over my credit card, then sign it.

"Nice to meet you, Verna!" Lacey calls as we leave.

She's got a Diet Coke and a bag of Cheetos, which she opens and digs into once we're back on the interstate. She offers me the bag.

Ah, what the hell. I grab some of the crunchy treats.

I try to eat healthy, other than that year after I got injured, when I ate my weight in junk food every week, not to mention I drank gallons of booze, trying to drown my sorrows. But I've gotten back to the way I learned to eat when I was playing, lots of protein and veggies. I've seen former players pack on the pounds, and I don't want to end up like that. I work out to stay in shape, and even still play hockey when I can. Truthfully, it's not just to stay in shape. I *have* to be active or I'd go nuts.

I'll have to find a beer league in L.A. to join.

"Tell me a joke," Lacey says.

I shake my head. "I'm not very good at jokes."

"You must know one."

"Okay. A chemist, a physicist, and a statistician go hunting."

"I can't imagine you hunting."

"I don't really hunt. Anyway, the chemist shoots at a deer and misses it by five feet to the left. The physicist shoots and misses by five feet to the right. The statistician throws down his gun and yells, 'We got him!'"

She frowns. "I don't get it."

"Because it's the mean of five feet to the right and five feet to the left, get it?"

"Oh. Yeah."

"I told you I'm bad at jokes," I mutter.

"Okay let's play more Would You Rather. Let's make it the sexy edition."

My eyes fly open. "Uh . . ."

"So . . . would you rather walk in on your parents having sex or have them walk in on you?"

"Oh man. Neither."

"You have to pick one."

I think through the pros and cons of each. Finally, I say, "I'd rather walk in on them."

"That took a long time."

"I like to be sure I'm making the right choice."

"Hmm. Your turn."

"I have no fucking clue what to ask."

"You did good with the beach versus hot tub question."

"Huh. Okay, would you rather talk dirty over the phone or send dirty texts?"

"Oh easy. Dirty texts."

Do I have that to look forward to? Oh wait. Fake marriage.

"Would you rather walk in on your best friend naked or have him walk in on you naked?"

"Phht. I've seen my best friend naked lots of times. And he's seen me."

"Oooh. Tell me more."

"We played hockey together. We changed and showered and got dressed in the same locker room all the time."

"Ah." She lays two fingers on her chin. "I'm picturing a

room full of naked hockey players. I like it. Never mind our game, I'm just going to close my eyes and fantasize for a while."

Jesus.

"Kidding," she says. "Who's turn is it?"

We go back and forth a while longer, and even though I struggle with some questions, I'm learning a lot about her. She likes bubble baths. She'd rather have her hair pulled than scratches on her back. She'd like to do a shot off my abs. And from our conversation with Charles, she likes oral sex. Hmmm.

This isn't doing much for my persistent semi. By the time we get to L.A. I'm going to be so hard I'll have to disappear into the bathroom for a fast hand job.

I glance at Lacey. Her cheeks are pink. Maybe she's a little turned on too?

No doubt there's some mutual attraction between us. After a few moments of thought, I conclude it's probably best to address this out in the open. "We're married."

"Thank you, Captain Obvious."

"You're a real smartass, aren't you?"

"I have my moments."

"Okay, I'm trying to be frank here. We're attracted to each other."

I fucking love the way her lips curl into a smile. "All right then, if we're being frank, yes. Yes, we are."

"Married people have sex."

"I've heard that."

I laugh. "You're not helping me."

"Are you trying to say you want to have sex with me?"

"Uh . . ." My tongue feels heavy. So much for being

frank. She's way ahead of me. "Yes, that's what I'm trying to say."

"How long till the next rest stop?"

I choke. "I didn't mean right this minute. Okay, well, I sort of do, but I was thinking bigger picture."

"Like, when we get to L.A. How many bedrooms do you have?"

"Three."

"Good. I don't think we should share a room."

"Oh."

"I'm not opposed to sleeping with you, though."

Jesus. But this is what I wanted. "That's what I was getting at. What are the terms of our relationship?"

"You're making this into a business deal?"

"Um . . ."

"A business deal that includes sex." Her eyes narrow. "I don't like that."

Hell. Does that mean sex is off the table? "I wouldn't say it's a business deal," I offer carefully. "More like we're doing each other a favor."

She tilts her head and considers that. "Okay. I can live with that."

"And I want to be clear: I don't expect sex as payment for the favor. But I wanted to know if, you know, if we both wanted it . . . if it would be okay to act on that."

She purses her lips, lifts her chin, and rubs her fingertips to her throat. "Well, I already said I'm not opposed to sleeping with you. But thank you for clarifying expectations."

Why do I feel like she's laughing at me?

9

———————

LACEY

Théo frowns. "I like having clear expectations."

"Always a good thing," I murmur solemnly.

He's so damn cute.

He should be annoying me, because wow, we're so different in some ways. He analyzes *everything*. He loves to plan. There've been moments where I worried he didn't have a sense of humor, but then he shows me he does. And he doesn't fake anything—he's honest. I like that.

So we do have some things in common—honesty. Humor. Shitty brothers.

I suspect Théo is way smarter than me, though. I may not be an intellectual, but I'm not stupid. I already know how to push his buttons.

I smile smugly to myself as I snuggle down into the super-comfortable seat of his Audi. Getting him to stop at that ghost town had been so much fun. Playing those crazy games too.

I'm also a teensy bit smug because he wants to have sex with me.

Whew. Because damn, I'm hot for this man.

There's something about him that just *gets* to me. The way he took charge when Ed and Lincoln were chasing us. The way he's so strong and controlled, yet there are hints of vulnerability when he talks about his brother and ex-girlfriend. The way he stops to analyze everything. Most of the time, ha. The way he's so freakin' smart. The way his lips curve when he's smiling against his will.

The fact that he wants to have sex with me makes me melt even more. I was only half joking about pulling over at the next rest stop.

For a while I'm quiet, my eyes closed, thinking about sex with Théo. I imagine getting my hands on his body, all those muscles. I imagine how strong he is and the things we could do . . .

My eyes pop open. "Hey. Why did you quit playing hockey? You're not old enough to retire."

His fingers flex on the steering wheel. "I had to. I got injured."

"Oh. That sucks. You're okay, though?"

"Sort of. I can't see well out of my right eye."

I blink. "Oh no. That's why you wear glasses?"

"Yeah. I had perfect vision before the accident."

I sink my teeth into my bottom lip. "What happened? Or is that too nosy?"

He lifts one shoulder. "It's fine. It was years ago. Puck bounced up under my visor and hit me in the eye."

"Oh my God." I cover my mouth with my hands.

"It was pretty scary. When it happened, everyone was

freaking out. They rushed me to the hospital for surgery. At first, I couldn't see anything, then I could tell when lights were off or on, and everybody freaked out because that was good. So there was hope I'd get my vision back. Of course, I kept hoping I'd get *all* my vision back and I'd be playing again in no time. But it took over a year and a half, and I'd been out of the game all that time, and I never got enough vision back to play professionally."

My heart contracts hearing his story, a pit in my stomach thinking about what he must have gone through. "I'm sorry," I say quietly. "That must have been awful."

"Yeah." A muscle in his jaw tics. This is still hard for him to talk about, obviously. "I'd just started my career in the NHL. Got drafted, got to follow in my dad's footsteps and my grandpa's footsteps—they played in the NHL. So did my uncle. And then it was over."

"You've obviously been successful, though. Just in a different way."

"Yeah. I love hockey. I knew I had to be involved in the sport somehow. I always liked numbers and stats—the guys used to make fun of me because I'd spout all these statistics. So I started my own analytics company. It took off, and teams were coming to me for advice on all kinds of hockey decisions. Then the Mustangs offered me a job as assistant GM, and it was a chance to really be back in the game."

I nod, impressed with his resilience. "That's really inspiring."

"Eh. Just did what I had to do."

My heart squeezes again. "I don't know. I think overcoming something like that is pretty remarkable."

His face relaxes, a smile touching his mouth. "Thanks."

Of course, this all makes me want to jump him even more. Damn.

We drive in silence for a while, then my phone rings. Like, actually rings, with a phone call.

I grab it. "It's Chris!"

Théo's eye widen.

I answer the call. "Chris! Where the hell are you?"

"Never mind me, where the hell are you?"

"Almost in Los Angeles."

"What the fuck are you doing? What do you mean you got married? To who?"

I ignore his questions. "Are you okay?"

"Yeah." He sounds surly.

"You took money out of my bank account."

"Stole," Théo says from beside me. "He *stole* money."

I shoot him a quelling glance.

"I'm going to pay it back," Chris says. "You know I will."

"I *don't* know that. I don't believe you, Chris. You've lied to me too many times. And what the hell? Trying to pimp me out to your bookies? That's low."

"That's bullshit," Théo puts in. "Despicable. Reprehensible."

"Who is that?" Chris demands.

"My husband."

"Jesus, Lacey! You're not serious."

"Oh, I am. This time you're going to have to get yourself out of your own mess." I pause. "Just be careful. Those guys came to the apartment looking for me. Or you. Or both of us."

"Shit."

"Yeah. We got away. I . . ." I almost choke up but swallow the lump in my throat. "Take care of yourself, okay? And stay in touch."

"Lacey. I'm sorry. Look, just come back and I'll show you—"

"I'll come back *when* you show me you can deal with this. Bye, Chris."

Théo nods approvingly, but his smile is gentle. "Was that hard?"

"Yes." I stare out the window, getting my emotions under control.

"But you did it, brave girl."

I nod. I did it.

We arrive in Los Angeles in the early evening, the sun setting and lighting up the sky orange and gold and pink. Théo changes freeways a couple of times and then we exit into Marina del Rey.

"I've only been here once before," Théo says, turning on the GPS in his phone for directions to his new home, and we find our way to Ocean Front Walk. His place is a condo in a triplex, a multi-level, modern concrete building with lots of glass, and it's so close to the beach there's sand on the sidewalk. He parks out front even though there's a small garage.

"I'll need the door opener to use the garage," he says, climbing out of the vehicle.

"Oh my God." I take a few steps away from car. The sun is setting over the ocean and the vista sucks the air out of my lungs. I actually break out in goosebumps, staring at the wide expanse of pale sand, the silvery ocean, and the flaming sunset tinting the turquoise sky and wispy clouds tangerine, peach, and pink. A squat, squarish lifeguard tower is silhouetted against the sky. "This is incredible. I don't want to move from this spot. Ever."

He laughs.

I reluctantly turn and follow him up a short sidewalk and high concrete steps to the door. He unlocks it and walks in, flicking on lights.

I follow, my eyes probably as big as hockey pucks, gazing around at the incredible interior. A wall of windows looks out over the beach and the vibrant sunset. He doesn't have a lot of furniture . . . brown leather couches and chairs, glass tables, lamps with black bases and modern shades. A big area rug covers the gleaming stone-tiled floor. "This is gorgeous."

"Yeah, it's pretty good. I'm going to grab my stuff out of the car."

"I can help." I follow him, and we bring in his suitcases and the cooler bag he had drinks in. I feel a twinge in my chest thinking about my lost suitcase with Pete in it. I guess I'll never see him again. Maybe someone will find the suitcase and keep it for me . . . I don't know. Oh well.

"Are you going to be okay for tonight?" Théo asks when we're back inside. "I'll take you shopping in the morning."

"I'm fine for tonight," I assure him. I wander to a set of doors in the living room and open them. They lead onto a terrace, also overlooking the ocean. There are a bunch of chairs and small tables and a shiny barbecue out here. "Nice." Back inside I check out the spacious kitchen, all glossy white cabinets, stainless steel appliances, and the same tiled floors. A vase of fresh flowers sits on the pale marble counter.

Théo sees me looking at them and smiles wryly. "Looks like my mom was here. She must have left those."

"That's nice of her."

"This can be your room." Théo gestures to a bedroom.

I peek in. "Whoa. Lots of white." The walls are white, the queen bed has a plain white duvet on it, a matching dresser and vanity in white, and white blinds on the window.

"It has a bathroom too."

"Awesome."

"The master suite is upstairs." He grabs his suitcase and hauls it up the open staircase, so I follow, curious.

The entire upper level is the master suite, with more floor-to-ceiling windows overlooking the beach. "You have room for a sitting area there." I wave a hand toward the windows. "Even with this massive bed."

I'm kind of afraid to look at the bed, because I know I'll think about Théo in that bed and hopefully me with him.

"Yeah. I might buy more furniture."

His bathroom is huge too, with stone walls, a generous shower *and* a tub, and a double vanity. There are doors to outside, so I go out there to find another terrace, this one with glass panels to shield from ocean breezes but not impede the view. Two lounge chairs face the Pacific, and behind them is a hot tub. "Holy crap."

"Pretty cool, huh?"

"Amazing."

"I'm going to order pizza. That okay?" He lifts an eyebrow at me.

"Yeah, sounds good."

Back downstairs, I take my backpack into my bedroom

and set it on the floor. I plop my butt down onto the bed and stare at my meager belongings. For a moment a sense of bleakness washes over me. I've left my only family to deal with criminals. I've left the only home I've known since I was about twelve when we moved into that apartment. I've left my friends and my hometown. I don't even have Pete.

I ran away from my problems because a hot guy was looking out for me.

It's been a long time since anyone looked out for me. No wonder I succumbed.

I blow out a sigh. Well, it's done. If I've learned anything in life, it's that you have to make the best of things. So here I am in sunny California, living right on the freakin' beach, with a gorgeous man. And hey, we're having pizza. Pizza is always good.

I send Karine another text message to let her know we arrived and I'm fine. She responded with the expected freak-out earlier, so I want to make sure she's reassured. Then I head out to the kitchen.

Théo must be still up in his room. I poke around a bit, finding dishes and cutlery. He's all set, I guess thanks to his mom. What the hell is she going to think when she finds out he's married? To someone she's never even heard of? We must be nuts.

Footsteps on the stairs alert me to Théo's presence. "Pizza ordered. Shit put away." He grins. "My mom's a lifesaver. I shipped most of my stuff here, and she came and put it all away. She even bought me new towels." He shakes his head.

"That's nice of her. I bet she's happy you're living closer."

"Yeah, I think she is."

"She's not angry about you working for your grandpa?"

"She probably tells my dad she is, but I don't think she's too upset about it. She's used to the shit that goes on in our family. Someone's always mad about something."

"Again, making me more and more look forward to meeting them." I give him a phony smile.

He laughs. "Sorry. They're not that bad. Just a lot of strong personalities and a lot of competitiveness."

I wander over to sit on the couch. The sun has set now so you can't really see much, but it's still lovely. "I can't wait for tomorrow. I'm going to run across the sand and right into the water."

"Yeah?"

"I've never been in the ocean. I came to L.A. once when I was eighteen, with some friends. We went to Disneyland. We saw the ocean but didn't really go near it."

"I have to go to work tomorrow. But I'll take you shopping in the morning to get some things."

"Is there a Walmart near here?"

"No idea. We'll find something." He grabs his phone and starts looking.

The doorbell rings with our pizza delivery so he drops his phone and goes to pay. I meet him in the kitchen, and he sets the big cardboard box on the counter. It smells amazing.

"I didn't realize I was so hungry." I pick up a plate.

"Same." He opens the fridge. "Oh, Mom, I love you." He pulls out a beer and holds it up. "Want one?"

"Oh yeah. I guess our hangovers are cured."

"I wasn't hungover."

"What was all the moaning and groaning and need for Advil about then?"

"Okay, I had a little headache." He grins.

He opens the beers and then we take them and our pizza into the living room to eat sitting on the big couch, which is lovely and squishy. He turns on the ginormous TV and zips through channels until he finds a sports channel. A hockey game.

"Playoffs are still on," he says.

"Ah."

After devouring a couple of pieces of pizza, I sit back into the couch with my beer. My eyes feel heavy and my body is weary. I did get some sleep, but apparently staying up all night has messed me up. I shift over closer to Théo and lean into him.

"Tired?"

"So tired." He puts his arm around me, and it's nice. He's warm, and big, and strong . . . I sigh with pleasure and snuggle in closer.

Except feeling his hard muscles and breathing in the scent of his skin, a spicy sandalwood, makes me tingle . . . and suddenly I'm not so tired.

I feel the change in him too, the way he goes on alert, the change in the touch of his hand on my hip. He caresses me through my sundress, slowly. My nipples tighten and melting sensation pools low in my belly. I shift and tip my head back to look at him.

God, he's handsome. I lift a hand to his face to stroke my fingertips over the stubble on his square jaw, then slide my hand into his thick hair. His eyes are dark behind his glasses, his sculpted lips only inches from my face.

I remember that kiss after we got married and how incredible it was . . . and my inner muscles squeeze up tight on a wave of lust. My lips part as I look at him.

"Lacey . . ." He cups my face with a big hand.

I melt even more. "Mmmm."

"Gonna kiss you now."

"Please." My eyelids drift down and I'm burning everywhere in anticipation of the touch of his mouth on mine.

It's magic. Delicious. Hot.

He gently touches his mouth to mine, then opens, and I part my lips wider, letting his tongue lick inside. A groan rumbles in his chest as his hand slides around to the back of my head to hold me. I clutch his shoulder and my head goes empty as I fill with luscious sensation.

He shifts my body closer, onto his lap, one hand going to my bare thigh, stroking up and down in a slow, erotic rhythm that has me hot and squirming, wanting his touch higher . . . everywhere.

Bing.

After a beat, Théo lifts his mouth from mine and growls, "What the fuck?"

"The doorbell." I'm a bit dazed.

Now there's a loud pounding on the door.

"Shit." Our eyes meet and he blows out a breath. "Hang on."

Breathing fast, I tug my skirt down as he answers the door. My body is pulsing and I need more of Théo.

"Dude!"

"Hey! Manny!"

I lean over to see who this is and watch Théo and . . . Manny grip hands and slap each other's backs.

No idea who this is. A relative? Friend?

"I thought I heard noises over here," Manny says with a big smile. "Bobby told me he'd rented this unit out to you. Talked to your mom the other day when she was here, and she said you'd be here this week. Welcome to California!"

"Thanks, man, great to be here."

"Can't believe you're gonna be my boss." Manny shakes his head. "But I always knew you were the smartest guy in hockey."

"Eh. Come on in. Want a beer?"

"Yeah, sure."

So much for our make-out sesh on the couch. I straighten my dress and tuck a strand of hair behind my ear as I stand.

"Oh hi." Manny pauses as he sees me.

"Lacey, this is Manny Martinez. He plays left wing for the Condors."

I smile at him.

"Manny, this is . . . Lacey." He pauses. "My wife."

10

THÉO

Wow, that feels weird, saying it.

"Holy shit!" Manny's eyes widen. "I had no idea you were married. When did this happen?"

"Last night." The answer bursts from my lips before I can even think.

"What?" He laughs in disbelief, as if I'm joking.

"Yeah. It was our last night in Vegas so we decided to tie the knot. Did the cheesy Vegas chapel thing and all." I catch Lacey's eye and she smiles because this is all true.

"Wow." Manny shakes his head and advances on Lacey. "Well, nice to meet you, Lacey."

"Likewise." They shake hands.

"Manny and I played hockey together in Wilkes-Barre," I tell Lacey. "And now we've both ended up here."

"Small world," Manny says. "Small hockey world. So, I'm, uh, interrupting your honeymoon, I guess."

"Ha. No worries. We're going to take a honeymoon trip

later, since I'm starting work right away." This is an outright lie, but oh well.

"I'd like to go to Italy," Lacey says. I can tell her tongue is in her cheek and I shake my head, trying not to laugh.

In the kitchen, I grab a beer for Manny. "Want another beer, Lace?" I call.

"Um, no thanks, I'm good."

I take one for myself as well, and we all sit again in the living room.

"What the hell are you watching?" Manny says.

"Nashville and Chicago."

"Fuck." Manny rubs his face. "We're out and I don't even care who wins. Haven't watched a single playoff game."

"Manny rents one of the other units in this building," I tell Lacey. "And the third one is occupied by Wyatt Bell, another Condors player. Bobby owns the whole place."

"Wow. A hockey building." She grins.

"Wyatt went home to New Brunswick," Manny says. "But he'll be back in a week or so."

Manny's one of the few NHL players from California. A lot of guys head back to where they're from when the season ends, but he's still here.

"So, are you eager to get started?" Manny asks me. "Ready to make some trades?"

His tone is light, but I see a little tightness at the corners of his mouth. I have to remember that having new management is probably causing the guys some stress. Everybody no doubt expects a lot of changes. And there will definitely be changes. I already know that from the research and analysis I've been doing, even before arriving here.

"We'll see," I answer. "Right now, I'm getting ready for the draft." The annual draft would be held at the end of June. I've got a lengthy to-do list between now and the start of training camp in September. Of course, the draft could involve a trade. Or more.

"Yeah, the good thing about having a craptastic season is we have the number two pick. That's pretty cool."

"We also have a second first round pick," I remind him. "Thanks to that trade for Filmore." Which was a huge fucking mistake, in my opinion.

"Yeah. And apparently there are some talented guys coming up."

"Apparently." I don't like to talk much about my plans, but I've done some preliminary investigation into this as well, and there are a couple of young guys I've got my eye on. "Sorry, babe," I say to Lacey. "Shop talk."

"That's okay! I want to learn more about hockey."

"Not a hockey fan?" Manny asks.

"Well, I grew up in Vegas and we only recently got an NHL team, so I haven't had much chance to be a fan. But I'm learning!"

"Vegas native, huh. Cool."

We catch up more on each other's lives, and then Lacey lays a hand on my arm. "I'm going to go to bed," she says softly. "Last night really tired me out."

Manny smirks, then covers his mouth with his hand.

"Okay. See you in a bit."

"Nice to meet you, Manny." She rises from the couch.

"I'm sure we'll see a lot of you. I can't wait to get out on the beach tomorrow."

"Yeah, nice to meet you too."

My body tenses as I realize Lacey's going to go to bed in her own room. What the hell is Manny going to think of that?

But Lacey's way ahead of me. Which doesn't happen very often. Not being a jerk, just honest. She climbs the stairs to the master suite.

All righty then. She's going to be waiting for me in my bed. Now I just need to get rid of Manny ASAP.

But Manny's not inclined to take off, and when I halfheartedly offer him another beer he accepts. Dammit.

Eventually he realizes he's keeping me from my bride and says good night. Fucking finally. I turn out the lights and sprint up the stairs into the master suite. It's dark. The light is on in the bathroom, but the door is open only a crack. I can make out Lacey's shape under the covers and as I approach the bed I hear her slow, even breathing.

She's asleep.

I exhale softly. Ah well. She's tired.

I wash up, ditch my clothes except for boxers, and slide into bed with her. She doesn't even stir.

IN THE MORNING WHEN I WAKE UP, LACEY'S GONE.

I roll onto my back and stretch my arms out, staring at the ceiling. Jesus, we've been married thirty hours and still no fucking.

Of course, we've only known each other about thirty-four hours.

I better cool my jets.

This isn't a real marriage, but I know she's interested. I just don't want to be that guy. She's been through some shit the last thirty-four hours. She needs someone to take care of her and make sure she's safe, not a horny jackass trying to jump her sexy bones.

After a shower I trudge downstairs to seek out hopefully coffee and food. I'm a big believer in breakfast, but I'm not sure how well my mom has stocked the kitchen. I find Lacey out on the deck in the early morning coolness, the air damp and fresh from the ocean. She's got a blanket wrapped around her, her feet tucked under her in the chair, a cup of steaming coffee in her hands, and she's gazing out at the ocean with a soft smile of wonder on her face. My chest pings.

She glances at me as I slide the door open. "Hey. Morning."

"Morning. Sleep okay?"

"Oh my God, I died. I slept *so* well."

"Good. I need coffee. And food."

"Your Keurig is on the counter." She holds up the mug. "Want me to cook something?"

"No. I mean, I can cook. You hungry?"

"I could eat."

"I'll see what we've got. Or maybe we can go out for something."

She stands, the blanket still draped around her, and I see she's wearing my T-shirt again, her legs bare. She follows me to the kitchen where I peruse the contents of the fridge and find eggs and ham and, yes, cheese. Omelets it is.

"What's the plan for today?" Lacey asks as she makes me a cup of coffee at the Keurig.

"After food?"

"Yeah. You're pretty obsessed with breakfast, huh?"

"The most important meal of the day."

"If you say so."

"Here's the plan."

"I knew you'd have a plan."

I pause.

Her lips twitch.

"Is that bad?" I ask.

"No. Not at all," she hastily assures me.

"We'll go find a shopping mall and get you some clothes and whatever else you need. Maybe a grocery store, if we need more food. Then I'll bring you back here and you can explore the beach while I go to work."

"Oh. You have to go to work already?"

"Yeah."

"Where do you work? I mean, I know you work for the hockey team, but you must have an office or something, right?"

"Right. The arena isn't that far from here, in Santa Monica. Which is why some of the guys live here, I guess. Our offices are there."

"Got it." She hands me my coffee. "What can I do?"

"Grate some cheese. Do you want toast?"

"No thanks. But I can make some if you want."

We're getting along just fine here for two people who barely know each other. This makes me smile.

"What's so funny?"

"This whole situation. Manny was surprised last night when I introduced you. I wondered what he was going to think when you went to bed in your own room."

"I thought of that," she admits. "I hope it was okay I went to your room."

"It was fine." I pause in whisking eggs. "I was disappointed you were asleep, though."

There's a beat of silence. "Sorry."

"Jesus, don't apologize! I wasn't trying to make you feel bad. I was just saying . . ."

She leans over and brushes her lips against my cheek. "Well, if it makes you feel any better, I was disappointed when Manny showed up and interrupted us."

My dick stirs in my loose athletic shorts. I consider the plan for the day and am briefly tempted to abandon it. *So not like me.*

What is this woman doing to me?

I focus on the food and not on her bare legs and gorgeous messy hair and what she's wearing under my T-shirt. My normal self-discipline serves me well as I make breakfast and we sit and eat it at the counter.

After we've eaten and cleaned up, I grab my phone to check for emails and sports scores and business news while Lacey goes to shower and get ready to go out. There are several business emails, the score from the game last night, news about the other teams in the playoffs, and a text message from my mom.

Hope you are settling in. We're having a welcome home party for you Saturday night.

Great. I text her back, thanking her for everything she did to get my place ready and saying I'll see her and Dad Saturday night. I assume JP will be there . . . ugh. Maybe with Emma. Double ugh. And what about the rest of the family? My uncle, Dad's brother, will likely be there. They're probably not impressed with my career choice either. And maybe my cousin Riley will be there—she works for the Eagles farm team as a goalie coach and lives here too.

I respond to some emails and then Lacey arrives wearing the same sundress she had on yesterday. She glances down at herself and grimaces. "Can't wait to get some new clothes."

"Let's go then."

In the car, I let my GPS guide me to a shopping mall not too far away. "My mom's having a party Saturday night," I tell her. "So get ready to meet the fam."

"Oh yay." Then she wrinkles her nose. "This is where I earn my keep, I guess."

I laugh. "Yes."

"That means I'll need to buy something to wear." She taps her chin. "Will it be a fancy party?"

"Yes."

Her eyes widen.

"No. I'm kidding. The only one in my family who likes fancy things is Chelsea."

Her brows knit. "Who's Chelsea?"

Gah. "Guess I didn't mention her name. My grandpa's wife."

"Oh, right." She nods. "Will they be at the party?"

"I doubt it, since my dad and my uncle aren't speaking to him. Or maybe I should say, they're speaking to him, but it's usually yelling and swearing."

"Sounds like so much fun," she murmurs.

"Well, remember, they're not really your family. You just have to pretend for a while."

"Right. So your brother and Emma will be there, I gather."

"I assume so."

"I'll buy something really sexy to wear and engage you in embarrassing PDAs all evening."

I cough. "Uh, we don't have to go that far. Just be yourself." I glance at her. "You're pretty charming."

"I am?" She smiles.

"You know you are."

The mall is a high-end one, and after we pass by a number of stores, Lacey says to me, "There's no Walmart here, is there?"

"No. Come on. Nordstrom has lots of things. I'm paying."

"No, you are not!" Her mouth falls open and she plants her Chucks onto the shiny tile floor of the mall.

"Yes, I am. I'm the one who ditched your suitcase. I owe you."

She sighs. "Fine. But I'm paying you back."

I'm not really into shopping, especially for women's clothes. Emma dragged me on shopping trips that bored me to tears, until I finally managed to get her to go without me.

She loved to shop.

Lacey is efficient, heading straight to the sale racks in a casual department for jeans, shorts, and T-shirts, always examining the price tags. We move to a dressier department for some other things. "A swimsuit," I suggest a while later. "For the beach."

"Right." She nods eagerly.

Finally, we arrive in the lingerie department. She shoots me a glance. "You, uh, don't have to hang out here if you don't want."

I can't help my grin. "This is my favorite department."

She huffs a laugh and shakes her head. "Fine." She quickly chooses a pair of pajamas, some panties, and a couple of basic bras. I note the size, and when she disappears into a change room, I browse through sexier offerings. She should have something prettier than basic beige. Nothing wrong with basic beige, but I like imagining Lacey in . . . well, lace. Pink lace would look good on her.

She returns a while later with a load of clothing in her arms. "These all work," she says. "Let's pay."

I add the pink lace bra and matching panties to the pile. Her eyebrows fly up.

"Just go with it."

Once we have a couple of shopping bags in our hands, I nod to the shoe department. "I like your Chucks, but you might need a pair of sandals or something."

"Right."

We soon have her outfitted with footwear. "Okay. Where next? Do you need to buy makeup or stuff?"

She laughs. "I do need a few things."

"There's a Sephora here."

Her eyes widen. "I love Sephora." She sighs. "But it's expensive. I can just go to a drugstore. And I do need toothpaste and shampoo."

"We can do both."

She sucks her bottom lip briefly as we stroll through the mall, and I can tell she's uncomfortable. I slide my fingers around her hand and squeeze. "Hey. We're doing each other favors, right?" She lifts her gaze to meet my eyes. "You're going to help me out at the party on Saturday. I'm getting something out of this too."

She nods slowly. "My life sucks."

I smile and stop, tugging her hand so she faces me. "I know. Right now it does. But it's all going to be fine."

The corners of her mouth lift in response. "Yeah."

We hit the Sephora and even though I'd rather hang out with the other dudes sitting in leather armchairs outside the store, I go in with Lacey. Mercifully she's quick in getting the things she needs and then we're out of the mall. I spotted a CVS on our way here, so we make one more stop, grabbing a few grocery items too, and then we're on our way home.

Home.

The sky is a clear blue above the ocean and I see Lacey look longingly at the beach as we get out of the car.

"Let's go," I say, once we've carried in our purchases.

She blinks. "Go where?"

"Down to the water. You know you want to."

"You have to go to work."

"Yeah. But I can take a few minutes to walk on the beach."

She toes off her Chucks and she's gone, out the patio

doors and running across the sand, her skirt billowing around her, hair flying in the gentle wind. I laugh as I lock the door and follow her, leaving my sandals on my patio.

Her joy fills me with a soft warmth, her laughter floating back to me on the breeze as she reaches the water and comes to a halt. She doesn't move when a wave washes over her feet, foaming around her ankles.

"Look! I'm in the ocean!" She holds her arms out and turns her face up to the sun.

"Yeah." I grin. "Pretty awesome, huh?"

"I love it!" Another wave splashes higher, and she squeals and dances out of the water. "It's cold, though!"

I grew up in Canada where my dad played hockey in Montreal until I was about six. Then he bought into a major junior team in Drummondville, Quebec, so we moved there. I played hockey in Moncton, New Brunswick, got drafted by the Pittsburgh Penguins and I played there after a couple of seasons in Wilkes-Barre. Grandpa and Chelsea have lived here a long time though, and I've visited them so many times I guess I've come to take the sun and the palm trees and the ocean for granted. Seeing Lacey's enjoyment of her first time at the ocean fills me with pleasure. I feel like making her happy and seeing her smile is gratifying. Contagious.

11

LACEY

"My life doesn't suck."

I say it out loud to myself, after I'm back at the condo and Théo has left for his office.

This may not be something I ever expected, but I'm lying here on a beautiful patio where I've been sunbathing in my bikini, looking out at the Pacific Ocean with the sun on my bare skin. I can pretend I have no problems—no bookies chasing me, no brother who's in debt trying to pimp me out, no negative bank balance, and no unemployment.

It's been so long since I had this feeling . . . just being able to relax and not worry about bills and debts and other people.

I could get a job here. I *will* do that. I at least can make some money so Théo doesn't have to buy my clothes.

I don't have a car, and this city is the kind of place you need a car, I think. But I'll figure that out. I'll figure it all out and then . . . and then . . . I'll be fine.

The ocean shifts and sparkles in the distance. Sailboats

bob across the water. Thin white clouds streak the bright sky, and the voices of some guys playing volleyball down the beach carry to me on the fresh breeze.

My life doesn't suck.

The water mesmerizes me. It's so huge and endless, the waves constant. I feel like I could sit and stare at it forever and maybe the solutions to all my problems would come to me.

Ha.

I can live in this moment, though. I've been doing that for so long, because worrying about my mom and Chris and what was going to happen and how we'd get out of debt was too much to bear, so I'm pretty good at it.

My thoughts turn to Théo. I've slept with him the last two nights, but "sleeping with him" is not a euphemism for sex. Dammit.

I don't think I've ever wanted to have sex with a man I just met the way I do with Théo. I haven't had a lot of men in my life. I had a boyfriend in high school, and I went out with a few guys after graduation, but my mom got sick when I was about twenty-one and my life was consumed by working three jobs at times to pay her medical bills, looking after her, and keeping Chris out of trouble.

There's something about Théo . . . he's a *man*. That probably sounds weird; he's twenty-eight, only four years older than me, not exactly ancient, but he has such a mature air about him, something solid and honest and real. He not only has a job, it's an *important* job. He has his life figured out and knows what he wants and where he's going, whereas I have no clue.

Maybe it's time for me to do that. To figure out what I want from life and go after it.

Théo said he'd be home around six, so I decide I'll have dinner ready for him, like a good wife. I'm afraid I'm probably going to be a terrible wife, but it seems like the least I can do for him after all he's done for me. And yeah, he's getting something out of this too, but right now it feels a little lopsided.

I'm in the kitchen snooping through cupboards when I hear the front door open. I turn with a big smile, expecting Théo early. "Hiiiii!"

A woman stands inside the door.

I freeze.

We stare at each other.

Uh . . . "Hi?" I offer. I'm acutely aware that I am wearing only a tiny red bikini.

She tilts her head and the way she does it reminds me of Théo. She's lovely . . . glossy, layered dark hair brushes her shoulders. She reminds me of Tina Fey. Except when she speaks she has a French accent. "Hello. I'm sorry. I didn't know Théo had someone staying with him."

She says Théo's name differently—Tay-oh. Not Thee-oh, like everyone else has been saying. Even he himself pronounced it Thee-oh.

"You're Aline, aren't you."

Her eyes widen. "Yes. Aline Gagnon."

Her French pronunciation of her name delights me and I smile.

"And you are . . . ?"

"Oh! I'm Lacey. Lacey Olson." I pause, thinking about

whether I should call myself Lacey Wynn. But we haven't had time to think about that, even if our marriage was real, and besides . . . Théo's mom's name isn't Wynn. Curious. "I'm, uh . . ."

Aline presses her fingers to her mouth and takes a step forward. "Are you Théo's girlfriend?"

"Weeeell." This isn't how I imagined meeting his mom, but might as well do this. "I'm his wife."

Aline gasps.

"I'm sorry." Now I move toward her, my hands out, wishing I had on more clothes. "I know this is a shock. This isn't how we wanted to tell you."

She blinks rapidly, her lips parted. "His wife. You're . . . married?" She takes in a shaky breath. "He didn't tell us . . ."

"I know. I'm sorry. But it happened really fast, sort of a last-minute decision because he was leaving Las Vegas and—"

"Oh." She covers her mouth and nose with both hands now, her eyes shiny. "Mon dieu, mon fils est marié!"

I have no idea what she just said, but she's about to cry and I don't know if she's happy or distraught. "We were going to tell you, uh, this weekend when we see you. I'm really sorry! Are you okay?"

"No, I'm not okay! My son got married to a woman I don't even know, without even telling us." She pauses. "I'm sorry. I'm sure you're a lovely person. You are beautiful." She studies me, her expression still pained. "I'm just shocked. And . . . and hurt. And disappointed." Her eyes tear up again. "I missed my son's wedding."

I nibble my bottom lip. "You didn't miss much. It was very quick. But it was all we needed," I add hastily.

She swipes fingertips beneath her eyes and takes a breath. "I apologize for becoming so emotional."

"No, it's fine! I totally understand." Jesus. This isn't good. Théo's mom hates me. As if they don't have enough tension in their family, now I've added to it. I clasp and twist my hands together. I've caused Théo more problems than I'm helping him with. *He's* going to hate me too.

Oh shit, now *I'm* tearing up. My bottom lip quivers.

"Oh, don't you cry too! I'm sorry!" Aline flies toward me, arms outstretched. "Please."

She wraps me up in an unexpected hug. Momentarily I stiffen, then cautiously hug her back. "You are my belle-fille." She draws back and smiles. "That is daughter-in-law. Translated literally, it is beautiful girl, or beautiful daughter. And that is what you are."

I suck in a shaky breath. Okay, maybe she doesn't hate me.

"I'm so happy for Théo that he has found someone. Someone to love. He can be difficult to love."

"I don't think so," I reply honestly. I mean, I'm not in love with him, but he's not *that* bad.

She beams.

"He *can* be a little rigid and picky, but—"

Aline laughs. "You do know him." She releases me and steps back. "I brought some food for dinner. I didn't know you were here, obviously." She goes back to the door and picks up a couple of shopping bags. "It's just a few things."

I take one of the bags and move to set it on the counter.

"You've done so much to help Théo get settled in. He really appreciates it."

She waves a hand. "I'm so happy he's living close now." She purses her lips. "I fear Théo doesn't feel the same about his family."

"He will." I nod firmly. "I know there are bad feelings, but family is family."

Aline tilts her head, again reminding me of Théo. "Just so," she murmurs. "What about your family? Were they at the wedding?"

"I don't have much family. My mom passed away a few years ago."

"Oh! C'est terrible. Pauvre enfant." Her eyes soften.

"Uh . . ."

"I apologize again. I don't speak French very often, but when I get emotional, I slip back into it. I'm sorry for your loss."

"Thanks. It was a difficult time. I never knew my father, and my twin brother, Chris, is . . . well, I'm not sure where he is."

She frowns. "You have quarreled?"

"Sort of."

"As have Théo and his brother." She grimaces.

"So I understand."

"Well. We won't get into that. Tell Théo I was here."

"I will. I'm sure he'll be sorry he missed you. And sorry about not telling you sooner that we got married."

Her mouth firms. "I now am angry." She notices my face, and her mouth softens. "Un petit peu. Not at you. We'll see you Saturday evening. Tell Théo seven o'clock."

"I will. Thank you again for all you've done."

I see her to the door where she gives me another quick hug and leaves.

I sag against the wall and close my eyes. Fuuuuuck.

Which is worse . . . Théo's mom hating me? Or Théo's mom happy for us . . . because what will happen when our "marriage" ends?

I HAVE DINNER READY WHEN THÉO ARRIVES HOME, WHICH was easy because of the roasted chicken Aline brought over. There were also side dishes of mashed potatoes, gravy, and vegetables, along with some fresh rolls that would be good for chicken sandwiches tomorrow with the leftovers.

"Wow, smells good in here," Théo says as he enters the kitchen.

"Dinner's ready!"

"Awesome. I'm going to go change. Be right back."

He went to work dressed in casual pants and a button-down shirt, but he returned wearing the black athletic shorts he'd had on this morning and a T-shirt. I've changed into a new pair of shorts and a T-shirt.

"Where'd you get this chicken?" he asks as we sit down to eat.

"Well. Funny story." I cut a piece of white meat. "Your mom stopped by with it."

He freezes, fork halfway to his mouth. "Say what now?"

My smile is big and tight. "Yeah. She brought over food, not knowing I was here. Let's just say it was a bit of a shock for her."

"No shit." He drops his fork onto his plate and stares at me. "You . . . told her?"

"Yep. She got a little . . . upset." I eye him warily. "I think she wanted to be at your wedding. Of course, doesn't every mom? So I totally understand."

"Shit."

"But it's okay," I continue quickly. "I think she was coming around to the idea."

"Shit."

"I know." I sigh. "She seems really nice."

"Yeah."

"I apologized." I fill him in on the conversation in detail.

"I'll call her tomorrow."

"And she said to come at seven o'clock on Saturday."

"Perfect." His tone is dry. "I wonder if she's telling everyone else or waiting to surprise them too."

I set my fork down and drop my head. "You regret this, don't you?"

He doesn't reply right away, and I peek up at him.

He moves his head side to side. "No."

Our eyes meet and that smoldering heat is back, burning over my skin, settling low inside me. My short breaths lift my breasts and Théo's gaze slowly drops there, lingers, then glides back up and lands on my mouth. My lungs burn and my lips part.

"I don't regret it," he says gruffly, breaking eye contact and staring at his plate. "But it's probably a bad idea for us to actually get involved."

I blink. Then I frown. "What?"

"I know there's this"—he waves a hand back and forth

—"attraction between us, but I've got a lot on my plate right now. I've got a family that's nuttier than squirrel shit. I've got a new job where people are already talking about how I only got the job because I'm the owner's grandson. I've got a million things to learn and just about as many decisions to make. I *have* to do this." His hands curl into fists and his voice is fierce. "I can't get distracted from what I need to do."

The heat scorching my body intensifies to mortification. I told him I wanted to sleep with him. Jesus. Why did I say that? But then, he'd asked if it would be okay to act on the lust we were both clearly feeling. "You've changed your mind," I say coolly. "When we were driving here yesterday, you seemed pretty into it."

If we both wanted it . . . would it be okay to act on that?

Well, I already said I'm not opposed to sleeping with you.

Oh my Gaga. I close my eyes. Why did I say that?

"That was a mistake." He rubs the back of his neck and looks away. "You make me do crazy things."

My eyes fly open wide. "You have got to be fucking kidding me."

His head snaps back around, eyebrows pulling down over his nose. "What?"

"You can't do that." I slide off my stool and stand, planting my hands on my hips and glaring at him. "Shifting blame like that. Be a man, for God's sake. Take responsibility for your own actions. I haven't made you do *anything.*"

His eyebrows fly up into his hairline. "No! That's not what I meant."

"So this is a business deal after all." Bitterness edges my voice.

"No. I told you. We're friends helping each other out."

"Friends." My throat squeezes up. I shake my head. He wants to be friends. How can he ignore this growing, sizzling lust? Or maybe it *is* just me.

FML.

"Okay," I finally manage to say, sounding sane and calm even though my chest hurts and my stomach cramps. I *think* I sound sane. "Friends. Got it. You're right. That's what we should do." I take a calmative breath and perch on the stool again. I stare at what's left of my dinner. Ugh.

I poke at my mashed potatoes while the air around us becomes thick and oppressive, the silence weighing heavy. All I want to do is run into my room and hide my head under the pillow and possibly never come out. "Did you ever make a volcano with your mashed potatoes?"

I sense his surprise and relief at my change of topic to something benign.

"Of course. Hasn't every kid?"

"Probably."

"One time I put some chocolate chips into leftover mashed potatoes, scooped it into an ice cream cone, put sprinkles on it, and gave it to JP."

A startled laugh obstructs my throat briefly. "Did he eat it?"

"Oh yeah." Théo grins. "He was pissed. It was hilarious."

"I once cut up a sponge into squares and spread Nutella all over it so it looked like brownies." I grin. "Chris grabbed one and started to chow down, and then he spit it out all over the kitchen."

"Ha! Good one."

Our eyes meet in shared amusement.

We both look quickly away.

I poke at my potatoes again. I try to eat, and when I think I've consumed enough that it doesn't look like I'm running away, I set down my cutlery and stand. "Well, I'm full. That was good. So nice of your mom." I carry my plate over to scrape the leftovers into the garbage and then slide the plate into the dishwasher. "I'm tired. Must have been our trip yesterday. I'm going to go wash up and read for a while before bed."

"It's seven o'clock."

"Wow, really? Feels like ten!" I start putting away the leftover food.

"Leave it," he says gruffly. "You're tired. I'll clean up."

I shouldn't leave it for him, but I do, because I'm desperate to escape the heavy atmosphere.

I close my door and throw myself facedown onto the bed. Jesus be a fence.

I lie like that for a while, letting thoughts spin through my brain. Eventually I calm down and roll onto my back.

Okay. He's right. If we had sex, I might feel like I was prostituting myself. I'm living in his house, letting him buy me clothes and necessities, like a kept woman.

Argh!

And yeah, yeah, I know I have to put on the act for his family. I can do that.

A slow smile tugs at my lips. I can *so* do that.

But fine, we'll be friends. I'll just ignore that tingly, flippy feeling I get when I look at him. Or think about him. Or touch him, or smell him . . . I can take care of my own needs, thank you very much.

Which I proceed to do, wriggling out of my shorts to lay there in my panties, sliding my hand down inside them to find my slick entrance, and getting myself off with a shuddering orgasm. I wasn't imagining Théo's fingers touching me. Nope, not at all.

12

THÉO

I'm at my office early Friday morning. Yesterday I organized a few things. I don't keep a lot of personal shit in my office, but I have framed team pictures from my days in Wilkes-Barre and my first (and only) season in Pittsburgh. I also have a stuffed penguin in the image of what used to be the team mascot.

The offices are quiet as I sip my Starbucks coffee and scroll through various hockey news sites. I pause at the article written by my uncle Asher. I snort because even though he's my uncle, he's two years younger than me, my grandpa's son from his second marriage. Asher's the other black sheep of the family who doesn't play pro hockey—he just writes about it for a new sports blog, covering both the Condors and the Eagles. Asher never wanted to play pro hockey, even though he was probably good enough. Unlike me, he had a choice and he chose something else. I admire that. Which is probably why, even though I'm supposed to be at odds with my grandpa and his family, Asher and I

have stayed friends. And now I'm working for Grandpa, so
. . .

Actually, it's technically not true that Asher and I are the only Wynns who don't play hockey. Asher's sister, Everly, also doesn't play hockey—but she works for the Condors Foundation. Just because she's a girl doesn't mean she may not have wanted to play hockey, because my cousin Riley, also a girl, does. Did.

I smile at one of Asher's comments. He's smart and knowledgeable about hockey, but he's also a good writer and his metaphors always amuse me. I'll have to suggest we go for beers sometime.

Okay. I've got a shit ton of work to do.

Ever since I made my decision to take this job, I've been researching and creating spreadsheets and charts and graphs to help me in my analysis. But there's much more to do. I flew into town a week ago to do exit interviews with all the players before they disappeared for the summer, but I know I'm going to have to meet with some of them again. It might involve going to them, wherever they're spending their summer, although there are a few players who've stayed in the area. I'll especially need to talk to the team captain, Jimmy Bertelson, also known as Big Bert, a veteran player and the undisputed leader of the team.

One of the first things I need to do is hire an assistant GM. I've already looked at who's out there and talked to some, and I've narrowed it down to a few candidates. I'd like to have someone more experienced than I am, because I know I'm smart and good at what I do, but I'm also smart enough to know what I don't know.

My mind drifts to Lacey.

Shit. I hurt her feelings last night.

I knew I was going to.

I sit back in my chair. After I left her at home yesterday afternoon, I was all sappy happy because she was loving the ocean so much. And I can't get all sappy happy about Lacey. When I got to my office and looked around, and the enormity of what I had to accomplish crashed over me, I realized I couldn't get involved with her. And by "involved," I mean bone her. This isn't a real marriage and it's not going to last; it's only until she needs to go back to Vegas, and then I'll tell my family things didn't work out and we'll all move on. So getting warm, squishy feelings about her can't happen.

I decided to tell her when I got home, even though I knew it was going to be uncomfortable and not only that, I'm sort of punishing myself too because she's sweet and sexy and I want to bone her so bad it hurts, and she's apparently down to fuck also . . . but I strengthened my resolve, determined to focus on my job because if I screw this up I'll pretty much have to give up using the last name Wynn and move to South America to live in a hut and ride a donkey.

I need to focus. As GM, I'll be facing tons of pressure from all directions—Grandpa, the players, the fans, and the media. I did the presser when they announced I'd been hired, and yeah, the media barraged me with questions, many of which focused on my lack of experience.

I figured the best strategy was to be honest. I *don't* have a lot of experience managing a team. I also want to be realistic about the team's potential, because not only is my job managing the team, it's managing expectations, and that includes the players' expectations and the fans' expectations. We're not going to win the Stanley Cup this year. We're going to need a long-term plan to get there.

I pull my laptop closer on the desk.

Not only is there pressure from everyone else . . . I'm putting huge pressure on myself.

This morning I'm meeting with Grandpa—my boss—and the head coach of the Condors, Joe Daneck. I wanted to get here early and work on a few things before that. I dive into numbers and the lists I'm compiling.

Others arrive at the office closer to nine o'clock—admin staff, Brock Thurlow, our director of hockey operations; Brenda Laurent, our chief human resources officer. I greet everyone and chat with them, sensing their wariness despite being friendly enough. I'll need to get to know all these people too.

I'm a numbers guy, so dealing with people isn't a strength, but I know that and I've worked on it. Managing means managing people . . . it's that simple. Getting the best roster possible on the ice. Making sure team staff are competent. Communicating with ownership—in this case my grandpa. Maintaining good relations with fans and the media.

And since I played hockey most of my life, I know what it's like to be on a team. Hockey is a team sport, and building the team that's *off* the ice is as important as building the team that's *on* the ice.

Grandpa arrives first, striding into my office with a big grin. I stand up and move around my desk for a hug and backslap. "Hey, old man. Or should I call you Mr. Wynn now?"

He laughs, a rough dry laugh. "Maybe you should call me that. Or how about Bob?"

"That's weird." I pause. "I'll call you Bob to other people. To your face I'll call you old man."

"Fair enough."

I gesture to the round table in the corner of my office and Grandpa takes a seat. He moves slower and more stiffly than I remember. I feel a clench in my gut at the idea of him getting older. Jesus, he's only seventy-two. *Only*.

I pick up the cup of coffee I got from the break room, my Starbucks beverage long gone, and join him.

"I bet you're chomping at the bit to get going," Grandpa says.

"I'm ready."

"I wanted to talk to you before Joe gets here. He has to go."

I blink at him. "What?"

"He's a losing coach."

"Maybe you shouldn't have fired Uncle Mark."

Uncle Mark had been the assistant coach for the Condors until he and my dad accused Grandpa of stealing money from them and sued him. I'm not making this shit up.

Grandpa scowls. "Are you fucking kidding me? How can I keep a man working for me who's suing me? He knew he was going to get canned when he did that."

Probably true.

"It may not be Joe's fault the team is losing." I sit back in my chair and regard Grandpa thoughtfully. "Maybe it's the roster he's got."

Grandpa narrows his eyes. "I've lost faith in him. He has to go."

I tip my head to one side and narrow my own eyes. "That's my decision."

Grandpa frowns. "I own this team."

Fuck me. Are we really going to start off like this?

Okay, he's my grandfather and I've known him my whole life. I'm not intimidated by him, as some might be. I love him and respect him.

On the other hand, this is my job, and I won't put up with interference by team ownership, no matter who they are. That caused a bit of friction in Vegas, but somehow I managed to take a stand and keep my job.

I need to do that now.

"And I'm the man you hired to run this team," I say to him, my voice low but forceful. "Full control. You said that. Remember?"

He scowls. "I never said that."

My eyebrows shoot up. "You did say that. Your exact words were that I'd have complete autonomy to rebuild the Condors as I see fit."

"Bullshit. I'm not turning complete control over to *anyone*. This is *my* team."

My jaw slackens and my heart drops. What the fuck?

I have a pretty damn good memory. I didn't imagine he said that. My fears that I'm being conned roar back, making my blood run hot. "I didn't take this job to be your happy-to-be-here yes-man." My hands clench around the armrests of the chair. "If that's the case, you can find someone else to be your yes-man."

I meet his eyes and lift my chin.

Grandpa stares back at me, and his expression shifts from belligerent to puzzled. "I don't want a yes-man," he says gruffly, quietly. "I want you."

I give my head a mental shake and inhale slowly. "You hired me to manage this team. If you don't want me to do that, I'm out of here."

"I do want you to do that."

I close my eyes briefly. What the fuck have I gotten myself into? "Then you have to let me do that, Grandpa. We'll talk and I'll listen to what you have to say because I respect your knowledge, and I'll take your opinions into consideration, but you told me I'd have autonomy. Do you trust me to manage this team or not?"

Now he looks bewildered. "I do. Of course I do. That's why I hired you."

"Okay." I suck in another long breath. "So you're giving me control to make decisions as I see fit?"

"You have to run things by me first."

I tip my chin down, then up. Does this mean we'll be arguing over every decision I make? Or is this a courtesy? Fuck, I'm so confused right now. "Fair enough."

At that moment, Joe arrives. He extends a hand with a smile that doesn't touch his eyes. "Good morning! Welcome!"

We shake hands and I motion for him to take another seat at the table. I move across the room to close the door. I feel off balance. I don't know what to think. Grandpa said he wants Joe gone. Then he said I just have to run things by him. As I take my seat again, my gaze shifts back and forth between the two other men, my nerves jumping as I wait for Grandpa to tell Joe he's fired.

Jesus.

"Tell us what you're thinking, Théo," Grandpa says, sounding clearer and stronger than he did moments ago.

"Sure." I nod, taking a few seconds to collect my thoughts. "So. This franchise has had a rough time the last few years. We need to change that around. We need to be a winning franchise. It's good for the community, it's good for the state, and it's good for the sport. Hockey's growing in popularity here in California, but it's important that we have a team we can be proud of. It's important to our fans, our organization . . . and it's important to me. I'm excited to be part of this."

Joe and Grandpa nod.

"I'm not one to make snap decisions," I say, although Grandpa knows this. "I plan to do a lot of analysis. Watch a lot of video. Run a lot of numbers."

"We already run a lot of numbers," Joe says.

Was that defensiveness? I eye him, keeping my expression neutral. "Great. I'm glad you're on board with that."

He starts talking about Corsi scores, and I hold up a hand. "I know Corsi used to be important, before we had a lot of other analytics, but I've found there are other stats that give us better information."

"Such as?"

"Such as, scoring chances. Scoring chances factor in shot quality."

Joe frowns.

"Scoring chances give us more insight into which teams are playing better than Corsi does. And they can also be used for more in-depth player valuation. Take Wyatt Bell, for example. He took only a hundred eighty shot attempts, but most of those have been scoring chances—like eighty-one percent." The numbers roll easily off my tongue; numbers have always stayed in my brain. "And more than half come from the slot or the crease."

"Uh-huh." His eyes narrow. "So you're saying we should judge players solely on their ability to produce and prevent scoring chances."

"Of course not, but it does give us much more quality information than Corsi does. You as a coach obviously want your players to create scoring chances, right?"

"Yeah."

"Especially high-quality chances in the slot or crease, as opposed to unsuccessful attempts from the blue line. But those count in the Corsi metric, which makes it less effective."

Joe doesn't look convinced but he shuts up. I feel like I need to take a stand here so he knows who's in charge, just like Grandpa, but also like Grandpa, he doesn't look happy about it.

I swallow a sigh. "I also plan to talk to a lot of people, including you, Joe."

He nods.

"Everyone here in the front office. The players, although I've talked to them already. The scouts. The draft is coming up in June, and we need to be ready to make some decisions. We have thirteen guys with contracts coming up. We need a plan to deal with that. Who we want to keep. Who we don't want to keep. And how we keep guys here that might be interested in jumping to a different team." I wait a beat. "A winning team."

"They're tired of losing," Grandpa says gruffly. "I don't blame them."

"You going to make a lot of changes?" Joe asks.

"I don't know yet. Change is hard. I think we're going to have to do some things differently, though. Maybe pursue some avenues that are less traditional than others. But we need to do the right things."

"Rebuild," Grandpa says with a sigh. "You're going to tell me draft and develop, aren't you?"

I smile. "Probably, yeah. There's no magic bean that's going to make us Stanley Cup champs next year."

"I know. But Christ, I'm seventy-two years old. I don't have a lot of time left."

"You have lots of years ahead of you," I assure him, even though I feel that pang again. "But I know what you mean. And even if our plan is to build slowly through drafting and development, I know we have to balance that with our needs right now." When the rules on the ice and on the business side of NHL operations changed in 2005, player development became even more important. With the salary cap, young players with entry-level contracts are now a key to success.

"That's why you get paid the big bucks," Joe jokes.

I do get paid big bucks. But I'm worth it.

Our meeting continues until nearly noon. Grandpa offers to take me for lunch, but I'd rather eat a sandwich at my desk and keep working.

Halfway through my turkey and avocado on sourdough, someone knocks on my open door. I look up see Everly, my aunt. Everly's about a year younger than me. I know, it's weird.

"Hey!" She smiles tentatively. "I just came to say welcome."

I smile back at her. There's always been tension between my family and her family. As I kid, I was kind of oblivious to it, but became more aware of it in my teenage years. Now things are even worse because of the big feud between Dad and Uncle Mark and Grandpa. My dad may be feuding with Everly's dad, but I'm working for her dad now and we need to be adults and get along. "Hi, Everly. Thanks. I'm stoked to be here."

She enters my office. She's all sophisticated in a gray pencil skirt, silky blue blouse, and heels, her dark, layered hair brushing her shoulders. The Condors Foundation is separate from the Condors Hockey Club, but works closely with the team to raise funds to support underserved youth in the area. Having grown up in California, the daughter of the Condors' owner, I have no doubt Everly has all the necessary connections not only in sports but in government, education, and other businesses. She's always been super together, mature from the time she was a toddler, smart, and confident.

"When did you get into town?" she asks.

"Wednesday night."

"And here you are, nose to the grindstone already."

"Oh yeah."

"You're taking time off for your parents' party on Saturday, though, right?"

I pause. "You're coming to the party?"

"Yeah." She elevates her eyebrows, the corners of her mouth lifting. "Your mom invited all of us. Not sure if everyone's coming, though."

"Everyone" means almost the entire family—the only one who doesn't live in California is my cousin Jackson, who plays for the Chicago Aces this year.

I wait for Everly to say something about me being married, but she doesn't. I guess Mom's keeping that as a surprise for everyone.

"Should be fun," I say dryly.

Everly laughs. "As much fun as a 7.0 earthquake."

Our eyes meet in shared understanding.

"Well, I'll let you get back to work, boss man." She walks to the door. "Let's do lunch one day."

"Absolutely."

Or not.

I like Everly. Maybe this is a chance for things to be less awkward between everyone.

Or not.

13

LACEY

I'VE HARDLY SEEN THÉO SINCE THURSDAY EVENING WHEN HE told me we should just stay friends. Without benefits. He worked late Friday and went to his office this morning too, even on a Saturday.

It's okay. I don't expect him to entertain me. So what if I don't know anyone here. I've been exploring the neighborhood. This afternoon, I'm walking on the beach, soaking up sunshine and sea air, loving the feel of sand beneath my bare feet, my flip-flops dangling from one hand.

"Byron! Byron, come back!"

The female voice shouting attracts my attention. I look up the beach and see a big dog loping toward me, a golden retriever, I think. His tongue is hanging out in a happy smile as he bounds, dragging his leash in the sand behind him. A woman is running behind him with no hope of catching him.

Instantly, I run toward him. "Byron! Hey, Byron, you good boy, come here!" He slows his pace and I drop to a crouch, extending my hands. He stops and eyes me. One hand still out, palm down, I grab his leash with the other hand.

"Did you escape, you rascal?" I ask him. He sniffs my hand and I gently rub under his chin.

"Oh thank you!" The woman chasing him arrives and halts. "Thank you so much!"

She's panicked, breathing hard, looking nearly in tears. I stand and hand the leash to her. "No problem. He's a gorgeous dog."

She swallows, then takes a deep breath and exhales. "He yanked the leash out of my hand to chase a bird. Jeez, Byron."

She's my age, I think, with long dark hair, smooth tawny skin, and dark eyes. She looks a lot like Jessica Alba. "You're a hero," she says to me. "A heroine."

I laugh. "Just happy to help." I eye Byron wistfully. "I love dogs."

"You don't have one?"

"Uh, no."

"I'm Taylor." She extends a hand. "We live just over there." She nods to a big beach house a few buildings down from Théo's.

"Hi, I'm Lacey." We shake. "We're neighbors."

"Really? Did you just move in?"

"Yes." I point to Théo's condo. "Right there."

"The hockey house."

I laugh. "Yes! I'm, uh, my husband"—wow, that's still weird—"is the new manager of the Condors."

"No kidding!" Her eyes widen. "Cool! I'm a big Condors fan. I met Bobby Ponomarenko a couple of times. I was wondering who would move in now he's gone."

We start walking on the beach together, Taylor's grip on Byron's leash firm as he trots along.

"I'm not a puck bunny," she adds. "Okay, maybe I am. Hockey players are hot."

Hmmm. "Yeah, I guess they are." Apparently, I've been missing out on something all the time we had a hockey team in Vegas. Théo is hot, that's for sure.

"How long have you been married?" Taylor asks.

"Three days."

She stops and gapes at me. "Seriously?"

"Yeah." I grimace. "We did a quickie marriage in Vegas before we left to come here."

"That is so romantic!"

Okay, I like this girl. "Tonight I'm meeting his family for the first time. Other than his mother." I tell her the story of Aline dropping in, and she laughs.

"Way to make a good first impression. I'm sure she'll love you, though. They all will."

"You don't even know me."

"I'm a good judge of character. And so is Byron. If he likes you, you're good people."

"Dogs always know," I agree.

We keep walking awhile, chatting and getting to know each other, then turn around back toward our homes.

"Guess I better get home," Taylor says. "I have a date tonight. New guy I met online."

"Good luck." We pause in front of her huge house. "You live alone here?"

"I live with my parents." One corner of her mouth turns down. "Don't judge me."

"Hey, I'm not." I hold up my hands. "I'm unemployed."

"But you're married." She sighs. "I make not bad money, but everything's so expensive here. I'm saving to try to buy a small condo somewhere eventually."

"It takes time. How old are you?"

"Twenty-four."

"Hey, same. Don't be so hard on yourself. You're probably barely out of college."

"Yeah." She nods. "That's true. I *just* finished grad school. Thanks. We should get together again. Maybe have lunch or something."

"That would be nice."

When I get home, I see Manny outside on his deck. "Hey, Manny. How's it going?"

"Good. You?"

"Not bad. I just saved a dog and made a friend."

"Cool. Come on over. Want a beer?"

I shrug. I've got nothing else to do. "Sure."

We hang out on his deck for a while, drinking a couple of beers and yakking. He's a nice guy.

"I better go get ready," I eventually say, rising from the comfy chair. "We're going to Théo's parents' place tonight for a big family thing."

"Wow. The whole Wynn family. That's like going to Buckingham Palace to meet the king."

I blink. "Uh. Who's the king in the family?"

He laughs. "Bob Wynn. Hockey royalty."

Jesus. I suck in a breath. "Great."

I spend the next hour getting ready, trying to calm the

birds' wings fluttering in my belly by taking slow breaths in and out. I hear Théo come in and I call out a hello from my closed bathroom door.

"I'm going to change," he calls back and heads upstairs.

I'm wearing one of the dresses we picked up the other day, which I hope is appropriate for both meeting the parents and wowing the ex-girlfriend. It's pretty bare and form-fitting, with narrow straps, V neckline, and just-above-the-knee hem, but it's a demure pink with deeper pink and gray flowers. I already have a tan from a couple of days in the sun and I add a little shimmery bronzer to my cheeks and décolletage to play it up.

I take one more peek at myself in the mirror, rubbing my lips together to spread my lip gloss and fluffing my hair, then exit the bathroom.

Théo's steps thud down the stairs. "Ready?"

"You bet." I flash a big smile.

His gaze moves over me, taking in my hair and the dress.

"Do I look okay?"

"You look amazing." His eyes linger on my shoulders. "Is that the dress we bought at Nordstrom?"

"Yes. It was on sale," I quickly add.

"Whatever it was, it's worth every fucking penny." He clears his throat.

"Thank you. You look good too."

He's wearing narrow beige pants, a white shirt, and a casual blazer in charcoal. His feet are bare inside brown loafers. He's so damn gorgeous I want to cry.

He hands me a small box. "Here. I thought this might be a good idea."

I take it slowly and open it. Inside is a gold ring—just a simple, polished band. "Right. Good idea."

"Hopefully it fits."

I remove it from the box. We didn't have rings the night we got married, so we skipped over that, and it feels weird to be doing this. I hesitate, staring at the ring. Getting married and saying vows seemed like fun that night, but putting my own wedding ring onto my finger makes my throat thicken. I'm not a girl who's dreamed about getting married; I've had to be too practical the last few years. But still . . .

I give my head a mental shake and push the ring onto my finger. "It fits."

"I got one too." He holds up his left hand to show me.

"Now girls won't try to hit on you because they'll think you're married."

"I *am* married."

"Well, not really. I mean, if you met someone and you wanted to go out with her, you could totally do that."

He frowns. "I'm not going to do that."

I get a little kick out of riling him a bit. "Okay."

He goes to the kitchen cupboard and takes out a little bottle of pills, pops one in his mouth, and washes it down with water. I've learned these are meds for his stomach ulcer. He doesn't have one anymore, but sometimes he takes them if he feels pain. "I think I could use one of those too." I press a hand to my stomach.

He grins. "Let's go. It'll probably take us an hour to get to Mom and Dad's place." He grabs his keys and a bottle of wine.

"An hour? Jesus. Where are we going?" I ask on the way out.

"Rolling Hills. They live closer to Long Beach, where the Eagles play."

This makes me shake my head. "Eagles. The hockey team. Right."

Traffic is crazy on the freeway, but I guess this is California life.

"Well, you're stuck with me now," I say once we're cruising. "I know you've been avoiding me."

He shakes his head, his lips twitching.

"How's work been going? Are you making progress?"

"I feel like I've accomplished nothing."

"I'm sure you have."

"I have a lot to learn."

"Do you know who's going to be at this shindig?"

"According to my aunt Everly, 'everyone.'"

"Eeek."

"I know. I feel the same way."

He doesn't look terrified; his grip on the steering wheel is relaxed and confident.

"Okay, so who's everyone? I need to be prepared."

"Well, you met my mom. Obviously, my dad will be there."

"Matthew."

"Right. And my brother, I assume. JP."

"And that bitch Emma."

He snorts. "Yeah. And my uncle Mark. He's divorced. I don't know if he's seeing anyone right now. His daughter, Riley, may be there. She's a goalie coach for the Eagles' farm team."

"Whoa. That's impressive. She plays goal?"

"She used to. She played for the Canadian national women's team."

I picture a woman who looks like Théo—six feet tall and muscular.

"Grandpa and Chelsea have been invited. Everly. Maybe she has a date, I don't know. And her three brothers, Asher, Harrison, and Noah."

"Crap."

"The only one who won't be there is my cousin Jackson. He lives in Chicago. They're still in the playoffs."

I'm memorizing all these names. I'm good with names, but this is a lot. I'm also trying not to freak out.

Théo's parents' home is a low bungalow that appears cute and modest—a white picket fence, a few trees, and lots of flowers. We approach the front door, painted a charming dark green, with matching shutters on the windows. There are already lots of cars parked in the massive stone driveway, so others must already be here.

Théo opens the door and steps in without ringing the bell, but an alarm system beeps and his mom appears in the foyer. "Hello! You're here!" She gives Théo a hug and a kiss on his cheek, then turns to me, beaming. "Hello again, Lacey." She hugs me too, enveloping me in the scent of expensive perfume.

"Here, Mom, this is for you." Théo hands her the wine.

"Oh, thank you, you didn't need to bring that. Come in, come in." She leads the way into the house.

The exterior is deceptive because inside the place is immense—a spacious living room on the right, a big family room, dining room and kitchen on the left, all open to each other. High vaulted ceilings create an airy feel. The furnishings are a sort of French country style that's elegant but relaxed.

And the rooms are full of people.

Gah.

"Hey, Théo!" a few voices call. Some are sitting on the big couches and chairs, others are standing. I have a vague impression of well-dressed, dark-haired people, mostly men, as Théo starts saying hi.

"Welcome to California," says one younger man seated on a couch. He stands and moves to shake Théo's hand.

"Thanks, Ash."

The door pings again and with a tight smile, Aline says, "That must be JP." She hurries off and returns momentarily followed by a young man and a woman. Aline's jaw is set and her eyes flash, but she's still smiling.

"Okay!" Aline claps her hands and calls out, "Everyone's here now and Théo has a surprise for you."

Oh, here we go.

I feel eyes on me. I smile. Théo takes my hand and leads me farther into the living room.

"What's your surprise?" asks a sophisticated-looking woman standing near the fireplace.

"I want you all to meet Lacey." He turns and smiles down at me. "My wife."

There's a shocked beat of silence and then a roar. The woman who spoke lets out a little shriek, the men all shout, and Aline smiles.

For a few moments, it's insanity as everyone swarms to congratulate us with hugs and handshakes. I don't know who anyone is, but I keep smiling.

"Okay, okay," Théo says. "You're going to scare the crap out of Lacey. Settle down and let me introduce her to you all."

"First let me get you drinks," Aline says. "We have champagne! Matt, can you open it now?"

"You bet." Théo's dad and mom head to the kitchen.

Théo starts introducing me to people. I recognize the names Théo mentioned earlier, glad I knew them ahead of time. When he gets to JP, tension thickens the air around us and Théo's jaw tightens.

"Nice to meet you, JP," I murmur.

"And this is Emma," JP says.

The blonde next to him extends a hand to shake mine. She's really pretty, with big blue eyes, long eyelashes, and perfect skin. "Hello, Lucy."

"It's Lacey." *Bitch*. "Lovely to meet you. Great shoes."

She glances down. "Thanks."

I actually *am* envious of the leopard Louboutins. They're fabulous.

I study JP. There's a definite family resemblance, and he and Théo are similar in size and build. And yet there's something different. JP is good-looking, but I don't feel any kind of tug of attraction like I do with Théo.

I catch the tense exchange of scowls between the brothers.

"Boys." An older man approaches us. "Good to see you both."

This must be Théo and JP's grandfather. And Théo's boss. I have to admit I'm curious to meet the patriarch of this big hockey family. The king. Ha.

"Hi, Grandpa," JP says with a smile. "It's been a while since I've seen you."

"That's not my fault," Mr. Wynn growls, shaking his grandson's hand.

JP's smile falters. "This is Emma. Emma, my grandfather Bob Wynn."

"You look familiar." Mr. Wynn eyes Emma with narrowed eyes.

"That's because the last time you saw her she was with Théo," Aline says tautly, still smiling.

The air goes static around us.

Emma grimace-smiles and shakes Mr. Wynn's hand. "Yes, we have met before."

Mr. Wynn stares at Emma then at JP.

"She's with me now," JP says.

Théo's watching this with what appears to be . . . amusement. Huh. I slide my arm through his and hug it. He glances down at me and winks. I meet his eyes and we share a look of hilarity. I'm surprised he's not more tense about this meeting. Although I do feel the hostility between him and JP.

"And this is Lacey," Théo says.

Bob Wynn is in his seventies and fixes me with a smile that's still . . . wow, sexy. In a charming devil kind of way. He's a big man too, although not as big as his grandsons, with a twinkle in his dark blue eyes as he greets me. "For Chrissakes, Théo, you could have told me you were married. Jesus."

I blink at his cussing. Not that I don't cuss. I love the F word more than any other. It just seems a bit odd in a first meeting. Nonetheless, my smile is genuine as he shakes my hand, studying me.

"You're beautiful," he says. "Good work, Théo."

I stop myself from wrinkling my nose, feeling a bit objectified, but I'll give him a pass since we just met.

"My wife, Chelsea." Bob indicates the woman next to him.

Chelsea's smile is warm albeit a touch reserved, and she extends a hand to me. I shake it, and her grip is firm and assured. I like that. I'm a little taken aback at the age difference between her and Bob, though. He's in his early seventies; she can't be much more than fifty.

She's beautiful, her blond hair cut in a chin-length bob of messy waves, her lips a shiny pale pink, blue eyes perfectly made up. If she did her makeup herself, she's good at it. She too is wearing Louboutin shoes that I could weep over and an expensive-looking black dress that flatters her slender shape. Huge diamonds sparkle on her left hand.

Théo's greeting to Chelsea is as reserved as hers, and I'm picking up all kinds of weird signals between them. Between everyone in this room, honestly. I don't know if I've ever been to a gathering with as many undercurrents of uneasiness and tension, despite the smiles and chatter.

I'm happy when Aline hands me a glass of champagne so I have something to hold on to, and I keep my smile pasted firmly on my face as Théo's dad makes a toast to us. Théo slides his arm around my waist and gives me an affectionate smile as we clink our glasses together then sip the bubbly wine.

I'm going to need a few glasses of this stuff.

I don't usually have problems meeting people or making

conversation. People are fascinating. But tonight, I want to stick close to Théo and be more of an observer. Because this whole family is intriguing.

Maybe I'd be more freaked out if I was actually going to be part of it.

I get the animosity between Théo and JP. The reason is standing beside JP, looking at Théo like . . . like she's a lion and he's a zebra she wants to attack and devour.

Lion and zebra? Whatever. She's got a hungry, longing look in her eyes and it's pissing me off.

I slide my gaze over to JP to see if he's noticed. He's talking to Riley and her dad, Mark. Riley, by the way, looks nothing like Théo, although she is tall, with long dark hair and a slender build.

Aware of Emma watching, I move closer to Théo, go onto my toes, and whisper in his ear, "Look at me like you want to bang my brains out."

14

LACEY

I feel Théo's startled twitch, but he smiles and turns his gaze on me. And oh my Gaga, he *does* look like he wants to bang my brains out. The heat in his eyes and the sexy curve of his mouth make my belly flutter. He lifts a hand and cups my cheek so gently, his thumb brushing at the corner of my mouth. "Did I tell you how beautiful you look?"

"Um, sort of." I flutter my eyelashes at him, our gazes connected. Heat expands around us.

It's not a pretense. Except neither of us is going to act on the lust blazing up inside us.

He slides his hand around to the back of my neck, pulls me closer, and kisses my forehead, and I melt even more inside. Gah.

Get a grip, girl.

I don't look directly at Emma, but I know she's still watching us and I can feel her displeasure. Good.

Gazing around the room, I see that the conversational

groups are along family lines—Théo and I are talking to his mom and dad, JP and Emma are talking to Mark and Riley, and a small group has formed of Bob and Chelsea and their four kids, and the girlfriend who's with one of the boys . . . Harrison, I think.

As if she's noticed too, Aline steps away and moves over next to Chelsea with a smile.

Théo follows his mom's lead, whether consciously or not I don't know, but I stick with him as he approaches Asher.

"Hey, man. I was reading your article today about the Condors."

Asher lifts a brow. He has the same Wynn bone structure in his face and build, his hair a lighter brown, cut short. "Don't punch me."

Théo laughs and claps a hand on his . . . um, his uncle's shoulder. "Not gonna. It was good stuff. I mean, it was bad, but honest. I make a point of reading your articles."

"Thanks."

"Why would you waste your time reading that?" Harrison says with a sardonic grin at Asher.

Asher shakes his head. "Asshole," he mutters to his brother.

"What do you get if you cross a sports reporter with a vegetable?" Théo asks. After a beat, he says, "A common tater."

Everyone groans. I laugh, though, 'cause it's dorky but kind of funny. Théo shoots me a grin.

"That's why *he's* the writer, dude," Harrison says, earning laughs from all.

"Writer," scoffs Noah, Asher's other brother. "What

kind of job is that? He watches sports all day in his underwear, then writes a blog post about what he watched."

Asher takes this in stride with a good-natured grin. "Sounds like the perfect job to me."

Somehow I suspect if anyone other than his own brothers made these jokes, he wouldn't be so laid back.

"Congratulations on the new job, Théo," Noah says. "I was surprised to hear you agreed to work for Dad."

Théo just smiles. "It's a great opportunity."

"Your dad can't be happy about it," Noah adds in a low voice.

"Nope." Théo shrugs. "It's my life. Besides . . . you play for the Eagles' farm team."

"I gotta take my jobs wherever I can get them," Noah says wryly.

"*Your* dad can't be happy about that."

"The trade happened before all this shit went down, so there's not much he can say now."

"True."

"Chelsea, would you help me bring out the food?" Aline asks.

Chelsea nods quickly. "Of course." I watch the two women walk over to the kitchen. Should I go offer to help as well? I'm torn between wanting to help and make a good impression on Théo's mom, and being terrified of leaving Théo.

I'll be brave.

I move away from Théo and join Chelsea and Aline. "Is there anything I can do to help?"

"Oh, thank you, Lacey. There are a lot of us so I'm

going to serve dinner buffet style. Could you take this baked brie and put it on the sideboard in the dining room?"

I take the dish she hands me. "I can handle more." I grin. "I've worked as a waitress. Load me up."

Aline laughs. "Well, okay, here." She gives me a platter of Caprese salad skewers—cherry tomatoes, bocconcini, and basil leaves drizzled with balsamic vinegar.

I easily balance the two dishes. "These look delicious."

Chelsea follows me with more dishes. "Aline is a fantastic cook."

"Oh my gosh, she made all these herself?"

"Most of it. I brought a few appetizers as well. But she made the entire dinner."

"Wow."

Chelsea and I help Aline load up the sideboard with some amazing-looking food, and then Aline announces everyone should come help themselves. The huge dining table is set, with flowers and candles in the center.

Théo's involved in a quiet but intense conversation with his father across the room. I hesitate to join them, as it looks private, but they end it and Théo approaches me with a grim smile to take my hand and lead me to the dining room. We fill plates and take seats at the table.

"Well, it seems like a long time since the whole family has been together," Bob Wynn says once everyone is seated. "Maybe my birthday was the last time."

"Some of us weren't invited to that," Théo's uncle Mark says with an edge.

"You wouldn't have come anyway," Bob retorts.

"Because you fucking fired me," Mark snaps.

I swallow and look down at my plate.

"Let's toast to Aline for all this amazing food." Matt lifts his glass.

Everyone toasts, then begins eating. For a while, things seem to be going well, with polite conversation about hockey, what the hockey players in the group will be doing over the summer, and compliments to the food. Several bottles of wine disappear as we eat, although Théo is nursing one glass of Merlot. I'm on my third. God.

Then Bob speaks up from the end of the table. "Seriously, JP, what are you thinking? You can't date your brother's girlfriend."

Awkward silence descends. I want to laugh. Emma sucks on her bottom lip.

"It's against the rules," Bob adds.

"So is stealing money from your sons." Mark Wynn stabs a piece of chicken on his plate.

The atmosphere thickens even more.

"Well, at least I don't steal girlfriends. Or cheat on my wife."

JP sucks in an audible breath. So does Mark. "Is that right?" Mark says tightly, glaring at his father.

"What are you saying?" Bob scowls back at him.

"I'm saying you remarried pretty damn fast after Mom died." He gives Chelsea a narrow-eyed look, and she flinches.

I reach for Théo's hand beneath the table and squeeze it. His fingers grip mine tightly.

Everly speaks up. "Well, I for one don't care who JP goes out with, but it is kind of inappropriate to bring her to Théo's welcome dinner."

"Don't be a bitch, Ev," mutters Riley.

"Don't call her a bitch," snaps Harrison.

Everly shakes her head at Harrison. She appears quite able to handle herself.

"Inappropriate?" Bob barks. "I'll tell you what's inappropriate. Inappropriate is two sons suing their father."

My eyes fly open wide. I glance between Matt and Mark. Their faces contract into lines of annoyance.

Théo stiffens next to me and picks up his wine. "Let's not talk about that here," he bites out.

"Good idea!" Aline looks around. "Does anyone want seconds? Please help yourselves."

"It's all delicious, Aline," Chelsea says.

"Thank you."

"What the hell are these?" Bob holds up a Caprese skewer.

Chelsea sets a hand on his arm. "Tomatoes and mozzarella cheese," she murmurs. "You like it."

"How's your mom, Riley?" Aline asks.

Riley glances at her dad. "She's great. She's been doing some work with the football team in Toronto. She has quite a few high-profile clients now. A couple of Olympic skating champions, a champion diver, and a few NHL guys."

Seeing my curious look, she adds, "My mom's a sports psychologist."

"You screwed that woman over," Bob says to Mark.

More uneasy glances are exchanged around the big table. Mark's jaw hardens.

Aline nibbles her bottom lip and closes her eyes briefly. I sense her distress.

"I'd like to make another toast," Bob says.

"No," everyone says at once.

Silence swells again.

"I'm so happy to have Théo living so close." Aline speaks with determined cheer. "And especially now he's married! I'm looking forward to getting to know you, Lacey."

I smile at Aline.

"What do you do, Lacey?" Riley asks.

"Well, I've had a lot of different jobs," I say. "I've worked in the hospitality business, also as a freelance makeup artist. I even worked as a budtender for a while."

There's a beat of silence as everyone takes that in.

"I need some good weed," Harrison says. "Can you hook me up?"

"As if you need her help for that," Everly says.

"You better not be smoking dope!" Bob bellows. "That's *really* against the rules."

"Come on, Dad, it's legal here now," Harrison says.

"I don't care if it's legal!"

"So, Emma, what do you do?" Aline interjects swiftly.

"JP, apparently," Everly mutters.

I hide my smile in my napkin while others all choke on laughter or maybe outrage.

"Everly." Chelsea chides her daughter, her fingers rubbing her throat, eyes darting around the table.

Everly's lips tighten.

"It's okay." Théo speaks up. "It's fine that JP brought Emma to dinner."

"Don't be such a pussy, boy," Bob snaps.

All the women at the table straighten.

Théo, to my surprise, grins. "Grandpa, that's not really an insult. Pussies are amazing."

I turn my head and stare at him.

Aline drops her head, fingers to her eyebrows.

"Yeah, Grandpa, that's not really woke," Harrison offers.

"Woke? What the hell?" Bob frowns.

"If pussy means weakness, that's just not right," Everly says. "A woman's vagina is incredibly strong and resilient."

"Not to mention powerful," Riley adds. "It has the ability to control men."

Asher and Noah snort.

"Seriously," she adds. "Pussy can make men do things like nothing else. And don't tell me differently, after the dumb things some of you have done for women." She levels a look at JP with raised eyebrows.

Théo clears his throat.

"I can't believe we're having this conversation." Aline looks to the ceiling.

"A penis isn't exactly a symbol of strength," Everly adds. "It may be strong and powerful, but it only lasts for a few minutes."

"You've obviously been with the wrong men," Théo says, earning laughs.

I nod in support of his stamina, although I sadly have no personal knowledge of it.

The tension has eased a little, but not for long.

"Anyway, I mean it," Théo says. "JP and Emma's relationship is their own business. I just hope they're as happy together as Lacey and I are." And he leans over to kiss my cheek. I flash him what I hope looks like a loving glance and briefly rest my head on his shoulder. But my insides burn at the thought that Théo's heart was broken by his brother and the woman he loved—loves? Ugh.

"Aw," says Everly, but she's smiling.

Théo stands. "If everyone's done, JP and I will clear the table." He shoots his brother a stern look. JP pushes back his chair.

"I'll get the desserts." Aline rises too.

Everyone pitches in and I plant myself in front of the dishwasher to help also, until we're all back in the dining room.

"Did you make all these, too?" I ask Aline, surveying the assortment of sweets on the sideboard.

"No." She smiles wryly. "I love cooking, but I hate baking. These are from La Belle Madeleine."

I have no idea what that is, but it sounds lovely. I take a selection of treats—something chocolate, a mini apple pie, and a pretty cookie. I love sweets.

Aline offers coffee and more wine. She's trying so hard to make this a nice evening.

Then everyone moves back to the living room. Aline shoos people away from the kitchen, telling us to relax. Like that's possible with this group. Théo takes a seat in a big armchair and tugs me down with him. There's room enough for both of us, but it's . . . cozy. I catch Emma's unhappy expression.

Okay, what the fuck is up with that? She's here with JP. She cheated on Théo with JP. Does she still want Théo? Does she want *both* of them? This is pissing me off.

Also I've had a lot of wine.

"I think we'll go soon," Théo says in a low voice near my ear. "Not sure I can handle much more of this."

"I know what you mean. Holy crap." This was crazier than I imagined.

"Gonna use the bathroom before we go. Be right back." He sets his empty glass on the small table beside the chair.

Everly, sitting near me on the couch, leans over. "It's good to meet you," she says to me with a smile. "Théo seems really happy with you."

I'm not sure what to say to that. "Thanks."

"We didn't know he'd even been seeing anyone," she continues. "Which is why we were all so surprised. I hope we didn't make you feel uncomfortable."

"This whole evening made me feel uncomfortable," I say without thinking.

She laughs, shaking her head. "You're not the only one. No wonder we're all single. None of us want to bring anyone into this madness. Théo's got guts."

If she only knew the truth. I shift in the chair and drain the last of my wine. "You know, I'm going to find the bathroom too before we leave."

Everly points the direction Théo went, down a hall.

I hike across the big room and turn down the hall, then stop dead.

Emma and Théo are standing in the dimly lit hall, close together, their faces nearly touching. She has her hand on his chest.

My stomach clutches and my breathing arrests. I put a hand on the wall beside me to steady myself. It feels like time freezes and this moment goes on and on. My head empties.

Théo spots me, his head whipping around. Emma's gaze follows.

"Lacey," Théo says calmly, moving around Emma toward me. "Are you ready to go?"

"I just need to use the bathroom first." Somehow I manage to speak.

Théo gestures to the room and I walk past him and Emma, giving Emma a hard look. Then I shut and lock the bathroom door and drop onto the closed lid of the toilet, burying my face in my hands.

I've never been so confused in my life.

I'm jealous.

How can I be jealous? Our marriage is fake. I don't really care about Théo that way.

I'm just doing such a good job acting, I convinced myself things are real. That's it.

If Emma still wants him, maybe Théo is happy about that.

Ugh.

Well, I can't hide in here forever. I use the toilet, wash up, and arrange my expression into relaxed and cheerful.

Théo is standing at the edge of the living room near the front door, talking to his mom and dad. He extends a hand to me as I walk up to them, taking mine and drawing me near to him.

So confused!

"Thanks for a lovely evening," I say.

"It wasn't really lovely," Aline replies wryly. "But you're

welcome. I look forward to getting to know you better." She moves and hugs me.

Théo's dad hugs me too, then turns to his son. "I still don't understand how you could take a job working for that asshole. He's the *enemy*, for Chrissake."

My eyes widen.

"Mark. That asshole is your father." Aline nudges him.

"He's losing his fucking mind," Mark mutters. "You have no idea what you're getting yourself into, Théo. It's a no-win situation. You'll never be able to run that team. The minute you do something he doesn't like, he'll fire you too."

Théo grimaces. "Well, thanks for the vote of confidence, Dad."

Mark scowls.

"Théo's super smart," I say, even though I'm in shock from what I just saw in the hall. "And talented and hard working. He can do anything he sets his mind to."

I feel Aline's pleasure at my words. Mark gives me a sharp, assessing look and I meet it head-on. He nods slowly.

Théo slides his hand into mine and squeezes it gently. We say good night and make our escape into the fresh night air.

"Jesus Christ." Théo blows out a breath as we walk to his car. "Sorry about that."

"Don't apologize. You were the sanest one there. Well, you and your mom." I pause. "And Chelsea."

"Chelsea? Are you kidding me? She's nothing but a gold digger."

I frown as I slide into my seat. I tug on the seatbelt while Théo goes around and climbs in. "I didn't get that impression of her."

"You don't know her."

"True. But . . ." I trail off. I guess I don't know her.

"She married a man twenty years older than her. What other reason would she marry him than for his money?"

"Maybe she loves him?"

He snorts.

"No really. It seems to me like she cares about him."

He dismisses my opinion with a shake of his head and turns on his GPS to direct us back to the freeway and his place.

"And what about Emma?" I ask, annoyance rising. "What were you two talking about in the hallway? Does she want to get back together?"

"Yeah."

I'm stunned into silence. I didn't really expect that. I sit quietly for a few minutes, as Théo doesn't offer up any more details. I watch city lights slide by outside the car.

I don't think he should go back to Emma. She fucked him over with his own brother. That doesn't bode well for their future together. I didn't get a good impression of her tonight, although we barely said two words to each other. I don't think she's good enough for Théo. I don't want him to be hurt again.

I guess showing up with me made her jealous enough that she realized she wants him back.

But if that's what he wants, I'm happy for him. So, I guess I'm not needed here anymore, if they're going to get back together. My stomach cramps up as I try to figure out what I'm going to do. Obviously, I can't stay with Théo. That would not make Emma happy. Back to Vegas it is then!

Pressure builds behind my eyes and I blink tears away, staring out the side window.

I'm going to have to go back there someday. I have an apartment there, other belongings. My brother, who I'm still worried about. My best friend. It's probably best if I just pussy up and deal with things. I'm not sure exactly how I'm going to deal with those thugs Chris owes money to, but I'll figure something out.

15

THÉO

I DON'T THINK LACEY HAS EVER BEEN AS QUIET AS SHE HAS tonight. She didn't say much at the dinner and she's gone totally silent now. Ha. As if I know her that well . . . in four days.

Wow, it seems so much longer than that.

I *do* feel like I know her.

I glance at her as I drive on the freeway. Her head's leaning against the window and her eyes are closed. I guess she's fallen asleep. That's why she hasn't said anything.

What an insane night. What was I thinking, dragging Lacey into my nutso family? No matter she needed to get out of town and I helped her do that, and tried to look after her and make sure she has what she needs—she doesn't deserve this kind of lunacy.

I have to admit, she was awesome tonight. She seemed to know when I was getting ready to blow up, and she'd reach out and squeeze my hand or take my arm. Or ask me to look at her like I want to bang her brains out, which honestly is probably the *only* way I can look at her.

Weirdly—what I thought I needed her for? JP and Emma? That didn't bother me at all. It was the rest of the family fucking drama that got to me. Everly and Riley sniping at each other. Dad and Uncle Mark cornering me and bugging me for taking the job with Grandpa. Then Dad on my case because I didn't get a prenup agreement drawn up before marrying Lacey.

Which was really fucking stupid of me, in hindsight. Not like me at all.

And JP . . .

I swallow a sigh. I don't even miss Emma. But I do miss JP.

We're not even two years apart in age. We've always been best friends. Sure, we're competitive, but the thing about having a family member who plays the same sport as you is that you push each other to be better. But we've always had each other's backs, and I still don't know how he could have done that.

I feel the loss of my brother more than anything, goddammit.

Even more than the fact that my dad doesn't think I can do this job. I'm not ashamed to admit I want him to be proud of me, like he was when I was playing hockey and winning championships.

Fuck me. I lean my head back against the headrest and sigh.

And Emma . . . following me to tell me she misses me and she thinks she made a mistake and now that I'm here in California too, maybe we could try again.

She was at the fucking party *with my brother.*

I'm pissed at him, but now I'm really pissed *for* him because . . . well, he's my brother. What the hell am I supposed to do now? Tell him Emma wants to get back together with me? He'd laugh in my face. But am I supposed to just let him stay with her, knowing what she's like?

Christ. As if our family wasn't fucked up enough.

Lacey talked to some of my family. Everly seems to like her. And Grandpa . . . he seems really taken with her. Or maybe he was just pissed at JP for showing up with Emma. That was actually hilarious. And Mom loves Lacey.

And why not? She's funny and sweet and genuine. Except for the lying-about-being-married part.

Even Dad gave her a look of respect when she defended me to him, and I . . . I wanted to grab her and squeeze the breath out of her for that.

The drive home is faster, the traffic lighter now, and I pull into the garage at the condo and park. I turn to Lacey and gently nudge her shoulder. "Hey, baby. We're home."

"Mmm." Her eyelashes flutter and she lifts her head. "Oh wow. Already?"

"Yeah."

She sits for a few seconds then reaches for her seatbelt. I jump out and hurry to open her door.

"I guess I was tired," she says quietly.

"I guess so. Don't blame you. The tribe is exhausting."

She gives a half-smile. "That they are."

In the house she heads straight to her bedroom. "G'night, Théo." She pauses. "Do you like to be called

Theo . . ." She pronounces it the English way, then the French way. "Or Théo?"

"Either." I shrug. "My family always called me Théo, but when I got into major junior hockey everyone assumed it was Theo, and I didn't bother trying to correct it."

"I like the French way. How your mom says it. Your mom's a doll."

"Yeah, she's okay."

"G'night," she says again, and shuts her bedroom door.

I don't move from where I'm standing in the living room. Something feels weird. Probably she hates my family. Understandable.

Okay, okay, I don't hate them all. None of them are bad people. Although I'm still not sure what the real story is about the missing money my dad and uncle have accused Grandpa of stealing from them. I can't believe he would do something like that, but they're pissed enough to sue him over it. Nothing says "I love you" like a lawsuit.

Also, did Grandpa really cheat on his wife? I never knew my grandmother; she died before I was born. I've only ever known Chelsea, and my parents have always regarded her as "the other woman" who married Grandpa for his money soon after he became a widower.

Fuck. Why did I take this goddamn job? I should have been looking for a job as far away from California as I could get. If only there was an NHL team in Alaska.

Sunday morning. I could go to the office. God knows there's enough to do.

When I come downstairs, Lacey's in the kitchen, making coffee, wearing pajamas—little shorts and a tank top. I stare longingly at her bare legs. Christ, even her feet are sexy, with shiny purple-painted toenails.

"Morning," she says, facing me.

"Morning."

Neither of us are morning people and we both love our coffee. I head straight to the Keurig and get myself a cup brewing.

Lacey leans against the counter, holding her mug in both hands. "So, I guess we need to talk."

"Not until I've had my coffee." I don't know what the hell she wants to talk about, but she knows I don't form words until I've had at least one cup.

"Right. Okay. I'll be out on the deck."

Yeah, I watch her walk out there because her ass in those little shorts is fucking hot and . . . those legs.

When my coffee's ready, I grab it and join her on the deck. The morning is foggy and cool, the ocean almost obscured by pearly white mist. I set my mug on the table then go back inside to grab a blanket for Lacey.

She gives me a startled look when I hand it to her.

"What?"

She just shakes her head. I get it. It's morning. No words.

She wraps herself up in the blanket and I take another chair, propping my feet on the railing. I'm wearing sweatpants and a long-sleeved tee, so I'm not cold. It's kind of cool, seeing the ocean in different ways. I'd love to see a big storm with crashing waves. That'd be killer.

We sip our coffee silently. Finally, Lacey speaks. "It never stops."

"What?"

"The ocean. The waves never stop." She takes another mouthful of coffee. "And it's so weird to think that way, way out there are other continents. Other people."

"Uh-huh."

"You can't even see them."

I nod.

"And there are whales out there. All kinds of living creatures. We can't see them either."

"That is true."

She sighs. "So."

Okay, this is it. The talk.

"I know I have to leave, since you and Emma are getting back together."

I spew coffee out my mouth and nose. I choke. I cough. I wipe my face. "What the fuck?"

"You said she wanted to get back together."

"*She* does. I don't." I shake my head vigorously. "Are you kidding me? After what she did? I'd never take her back."

Lacey bites her lip. "Are you sure? Maybe you could have a second chance with her."

I frown. "I don't want a second chance with her. That was never what this was about. I just didn't want to feel like a big loser walking into that gathering with her there and everyone feeling sorry for me."

"I don't think you needed me for that," she says quietly.

I tilt my head. "You're probably right. Having a

beautiful woman on my arm doesn't make me a better man."

"You were the better man because you were gracious about it."

"But I did need you there."

She rolls her head against the back of the chair and looks at me. "You did?"

"Yeah. I almost lost it a few times. When Dad and Grandpa were barking at each other. When Everly and Riley were snarking at each other. When Dad insulted me. And about ten other times. Having you there calmed me down."

She blinks. "I knew you were getting pissed."

I huff out a laugh. "Yeah."

"So you're not getting back with Emma?"

"Fuck no."

"I was going to leave today. Since I wasn't needed anymore."

I frown. "No. You don't have to leave. I . . . I do need you."

She sinks her teeth into her bottom lip and holds my gaze. I can only be honest. I was stupid to think I need a hot wife to feel better about myself with my family, but the truth is, Lacey makes me feel better about myself just by being here and it has nothing to do with my family or Emma and JP. It's just . . . her.

"Okay," she says. "I won't go. Yet."

Relief flows through me, but still I frown. "Yet?"

"Well, we both know I have to leave at some point."

I nod slowly. "Yeah." That is true.

She sits up straighter and shifts in the chair so she's

turned toward me and not facing the ocean. "I have questions."

"About?"

"Your family. Oh my God! They're crazy!"

I laugh. "I think I told you that."

"What are you going to do about Emma? Are you going to tell JP?"

"I don't know." I rub my jaw. "Still thinking about that. Don't really want to get involved."

"I understand that. But maybe he should know he's dating a . . . a . . ." She flounders.

"Yeah, I thought of that too. But . . . I expect he'll find out himself."

She purses her lips. "True. Okay, do you really think Chelsea only married your grandfather for his money? That's nuts."

"That's what my parents always said. My grandma came from a really wealthy family. When she died, she left a shit ton of money to Grandpa and to my dad and my uncle. Not to mention, he did pretty well with his hockey career, although back then players didn't make the kind of money they do now. But he owned a hockey team and had lots of money, and then he married this hot woman who was twenty years younger than him, and it wasn't long after Grandma died, which is why Mark was insinuating that Grandpa was having an affair with Chelsea before Grandma died."

"Holy shit." She sips her coffee. "But they have four kids together. I don't think a gold digger would have four kids."

"Fair point, I guess."

"Are your dad and uncle really suing your grandpa?"

"Yeah. They can't talk about it though, because the lawyers told them not to."

"Because he stole money from them? That's messed up."

"He says he didn't. They suspect it was actually Chelsea, because they think she married Dad for his money. So yeah, there are some bad feelings there."

"No shit." She shakes her head. "And what's with Riley and Everly?"

"I don't know. But Uncle Mark and his kids have never liked Chelsea or her kids."

"That's sad."

"I like all of them, but when we were growing up, we—Riley, Jackson, JP, and me—knew our parents didn't like or trust Chelsea."

"And your uncle Mark—what's up with him? Did he cheat on your aunt?"

"I don't know." I grimace. "They got divorced a long time ago and I don't know the details."

"Wow."

"I need breakfast."

"Of course you do."

"Let's go out."

She shrugs. "Okay."

We go inside to change then go for breakfast at a Venice Beach café on the boardwalk with a view of the beach and palm trees. Lacey orders an omelet with avocado, cheese, and bacon.

"I'm going to eat avocado every day while I'm in California," she announces. "It's my mission."

"Sounds like a worthy cause." I order classic eggs Benedict.

"This is lovely." She picks up her orange juice and leans back in the chair to stare out at the beach. "I love the smell of the air. The feel of it. It's so soft."

I study her across the table, taking in her glowing skin, masses of shiny hair, and luminous smile. "The air is soft?"

"Yes. Can't you feel it?"

I grin. "Sure."

"You're patronizing me." Her lips curve into a smile.

"No, I'm not." I lean forward, wanting to kiss those lush lips. "You're entertaining me."

"So, you're laughing at me."

I shake my head, reading the teasing glint in her eyes. She knows how to push my buttons. Impressive. "I'm laughing with you, and you know it."

"Okay. Can we go for a walk on the beach after this? Or . . ." She hesitates. "Do you have to go to work?"

I sigh. "I should."

I sense she wants to protest, but says nothing. I appreciate that. Emma used to nag me about how much I worked.

I find myself talking to Lacey about some of the issues I'm facing with the team as we eat our delicious breakfasts. She doesn't try to solve the problems for me, obviously, but her intent listening and the questions she asks help me process things.

After breakfast we go home, and I find myself saying, "Okay, let's go for a walk."

Lacey's face lights up and that makes a warm glow spread through my chest. We walk close to the water on the firm, damp sand, Lacey pausing to pick up shells or unusual rocks.

"This one's shaped like a heart." She holds it up then pockets it.

Her joy in such a simple thing makes my heart turn over in my chest. I spot another heart-shaped one, which I pass to her. I keep walking with my head down, watching for others.

"Byron!"

Startled, I look up at Lacey's shout. She's greeting a dog, a beautiful golden retriever. Byron? What the hell?

Byron seems happy to see her too, trying to lick her face, and she's laughing. I glance over at the woman with Byron, who's smiling.

"See, he likes you," the woman says.

"You're such a good boy, aren't you. Such a handsome boy." She rubs Byron's ears, then straightens and looks at me. "This is Byron. And Taylor. My husband, Théo."

Taylor reaches out to shake my hand. "Nice to meet you, Théo. I hear you've moved into Bobby's house."

"Yeah." Perplexed, I glance back and forth between Lacey and Taylor. "You two know each other?"

"We met yesterday out here." Lacey turns to Taylor. "How was your date?"

"Omigod, the worst!" She rolls her eyes. "Dinner went okay, but just as we were leaving the restaurant, he took off running down the street."

"What!"

"I started running after him, asking what was wrong, and he yelled 'Cops! I have a warrant out for my arrest!' So

I stopped and the police ran past me and arrested him. Apparently he was dealing crack cocaine."

Lacey's mouth drops open and she stares at Taylor. "That *is* the worst!"

"I know, right?" Taylor shakes her head. "I have no luck with men."

I'm speechless.

"You want to come over for margaritas?" Lacey asks her. "I'm going to make guacamole because I'm on a mission to eat avocado every day."

She's already had avocado today, but I like guacamole.

"Sure. Let me take Byron home."

"No, bring him! I love him." She pets Byron then turns big eyes on me. "You should get a dog."

"Let me think about that. No."

She laughs. "What? You don't like dogs?"

"Sure, I do." I hold out my hand so Byron can sniff my knuckles. "I just don't have time for one."

"Bah."

Within a short time, we're at home, on the patio, drinking margaritas and eating chips and salsa and guacamole and Manny has joined us and there's music playing. And I should be at the office, but I'm not, because I'm laughing and drinking tequila and I haven't been this relaxed and happy in a long time.

"You think *your* family's weird," Manny says. "My grandma has fake plants but she puts them in real dirt."

Taylor laughs. "That's hilarious! My grandma—bless her soul—used to turn off the TV when she was undressing because she didn't want the men on TV to see her naked."

We all laugh uproariously. The tequila might have something to do with it.

I can't take my eyes off Lacey—her smile is radiant, her jokes make me laugh, she's absolutely fucking gorgeous. And I can't have her. Christ.

Then Taylor tells Manny about her date last night. He commiserates. "I once had a date with a woman and when I showed her a picture of my dog, she said 'I hate dogs' so I got up and left."

"You have a dog?" Taylor's eyes light up.

I meet Lacey's eyes. Taylor and Manny seem to be getting along great.

She grins at me and holds up her margarita glass. Okay, it's a wineglass, but whatever. I'll have to get some margarita glasses.

We end up cooking chicken breasts and veggies on the grill, then Manny and Taylor head home, eyeing each other like they both want to say something but don't.

"They'll totally get together," Lacey says as we clean up the kitchen.

"You think so?"

"I know so."

Her confidence and pleasure in her prediction for her new friend is a total turn-on. Don't ask me why. I want to crowd her against the counter and kiss her until neither of us can breathe and she's begging me to fuck her.

Jesus.

I dry my hands on a towel and hang it inside the cupboard.

"Let's go in the hot tub," Lacey suggests.

I gaze at her for a moment, remembering our drive

from Vegas to L.A. and her telling me she'd rather have sex in a hot tub than on the beach.

I swallow a groan. This is probably an epically bad idea. If I'm having a hard time keeping my hands off her, it's not going to be any easier sitting in a hot tub half naked.

"We haven't tried it out yet," she adds.

I try to run through pros and cons and identify alternatives. If I say no, her feelings could be hurt. Or not. Maybe she'd rather be alone. If I say yes, I'll be . . . aw, fuck it. "Okay."

"I'll go get my swimsuit on!" She darts away into her bedroom.

Once again she's got me doing things I know I shouldn't do. And the weird thing is . . . I don't even care.

I don't want to analyze this too much, which is also weird, because I live for analysis. Maybe sometimes it's better to just not dig too deep.

Or maybe I'm a coward.

Whatever. I jog upstairs and change into a pair of board shorts. The hot tub is outside my bedroom so I head out and lift off the cover. Steam rises into the air along with the scent of bromine. I turn on the jets and the lights, and let the water churn for a few minutes while I wait for Lacey.

She appears in my bedroom door, and all the air leaves my lungs. I can't fucking breathe. Her red bikini doesn't cover much, and she's absolutely goddamn gorgeous. Her hair is piled on top of her head in a bunch of loops and she drops a towel onto a chair and smiles.

The sun is setting and the solar lamps on the deck are illuminated, the sky above us a deep blue with a few stars winking here and there. Lacey walks toward me and I can't speak, can't think, still can't breathe.

16

THÉO

"THIS IS GOING TO BE SO NICE." LACEY DIPS A HAND INTO the water. "Hot."

"That's the idea." I clear my scratchy throat.

The hot tub is built in, with two steps up to it. Lacey climbs them, giving me a stellar view of her ass, barely covered by the scrap of red Lycra, then lowers herself into the water and wades into a corner. She lets out a long sigh as she sinks into a seat. "Lovely."

I leap in and submerge myself to hide the wood I'm suddenly sporting. The hot water closes around me. I'm in the opposite corner to Lacey, nowhere near enough to touch her. Except our feet. My toes brush hers when I stretch my legs out.

She leans her head back and closes her eyes. "Oh my God, this is wonderful."

"It's pretty nice."

"I can just feel the tension melting out of me."

"Yeah. Wait. What tension? We had fun today."

"Oh, you know. Just normal stuff."

"Like what?"

She sighs. "I'm still worried about Chris."

"Have you heard any more from him?"

"I texted him yesterday, and he did reply and said he's fine. I think he's mad at me."

"He has no fucking right to be mad at you."

One corner of her mouth kicks up. "I know."

"When we left Vegas, you were pissed at him for trying to pimp you out and disappearing, and you were strong enough to cut him loose to stand on his own two feet."

"Yeah. But I still worry about him."

I wade through the water over to crouch in front of her. I take her hands and squeeze them. "You're being the strong one, you know. You're doing the right thing."

"As long as he doesn't end up dead."

Ugh. That *is* a concern. I wish I could fix things for her. "He won't. And I for one am glad you're here, and safe."

She leans forward and plants a kiss on my mouth. My body zooms to attention, going still other than my dick which swells and twitches. It's a chaste, closed-mouth kiss that lasts a few seconds, then she draws back and says, "Thank you."

I stare at her, my body tingling, blood rushing hot through my veins. Her expression changes, her eyes darkening, her lips parting. I study that mouth. I want to feel it on mine again. I want to taste her. I want her warm wet curves pressed up against me, especially one part of me that's throbbing with need.

"Théo . . ."

I shift closer, sloshing water, to find her waist. I clasp my hands on her and her knees part to let me closer. I'm weirdly weightless in the water. She sets her hands on my shoulders.

"Kiss me again," I quietly order.

Her eyelids drift down and she leans forward. Our mouths come together in another kiss, this one gentler, our lips clinging, until I open mine on hers, coaxing her to open to me too. I lick inside, tasting her sweetness, swallowing her soft moan.

Her fingers tighten on my shoulders and I break the kiss to tilt my head and go in deeper. I ease her forward on the seat of the tub until I'm wedged between her thighs and my aching cock is pressed against her soft pussy.

"Oh." She breathes against my mouth and then she slides closer still, winding her arms around my neck, pressing her breasts against my chest, hooking her heels behind my back.

Christ.

My hands wander over her, up and down her sides, around to her ass and I pull her even tighter against me, thrusting my hips a little. She makes a needy sound in her throat. The glowing water bubbles and swirls around us. My blood is swirling and rushing through my veins too, straight to my cock, which is so goddamn hard it hurts.

I move my mouth off hers and drag it over her jaw and her head falls back as I kiss her neck, then her throat. Those sweet tits are right in front of me, barely covered by the bikini top.

"We're not supposed to be doing this," she murmurs as I lick the hollow of her throat. "You said . . ."

I sigh. "Yeah. I did."

She lifts her head and focuses lust-hazed eyes on me. "Do you want to stop?"

"Christ, no."

"Me either."

"Then let's not." I kiss her again, deep consuming kisses that she responds to with clutching hands and needy sounds.

Lust punches through my stomach, every nerve ending in my body on fire. My cock is a throbbing spike.

When we pull apart, nearly gasping for breath, our eyes meet. It's like a spell, holding us in place. My heart pounds.

Lacey lifts her hands to behind her neck and unties her bathing suit top.

My breath stalls in my chest, my lungs deflating.

Inch by inch, she lowers the top, revealing perfect, firm round breasts tipped with the most erotic nipples I've ever seen, perfect hard little nubs.

"Jesus," I rasp. "You're beautiful."

She gives me a shy smile and I reach for her, cupping the resilient flesh, squeezing gently, the feel of her in my palms making me ecstatic. Blissful. I catch her nipples between my thumbs and forefingers and squeeze, tugging them out.

She whimpers.

I watch as I play there, pinching and pulling, her nipples going a gorgeous deep rose. Her eyelids droop and her breath is choppy. Her arms go lax in the water and she whispers, "Oh God, that feels good."

Yeah, it sure as hell does. Electricity pours into my body, zapping and jolting me, my need for her burning inside me.

I reach around behind her and undo the back of the

bikini, then toss it over the side of the hot tub. "Nobody can see us up here."

"I don't know." Her eyes flicker toward the glass panels at the front of the deck, facing the ocean.

It's all dark out there, and we're on the second story. I shake my head. "No."

"Okay."

I grasp her waist and lift her. She lets out a little shriek, grabbing my arms. I plant her butt on the side of the hot tub and hook my fingers into the bikini bottoms to drag them off.

"Pretty sure Bobby intended this tub to be used in the nude."

"You think?" Her slow smiles sets my groin on fire.

"Yeah." And I tug the laces of my board shorts to loosen them and shove them down over my hips. They float away in the bubbling water.

Lacey's gaze drops to my dick, which expands even more. "Oh. That's nice."

"Yeah?" I give my shaft a firm tug.

"Yeah." Her tongue slides along her bottom lip.

I move closer, sloshing water, parting her thighs. Then I glance over where I left my towel. "Hang on." I wade over to grab it, fold it into a thick pad and set it beside her, then lift her onto it. The wall of the house is only a foot or so away and I ease her back to lean against the smooth cement. Then I lay my hands on her inner thighs again and press them open.

I drink in the sight of her beauty—perfect feminine bliss, plump, smooth flesh with a neat patch of light brown hair above it. "Gorgeous."

"Th-thank you." She's flushed everywhere now, her chest, her throat, her face. Her eyes glitter and she reaches out a hand to touch my chest.

"Are you okay there? Is that towel enough padding?"

"I'm okay." Her voice is breathy. "Are you going to touch me?"

"Oh hell yeah. I'm going to touch you. I'm going to lick you. And suck on you. Until you come on my face."

She shivers. "Oh my God."

I caress her inner thighs lightly, sliding up and down, closer and closer to her center, studying her with focused intensity. Then I lean in, closing my eyes, and breathe in her scent. "I need to taste you," I whisper.

She whimpers.

I kiss her softly, over the smooth skin of her plump outer lips, sucking gently, letting my tongue linger. Then I use my thumbs to part her lips and I slide my tongue through heaven.

She twitches, one hand gripping my hair. "Ohhh yeah."

I lick her more, up, down into the crease of her groin then back to her center, probing with my tongue, swallowing her essence. Then I flick the tip of my tongue over her clit.

She jolts again, yanking my hair. I fucking love it.

Her body is quivering, quaking. I go for it, laving her swollen bud, sliding a finger inside her to curl against her inner wall. She cries out again, and again, shaking harder, and I suck her clit into my mouth.

Her fingers pull my hair again as her body spasms, clutching around my finger, and she makes the sexiest gasping noises I've ever heard.

I gently lick her more until she relaxes a little, then lift my head. "Okay?"

"Oh my God." Her head rests against the house, her eyes closed. "Oh my God."

I kiss my way up over her abdomen, between her breasts, and then I kiss her mouth softly. "Making you come is my new favorite thing."

She gives a choked little laugh and kisses me back, then sets a hand on my chest to push me away and slides back into the water.

"Are you cold?"

"No."

"Okay, good, because I'm taking you out of here. I'm going to fuck you." I pause. "Okay?"

"Oh God, yes, please."

I lift her out again and lead her over to one of the lounge chairs, which have nice thick cushions. She lays down and smiles at me as I kneel on the cushion between her legs. Then I pause. "Hold on. Gotta grab a condom."

I zip into the bedroom and grab one, rolling it on as I hustle back out there.

"We're married," she murmurs as I rejoin her on the chair. She reaches for my hips. "We shouldn't need that."

"We can talk about that later."

"'Kay."

I can't take my eyes off her, so beautiful, her smile heartwarming, her body supple and smooth and perfect. I stretch out over her to kiss her again, first her mouth, then her throat, then the tops of her breasts. "I love your tits," I mumble before taking a nipple into my mouth.

I sense her smile. "Thank you." She cups the back of

my head as I suck on her, her nipple stiff against my tongue. I love how her breath hitches, how her hips roll up against me as I tug and draw on the budded tips, one, then the other, until she's shaking again.

I slip a hand between us to find her wetness, and yeah, she's wet. So wet. I push back up onto my knees and carefully find her entrance with the head of my cock. I look up to watch her face and see her watching me too, eyes dark and glittering, her lips parted hungrily. "Okay?"

"Yes. God, yes."

It takes a bit to work myself all the way inside her. She's tight, gripping my cock, almost making me lose it. I grit my teeth, sensation flowing through me, hot and electric. My skin prickles all over, pressure building. A groan rumbles up from my chest as I'm finally, finally seated inside her, all the way, and she throbs around me in an erotic rhythm. I go still, holding on by a thread, my body pulsing and hot everywhere.

Then I move. I hold her thighs and rock into her, my cock sliding in and out in a sublime tempo, trying not to go too fast but dammit, I can't, I can't hold back. My eyes meet hers, which go wide as we move together, both of us feeling something . . . huge. Something . . . unexpected.

I find her clit with my fingers, brushing over it. She sucks in a shaky breath and her chin lifts. "Yes . . ."

I want her to come again. I want her to come on my cock, I want to feel her orgasm all around me. And she does, crying out, shuddering, squeezing me so tight. Now I do lose it. With a shout, I release her legs and stretch out over her to pound into her. She grips my shoulders, still making soft little sex noises and we come together, fiery sensation ripping through me and exploding.

A while later, maybe a few hours, I don't even know, I lift my head to peer down at her.

"You better not accuse me of making you do that against your will."

I choke on a laugh. "Ah, no. I was completely willing." I smile. "So were you."

"Yeah. Thank you for asking."

"Of course." I frown. Nobody's ever thanked me for asking before. Hell, you have to make sure the woman wants it or it's not gonna be good for her. "Will you sleep in my bed tonight?"

"I think I have to, since I'm pretty sure I can't walk downstairs."

I grin. "That good, huh?"

"Oh yeah." She drowsily turns her face to mine and kisses me.

"Maybe we should shower before we go to bed. So we don't smell like the hot tub."

"Mmkay. You'll have to hold me up, though."

"I can do that." Christ, I can't wait to get her in the shower, all soapy and naked, my hands all over her. Better take it easy on her, though.

"Also just so you know, this shower isn't going anywhere. I mean, sex-wise."

"Uh . . ."

"'Cause sex in the shower doesn't really work. Water does not work as lube. Nope. It just washes away all my girl lube."

Jesus. "Um, yeah, I'm aware of that."

"'Kay, good."

I roll off the lounge chair to turn out the lights of the hot tub and flip the cover over it, then pull Lacey up from the chaise. She lets out a squeal when I bend and pick her up in my arms. "Show off."

"What am I showing off?"

"How strong you are."

I pull open a door and stride into my bedroom.

"You lifted me right out of the hot tub," she adds. "How do you stay in such good shape if you don't play hockey anymore?"

"I work out. And I still play hockey sometimes. Just for fun."

"Hmm."

I set her on her feet on the tile floor of my bathroom and open the shower door. It's a huge shower, and there's even a bench. Once I get the water going and it's hot, I lead Lacey into the shower, close the door, and gently push her down onto the bench.

"This is beautiful." Her voice is still slurred a bit.

"Yeah, I like this shower." I grab one of the showerheads, the one that's also hand held, and direct the warm spray onto Lacey.

"I was really just joking." She smiles. "I can stand up."

"Relax." I replace the showerhead, grab a bottle of body wash, and squeeze out a generous amount. "I'm dying to do this."

"Mmm. Go ahead. Play with my soapy boobs."

I choke. "Thanks."

"Obviously, they feel amazing, I know. Go ahead and

feel me up." She leans her head back and her smile goes sultry.

Christ. She fucking kills me.

I run my hands over her shoulders and down her arms, taking my time so I can enjoy the feel of her. I glide back up, down her chest, over her tits. Yeah, she's right—nothing feels better than slick, soapy breasts with hard little nipples. I mold and squeeze them, then continue my path of washing her, all the way down to her feet, then back up to the juncture of her thighs. I ease them apart and gently slide my hand between them, over her soft, swollen pussy.

She makes a sound that's half moan, half sigh. My fingers slip and probe but I don't do more than that before I pull her to stand, turn her, and wash her back from the nape of her neck, which I can't resist kissing, down over the curve of her spine, the swell of her delectable ass cheeks and the backs of her legs. I linger on her thighs and knees when she quivers, filing that response away for another time.

Then I rinse her off and let her sit again while I stand beneath the other showerhead and wash myself while she watches. That's hot as hell, her eyes following my hands over my chest and abs, down to my junk, soaping up my balls. Pretty sure she thinks it's hot too, so I turn in a circle to rinse myself off, giving her the full view.

When you're used to showering with a bunch of guys nearly every day, walking around naked in the locker room, any self-consciousness about your body is long gone.

I crank off the water, smiling at the languorous, lusty look on Lacey's face. I'm glad she's relaxed enough to sit there naked and let me watch her too as she observes me.

Thick towels hang on the wall just outside the shower and I pluck one off the hook to gently dry Lacey, then wrap it around her. I tuck the corner between her breasts as she reaches up and pulls her hair tie out. Her thick, wavy hair tumbles down around her shoulders in masses of gold and honey and caramel brown.

"Oh yeah." I groan. "Love that hair."

Her smile turns seductive. "I remember. The hair fetish."

"Yeah." I reach for another towel.

She moves closer and traces a finger down between my pecs. "Tell me what you want to do with my hair."

17

LACEY

Théo is so damn sexy I could just about explode with wanting him.

I've never felt so cared for . . . so . . . *cherished*.

Reaching for my hair, he lets out a groan. "This." He slides his hand into it and twists, wrapping his hand and tugging.

My eyelids feel weighed down. Thick liquid heat slides down through me, converging between my legs.

He uses my hair to pull me closer and touches his lips to mine. "I want to feel your hair on my thighs when you have your mouth on my cock."

I inhale sharply, my inner muscles squeezing.

"And on my stomach." He brushed his mouth over mine again. "And wrapped around my cock."

The images are making my inner muscles squeeze tight. "That sounds very dirty."

"Oh yeah. I have a lot of dirty thoughts about you."

"Did one of them involve sex in a hot tub?"

"As soon as we got here, it did."

I smile and melt against him. He pulls my hair again, tugging my head back to expose my throat. I close my eyes as he slides his tongue over the hollow of my throat, around my neck, and sucks gently on my skin.

"God . . ." Desire swirls inside me, my pussy aching, my clit pulsing.

He releases his grip on my hair, but his hand stays there and the other joins it, holding my head as he tilts it and kisses me . . . long and deep and wet. Then he turns me and nudges me into the bedroom and toward the bed.

"Are we going to sleep?" I ask.

"Not yet."

"Good."

He's turned me on so much with his words and his touch, I'm practically vibrating. A few minutes ago I'd been ready to crash I was so satiated and limp from two wrenching orgasms, but I guess I'm greedy because I want another one.

But first I want to act out his fantasies.

I drop my towel and climb onto the bed to wait for him. His towel hits the floor also. Sweet Jesus on a pita, he's beautiful. I've never been into guys with huge, bodybuilder muscles, and I find him *so* attractive—lean, ripped, definitely with muscles in his arms, shoulders, and legs, but not massive. "I want to lick your abs."

"Go right ahead."

"Come lay down here."

He stretches out on his back on the bed, and my mouth is literally watering. I sweep my hands over his chest, moving to kneel beside him. Then I bend my head and kiss the muscles on his chest . . . softly, moving over his body until I reach a nipple. I lick him there and give his nipple a quick suck, not sure how he'll react. Some guys like it, some hate it.

He groans and his fingers curl into the duvet.

I move to the other one and suck it too, then kiss my way down his body. Yes, I lick his abs, running my tongue over the ridges, around his navel, then to the tender skin below that. He's taut here too, but obviously sensitive as the muscles quiver at my touch. He makes another low sound of desire.

I'm so close now to his cock, his lovely, thick cock. I lay kisses in the crease of his groin, spreading my hands on his thighs. His hair is silky-rough, the muscles hard. I rub my palms over him, savoring the sensation, then teasingly I skim my hands lower, to his knees, then the insides of his thighs.

"Christ, Lacey." His voice is strained.

His cock is on his belly, stiff, flushed, and dripping, the most erotic thing I've ever seen.

I torment him more by gently scraping my fingernails up his inner thighs. His legs part for me and he's nearly panting. I brush my fingers over his balls, then dance them over his hips.

"Do it," he begs. "Touch me."

"I will." I bend over to kiss his thigh, then slip my fingers under his balls and gently squeeze. His groan encourages me, so I bury my face in his groin again to kiss him there, breathing in his scent. We just showered, and he smells clean and spicy, overlaid with a hint of arousal.

I love the feel of him, so full and tight. I want more.

I curl my other hand around his shaft and he emits another guttural sound. I stroke him, watching my hand move on him with fascination. So damn beautiful . . . so male and vigorous.

I want to taste him too. I open my mouth and close my lips over the tip. His hand is on my lower back now, caressing me there, down to my ass, so I lift it up a bit and there . . . he slips his fingers into my pussy from behind as I suck on him.

"Fuck yeah."

I let my hair fall all down around him, dragging it back and forth as I move on him. I cup his balls, run my lips up and down his shaft, pausing to lick around the head, then going back down.

"That's fucking amazing," he groans. "Your mouth . . . lick my balls, baby."

"Mmm." I do that, even sucking on them, my hand taking over for my mouth on his cock, sliding up and down.

His fingers in my slick pussy are distracting me, especially when they flick over my clit, which is straining for attention.

"You're so wet," he says, pushing a finger inside me. "Love that."

"God, I love it too." I lift my head for a moment, eyes closed, reveling in the sensation his touch evokes in me, heat spiraling through me. Then my entire body jolts as he brushes his wet fingers over my back entrance.

It feels shockingly good, but I've never done that and I jerk upright.

"No?" He pets my pussy. "Sorry, baby."

"No, no, it's okay . . . I just . . . I've seen your rodzilla and there's no way that's going in my butt."

He choke-laughs. "Okay. We'll save that."

I suck briefly on my bottom lip and nod, meeting his eyes. Our gazes lock in a blast of heat that sears me right to my core. I can't look away. At this moment I think I'd do anything for this man. With this man. Even butt sex. "Okay."

I take him in my mouth again, loving the feel of him, so solid and warm and pulsing. I love how much he loves this, the noises he makes, the way he gathers up my hair and holds it at the back of my head.

"Love the feel of your hair," he says. "But I want to see you sucking me . . . fuck, that's so good. I'm close . . ."

"Mmmm." I want all of him and it's only a moment before he comes, his singular taste on my tongue, and I swallow it down. And want more. I give him a moment and then slowly slide off him, swirling my tongue around the head, then licking my lips.

"Jesus." He releases my hair and I slide up beside him and sprawl on the bed facedown. My jaw aches a bit and I'm still drained from my own orgasms. His hand lands on my lower back and stays there, warm and heavy, the weight comforting.

A while later, through a drowsy haze, I feel him shifting me and moving the covers to pull them up and over me, then snuggling me, his body curved around mine.

I vaguely hear Théo get up in the morning, showering and dressing for work. I shove my hair out of my face and try to sit up. Théo bends over and kisses my forehead. "Stay in bed, if you want."

There's nothing I love more than staying in bed in the morning. Well, now that I know what sex with Théo is like, staying in bed comes second. If he stayed with me though, it would be heaven on earth. So I flop back down, pull the covers up to my chin, and close my eyes.

"See you later, sweetheart." He passes a hand over my hair.

I smile. "'Kay."

Moments later I hear him leaving the house, his car starting and then pulling away.

I sigh. This bed is lovely . . . luxuriously soft yet supportive, with silky sheets and pillows that smell like Théo. I roll over and breathe in the scent of him.

For a while I hover between sleep and wakefulness, delicious sex dreams floating through my mind. Wow.

I could lie here all day like this.

Except . . . as I become more alert, my eyes opening to stare at the ceiling, the fact that Théo has left the house because he has a job to go to makes me feel . . . useless. I haven't been unemployed since I was fifteen.

Feeling like a slug, I throw back the covers and slide out of bed. I'm naked, but I'm home alone, so I pad downstairs to shower and get dressed. I feel my thigh muscles as I walk, which is a reminder of last night's activities and how hot they were. And I get a little hot again, thinking about that.

I spend the day walking on the beach, wandering the neighborhood, and playing with Byron when Taylor gets home from work. I eat a solitary dinner, as Théo texts me he's working late. And the next day is much the same.

Wednesday morning, I sit at the kitchen table with my phone and a cup of coffee, scrolling through social media and news sites. A text message notification pops up and I tap it. It's from Théo's mom.

> Hi Lacey! Théo gave me your number, I hope you don't mind. I was wondering if you'd have lunch with me today?

Eep. My eyes pop wide open. I sit back in the chair. Well, it's not like my schedule is already full. I can't even think of an excuse to make. So, what the heck. I send her back a message saying I'd love to.

She says she'll pick me up, since she knows I have no car. That has to change. And I need to find a job. Even if I'm only going to be here a short time, I need to do something. To be productive. I'll figure it out.

Since I have time, I go for another walk on the beach, letting the wind dry my hair, inhaling fresh sea air. There's something so calming and centering about the ocean. When I'm almost back at Théo's place, I plant my butt in the soft pale sand near the lifeguard stand, wrap my arms around my legs, and stare at the water.

Théo and I have slept together every night, and it's amazing. I just wish I saw him more *out* of bed. Or maybe . . . I just need something more to occupy my time.

I knew we were going to do the deed at some point. We'd both admitted we were attracted to each other, and the sparks between us were only increasing even though he'd said we shouldn't get involved that way. I hope he's not angry about it. I don't think I pushed him into it. But I was definitely willing.

I smile, resting my chin on my knees. Oh yeah, I was willing. And I'm willing to do it again. And again.

Seeing him with his family over the weekend only intensified the attraction. It made me feel . . . protective of him, which is weird. But also admiring. He was calm and unwavering in the face of criticism about taking this job. He kept a sense of humor despite the tension that buzzed the entire evening. He's so smart and knowledgeable about what he does, his family—even the older generations who've been in the hockey world a lot longer than he has—listened to his every word.

That all made me want him even more. And when we had sex . . . it was more intense than I'd expected.

I shake my head and stand, brushing sand off my shorts. I better get ready for lunch.

I change into a sundress and flip-flops, hoping this is appropriate. I use some product on my hair to tame the frizz—it dried into nice waves, but it's a little wild.

Aline Gagnon rings the doorbell this time, instead of just walking in. I smile as I answer the door, remembering that. "Hi. Come in."

"Hi, Lacey. You look so pretty. What a cute dress."

"Thanks. I just need to grab my purse and I'm ready to go."

"Perfect."

Soon we're driving along Pacific Avenue, with the top of Aline's little BMW convertible down, the sun on our faces and the wind in our hair.

"What a lovely day," Aline says, big sunglasses perched on her nose.

"It really is. I love Las Vegas, but I'm enjoying the ocean and the cooler temperatures."

She's a confident driver. She pulls up at a big hotel right on the beach and lets a valet take her car. I'm a little in awe of her ease with this, and follow her into the elegant lobby.

"We'll go to the café here," she says. "It's more casual."

I hope that's not because I'm not dressed right for the other restaurant.

Even the café is lovely. We're shown out onto a patio overlooking the beach, with glass panels blocking the breezes. Big potted palms fill the spaces between wicker tables and chairs with comfortable striped blue cushions. From here we can see people walking and running on the boardwalk and the Ferris wheel of the Santa Monica Pier.

The beauty of it all makes my chest hurt. I don't even know what I'm doing here.

"Let's order prosecco," Aline suggests.

"That would be nice."

With flutes of bubbly wine in hand, we peruse the menu.

"I think I'll have the grilled salmon salad," Aline says. "What are you thinking of?"

My eyes skim over the prices. I still have some cash, so I can afford this, but wow, it's expensive. I don't want to assume she's paying for lunch. "I think I'd like the ahi niçoise salad."

"Oh, good choice, I've had that."

We set our menus aside. "You've obviously been here before."

"Yes, I love this place. We used to stay in this hotel when we visited Bob and Chelsea, before we moved to California."

"Ah. It's beautiful."

"And a nice location. The boys loved going to the beach and the pier when they were little."

We order and then Aline says, "I thought this would be a nice chance to get to know each other, and I'm sure Théo's busy at the arena."

"Yes, he apparently has a lot on his plate."

Her forehead furrows briefly. "I'm sure. That team is a mess. He's got a challenge on his hands, but then, he's always loved a challenge."

"He's been through some tough times." I'm thinking of his eye injury.

"Yes." She studies me. "He's told you about his accident, obviously, and having to give up playing."

"Yes. It must have been hard for him. But I admire what he's done."

She smiles warmly. "So do we. He didn't always have things easy as a youngster either. He was so smart, people treated him like a . . ." She searches for a word. "An oddity. Nobody expected him to be athletic, even though he comes from a family of athletes." Her eyes shadow. "He endured a bit of bullying." She sighs, sounding pained. "There's nothing worse than when your children are hurting and you can't fix it or stop it. I tried." Her brief smile holds sadness. "But he was determined to prove those bullies wrong, and he excelled at hockey too. I think that made it even more painful for him to have to give that up."

My heart squeezes, thinking of an unhappy little Théo,

his accomplishments even more impressive after hearing this. "Luckily, he has brains as well as athleticism."

"Yes." She shakes her head, a rueful smile perched on her lips. "We don't know where he gets his brains from."

"I'm sure you and your husband are both very intelligent."

"Well, we're not stupid." She laughs. "But Théo's mathematical genius is remarkable."

"Not to mention he's very hard working."

"C'est vrai. True."

Our server refills our wineglasses.

"So." Aline looks around the café. "You like this hotel?"

"It's gorgeous." I can only imagine how much it would cost to stay here. Maybe even more than a basic room at the Wellborne, where I used to work. Although the penthouse suites at the Wellborne are about two grand a night.

"I'm so glad you think so! You know"—she leans forward—"they do weddings here."

I blink. "This would be a lovely location for a wedding."

"Yes!" She beams. "Matthew and I were thinking that we would like to give you and Théo another wedding. Since none of us were there when you tied the string."

"The knot," I say automatically, my mind emptying. *What?*

"Oui. Yes. Tied the knot."

"I, uh, I don't know . . ."

"I'm sure Théo will agree," she rushes on. "Men don't care as much about things like that, so I wanted to talk to you first. It would be such a pleasure to have a wedding here for you, and for the whole family. Weddings bring people together."

I slowly move my head side to side. "I don't think a wedding is going to fix all the problems in your family."

Her bottom lip pushes out briefly and she drops her eyes. "You are probably right." She sighs. "This family is very . . . messed up."

I huff out a laugh. "Um, yeah."

"But still . . . think! Wouldn't you love to have a beautiful dress and flowers? All the people you love around you?"

I sadly reflect on the fact that I don't have that many people I love to surround myself with. Chris and I are on the outs. I have one best friend back in Vegas, a good friend in Miami I haven't seen in years, and a few other girlfriends I see from time to time. But that's about it.

Wait, wait, wait. This is ridiculous. Théo and I aren't going to stay married. This would be a huge waste of time and money. In fact, I'll be back in Vegas before it could even be organized.

A rock settles in my gut. I study Aline's hopeful face. What the hell am I going to tell her?

18

LACEY

"Well, hello."

I look up and see Everly Wynn standing next to our table. As at the party on Saturday, she's polished and elegant, her hair in stylish layers, wearing a sleek sleeveless dress in a gorgeous coral color and nude pumps.

"Hi!" My exuberant greeting startles her. I'm just so happy at the interruption and not having to answer Aline right now. "So nice to see you! How are you?"

"I'm well, thanks." She looks at Aline, who smiles.

"Are you here for lunch too?" Aline asks.

"Yes. I was supposed to meet a client, but he just texted me he can't make it after all."

"Oh, you should join us!" I pipe up.

Aline's smile doesn't falter, although I sense the wariness between the two women. Not dislike or even awkwardness, just guardedness. "Of course!"

Everly hesitates, then hitches one shoulder. "Okay."

Immediately one of the café staff appears with a chair for her and she sits.

"Well, this is nice," I chirp, guzzling my prosecco. "I get to see both of you."

The waiter refills my glass instantly.

"Who were you meeting with?" Aline asks Everly.

"Dan Diaz." She says to me, "The mayor of Santa Monica."

"Oh. Wow."

"We're working on a new partnership between the city and the foundation," she adds. "I think it's going to be amazing."

Right. Everly runs the Condors Foundation. And lunches with the mayor.

"Would you like to see a menu?" The waiter is here.

"We've already ordered," Aline tells Everly.

"I'll have the coast burger," Everly says without needing a menu. "With fries. Thank you, Liam." She smiles at the waiter who bears a striking resemblance to Ryan Gosling.

"Of course." He smiles back, plucks the menu away, and disappears.

"Well." Aline picks up her wine and drains it too. "This is so nice. Tell us more about yourself, Lacey."

Great. Just what I don't want to do. I shift in my wicker chair. "Um. Well, I told you my mom passed away a couple of years ago. She had ovarian cancer." I pause. "I never knew my father."

They both nod without judgment, so I continue. "I have a twin brother, Chris. He's a little angry with me right now." I drop my gaze to my wineglass. "He has a gambling addiction, and I finally refused to keep bailing him out."

"Oh no." Aline's eyes warm with sympathy. "Addictions are a terrible thing. They make us feel so powerless to help someone."

"Yes. Théo was very supportive in my decision. I know I can't help Chris . . . he has to help himself."

"I'm glad you and Théo have each other," Aline says softly.

"Are you planning to work now you're here?" Everly asks me.

"Yes, I'd like to do something." I wrinkle my nose. "I've definitely been feeling at loose ends this week, with Théo so busy."

"We always need volunteers," Everly says. "If you're interested in getting involved. The players' wives and girlfriends do a lot of charity work and help contribute to the foundation, and I'm sure they'd welcome your help."

I tilt my head. "Hmm. Yes, I could do that. Obviously, I haven't met any of the wives and girlfriends. I've only met one player—Manny—who lives in our building. I gather most of them aren't around in the summer."

"Yes, many of them go spend time with their families."

"When does the season start?"

"Officially, October. But they'll start arriving back in town in August for training camp."

"That's still so far away."

"Yes, our activities do slow down over the summer. We can talk more about ways for you to get involved."

"Thanks, I'd like that."

I let Everly and Aline chat more, gradually joining in the conversation. I learn that Everly has a wicked sense of humor and I admire how she digs into her huge hamburger and fries with no shame.

"I'm on a low carb diet," she tells me when she sees me eyeing her food. She picks up a fry in her fingers.

I raise my eyebrows.

"When I feel low, I eat carbs." She grins.

I laugh. "Hey! Me too!"

"Why do you feel low, Everly?" Aline asks with a slight frown.

Everly shrugs. "Just joking."

We also discover a mutual love of knitting. "It's great for stress relief!" I say excitedly. "I wasn't able to bring my knitting things with me."

"Why not?" Everly's forehead furrows.

Ugh. "Long story," I say lightly, waving a hand. "Is there somewhere near here I can get needles and yarns?"

"Oh yes, there's a great shop on Ocean Park Boulevard. I can take you there."

I assume she's throwing out a polite non-invitation, but she actually arranges to take me there tomorrow after work.

"I'm sorry I don't have a car," I say. "But I can probably figure out how to get there by bus and meet you there."

I learn that she lives in a condo not that far from Théo's place, in Venice Beach. "I'll pick you up," she tells me.

"Okay, thanks."

We finish our lunches and I reach for my purse, but Aline and Everly wave at me and argue over who's paying. Everly gives in graciously and lets Aline buy us all lunch.

"I better get back to the office." Everly glances at her watch.

We walk through the lobby to the hotel entrance. Aline

gestures to Everly to have her car brought first. "Since you have to go back to work."

"I *am* the boss," Everly says with a smile. "But thanks." As we wait, she tips her head to one side, looking at me. "I'm glad I ran into you. It was a fun lunch."

"Yeah, me too."

She gives me a small hug.

With her gone, I turn to Aline, my insides knotting, knowing she's going to bring up the wedding again. She doesn't until we're on our way back to Théo's place.

"Think about the wedding idea," she says. "It would be so much fun. I don't have a daughter, and I've always waited for the day we'd have a wedding in the family."

My heart sinks. We took that away from her. But probably someday Théo will get married again, for real, and she'll get her wish.

Ugh.

"I'll think about it," I say, relieved that I don't have to disappoint her right now.

"Everly gets to take you to the wool shop," she says when she drops me off. "We should go shopping too. Maybe next week? We could go to South Coast Plaza."

Yikes. I did not expect all this family inclusiveness. But it's . . . nice. I smile at her. "Okay, that would be fun."

"Thank you. I'm so happy to have a daughter!"

My smile widens at her infectious delight. We exchange hugs too on the sidewalk in front of Théo's condo, and I wave as she drives away.

I enjoy the feeling of well-being that settles inside me after a fun lunch with the two women as I gather up laundry from my room and Théo's, sort it, and start a load in the washing machine, then take my Kindle out onto the patio with a glass of iced tea to read for a while and think about what I can do while I'm here.

I make dinner for two, even though I'm pretty sure Théo won't be home until late again. He surprises me though, showing up shortly after six, just as I'm sitting down to eat.

Seeing him, my heart bumps like a teenage girl running into her crush. "Hi!" I jump up. "Dinner's ready."

"Awesome. I'm starving."

I hustle over to the stove and fill a plate for him with the pasta dish I made, linguine with red peppers, asparagus, and parmesan. I even whipped up some garlic buns.

When I turn back to him, he's holding up a . . . penguin.

I halt in place. I blink. "What's that?"

"It's the mascot for the team I used to play for. I brought it home for you." He grimaces. "I know it's not Pete, and it's not from your mom, but I thought you might . . . like it."

My chest swells and tightens. I can't breathe as I stare at the soft stuffed toy. I set his plate on the counter and reach for the penguin. "Thank you." My mouth quivers as I stare down at it. It's not Pete . . . he's right. But I almost can't bear the emotion filling me because he brought me this.

I blink back tears, set the penguin on the counter, and pick up Théo's plate. Like a happy housewife of the 1950s, I set the plate in front of him and fetch him a glass of water. "Here you go."

He eyes me. "You don't have to wait on me."

I roll my eyes. "Please. I know that." I sit and sigh. "I have nothing else to do."

His lips twitch. "Bored?"

"A little."

"I hear you had lunch with my mom today."

I frown. "How did you . . . oh. Everly?"

"Yeah." He twirls pasta onto his fork. "The foundation offices are in the arena too. She stopped by to give me shit for working late."

I blink.

His smile is crooked. "She said I shouldn't ignore my new bride, especially since you don't know anyone here and you seem a little at loose ends."

"I'm fine." I pause. "But I am happy you're here."

Our eyes meet. Heat fills my belly and my skin tingles.

His slow smile has my panties dampening. "What do you want to do after dinner?"

My mind goes straight to the gutter. Or rather, the bed.

"Maybe a walk on the beach?" he suggests, eyes gleaming.

I smile back. "I never turn down a walk on the beach."

"You're obsessed with the ocean."

"Yeah, I kind of am." I stab a piece of asparagus with my fork.

"This is really good."

"Thanks. Um. Your mom wants to give us a wedding."

He freezes. "She wants what now?"

One corner of my mouth lifts. "She wants us to have another wedding. She took me to Shores for lunch and told me what beautiful weddings they do there and that she's been waiting and waiting for a family wedding and missed out on ours."

"Jesus Christ."

"I know." I poke at my food. "I didn't say yes or no. She asked me to think about it. I didn't want to hurt her feelings."

He scrubs a hand over his face. "Yeah." Then he shakes his head. "I'll deal with it."

"Whew. Okay." I blow out a quick breath of relief. "How was your work today?"

"Well, I'm learning a lot."

"About the team?"

"Yeah. I've been watching tons of video and crunching numbers."

"The night I met you, I thought you were an accountant. Then I thought you were a hockey player. Turns out you're a number cruncher after all. But I don't get what kind of numbers you're crunching."

"All kinds of things. Analyzing the video and then the data helps us know more about individual player performance, also how specific lines perform together and how the team performs."

"It's so technical." Once again I feel a surge of admiration for him.

"It is."

"I guess when I think about hockey or sports, I just think about how many goals they score or how many games they win."

"Yeah. That's what it all comes down to. But I'm trying to make decisions like how much a player is worth paying or if the player is even worth keeping on the team. And when we get into the season, the numbers will help the coach make decisions like which players should play together, who should kill penalties, who goes on the power play. We can use stats to predict what will happen with teams we play against—which ones are likely to outscore us. Or not."

Honestly, talking about numbers and stats should make my eyes glaze over, but I find I'm fascinated by this. When I thought about hockey (not that I ever thought about hockey much) it was as a fast, physical sport with guys slamming each other into the boards and taking pucks to the teeth. I had no idea there was so much strategy to it.

I let Théo keep talking about it as we clean up then go for our walk, asking probably stupid questions and letting him patiently explain things to me, like what Corsi and Fenwick and expected goals scores are.

"But you can't rely on just numbers," he adds, my hand clasped in his as we stroll along the sand. "You have to rely on your eyes too, to get a complete picture. There's a saying about stats . . . they're like a bikini."

"Uh . . ."

"What they reveal is interesting . . . ." His eyes wander over me, leaving heat in their path. "But what they cover up is crucial."

"Ha."

"Sometimes our eyes lie . . . and the numbers prove it. But sometimes the numbers are misleading too."

"And you know hockey, so you can use your eyes too."

"Yeah." He swings my hand and gives me that slow, sexy smile. "Even though I have one shitty eye."

My heart bumps. "But you can see fine with your glasses."

"Yeah, I can."

"Your mom said that kids bugged you about being smart when you were a kid."

He grimaces but shrugs. "Yeah."

"But you showed them."

The smile is back. "Yeah, I did. But you never totally lose that feeling of being . . . different. I felt like something was wrong with me."

"I can't imagine you feeling that way." I eye him. The sun is low in the sky, making his tanned skin golden, emphasizing his strong bone structure. Our shadows stretch long across the sand. "You seem so confident and together."

"Well." For a moment he says nothing. "I am confident in my abilities. But I like to analyze things—maybe too much sometimes. I always want to understand why things happen. Why kids bugged me when I was younger. Then when I got injured, I couldn't figure out why that happened to me. Why something I loved was taken away from me. Then it happened again . . . with Emma."

I flinch at hearing that he'd loved Emma. But I try to keep my face composed.

"And with JP," he adds. "He was my best friend. He... stuck up for me when kids teased me. He was there for me when I got hurt. I couldn't figure out how he of all people could have done that to me."

My chest aches for him, for the hurt he felt.

"So in the end, what I came up with is . . . I don't deserve the things I want."

I stop walking, my mouth dropping open. His hand tugs mine and he stops too, turning to face me. "That's crazy," I announce.

He gives a soft laugh. "You have a better explanation?"

"No." I frown.

"I know, I know. It's hard to stop those thoughts

sometimes. I try not to want things too much, in case they get taken away. But . . ." His eyes shadow. "I really want this job. And I want to do well at it."

My heart squeezes almost painfully at the hints of vulnerability in his words, his fear that this too will be taken away from him, his hesitancy to even say it out loud. "You will." I reach up to cup his face with both hands and go onto my toes to kiss him. "You will."

He clasps my waist and says lightly, "I appreciate your faith in me."

I wind my arms around his neck and kiss him deeper, the ocean breeze blowing my hair all around us. He pulls me closer against him and I exult in the feel of his big, hard body against mine and his arms around me. I can't explain why I have faith in him. But I guess that's what faith is, believing in something without any real evidence. I don't really know if he's good at his job, despite how smart he seems and how his family listened to his every word when he talked about hockey and how his grandfather hired him for a reason.

But I do believe in him.

19

THÉO

"Belmont has to go."

I shake my head at Grandpa. "I disagree."

"Are you kidding me? He was struggling at the end of the season. Hardly any goals."

I smile. I'd rather deal with exact numbers than "hardly any," but this is one of those situations where you need your eyes *and* the math. "He was playing at about the same effectiveness in the offensive zone at even-strength as he did the year before, with similar scoring-chance numbers, but getting a higher percentage of his shot attempts from the slot on net, and a high proportion of them were off the rush. Part of the reason he didn't put up points is the team overall wasn't scoring." I give Grandpa a pointed look. "At five on five, they scored on 5.04 percent of their shots on goal, the second-lowest in the league."

Grandpa frowns. "I think you're trying to baffle me with bullshit."

I laugh. "No, I'm not. These are the things we need to consider."

"All that data shit just goes over my head," he complains.

Grandpa's an old-fashioned hockey man, and cap compliance and statistical analysis aren't areas traditional hockey men are very knowledgeable about. "His line mate wasn't scoring either," I add. "But the reason I'm not worried about Belmont's lack of production is his dominance in gaining the zone. He's an elite player at gaining controlled entries, and his attacking style off the rush makes him a dangerous player once the puck crosses the blue line. He's also pretty decent at creating offense off dump-ins; I've been watching video of him and comparing him to some of the best scoring-chance producers off entries, and he's right up there."

"Jesus. Are you serious?"

"Serious as taking a puck to the nuts."

Grandpa barks out a laugh.

"Look, he may have been in a slump, but I think we need to be patient with him because he does all the right things to create scoring chances. Now, Jablonski, on the other hand—"

"I like him," Grandpa interrupts.

"Great. I like him too. But with him, the numbers don't lie. He's not worth the money we're paying him."

Grandpa sighs. "Are you ever going to listen to me?"

"I'm listening to you. If you're asking am I always going to do what you want . . . then, no. Not always. Also, we have to talk about Joe."

"I told you he had to go."

"And he does. But not just because we were losing." I rub the back of my neck. "He doesn't respect me or what I'm telling him." I'd had that feeling from our first meeting. "He doesn't agree with the kind of analytics I want to use. We need someone who's on board with that."

"Fuck. Like who? You got someone in mind?" He gives me a shrewd look.

"Actually, I do. Dave."

Grandpa frowns. "Dave Martin?"

Our assistant coach. "Yeah. We've talked a lot and I think he's ready to move up."

"He's too new here. I just hired him."

He hired him to replace my uncle Mark, who he fired.

"You have other ideas? You wanted to replace Joe right from the start. Who did you have in mind?"

"I was thinking about Ben Gardner."

My jaw drops. "Are you fucking kidding me?"

"I like him."

I rub my forehead. "Grandpa, he got fired by the Blades for running an illegal sports gambling ring."

"He did?" Grandpa's eyebrows draw together.

I give him a long, searching, incredulous look. "You had to know about that. The whole sports world knew about that."

"Right, right." He shakes his head. "Okay, never mind him."

Okay. Jesus.

"When is Scott starting?"

"Monday."

I hired an assistant GM the other day, after talking to a bunch of candidates and doing a lot of research. Then Scott flew to L.A. and we had lunch, which turned into nearly three hours because we got along so well. I can't wait till he gets here and I've got someone I can delegate things to, someone who thinks the same way I do I can bounce ideas off. He also has tons of experience managing an AHL team and a few years working in the NHL as assistant GM in Vancouver.

I get back to work in my office. I'm starting to put the puzzle pieces together. The contracts we want to negotiate and the ones we don't.

There are ten players I need to figure out what kind of future they have with us. Bertelson and Bell are definite cornerstones and we need to offer them big contracts. Bell has proven himself as a top four defenseman and will also need to be paid as one. The other guys are all well regarded in the club, but there are better established players ahead of them, and up-and-coming prospects behind them. I've been watching video of our farm team too, and I'm impressed with a few of the young guys.

Then there are the bigger contract veterans. To be honest, some of those contracts now seem at best cumbersome when it comes to the salary cap, at worst, terrible deals for us. I'm already looking at trading at least a couple of those contracts to make room for pending restricted free agent deals.

It's complicated as fuck, but I love putting the big picture together, moving things around, adding up the numbers and making it all work. I'm not there yet. But I will be.

I immerse myself in my spreadsheets, plugging in numbers to see the impact, and time flies by. But I've set an alarm on my phone to remind me when to go home.

I've never done that before. In the past, I'd stay in the office all night. Hell, that's why I had a couch in my office— so I could grab some sleep, saving time by not having to drive home and back to do so.

But Lacey's at home. And that makes me happy to go there.

It's Friday night and I told her I'd pick up pizza and beer and wine on the way home. I grab my phone and check it as I walk out of the arena.

Oh for . . . I have a text message from Emma.

> I still can't believe you're married.

My feet come to a halt. I frown at my phone. I can't believe Emma is texting me. Why is she doing this? Did I not make it clear to her that night at Mom and Dad's that I wasn't interested in resuming things with her?

As usual, I sort through various options in my head. Do I reply and tell her not to contact me anymore? Do I ask her what she wants from me? Do I ignore her and hope she gets the message? What is up with her and JP?

I still don't know what to do. My usual problem-solving skills don't seem to be working at optimum capacity when it comes to my brother and his love life. So for now I choose to do nothing.

But when I'm starting my car, another message arrives.

> I miss you.

Ignore.

> Do you miss me too? Remember the good times we had . . .

Oh, for Chrissakes. She's not going to stop. I need to deal with this. I'm just going to be blunt and to hell with it.

> Please stop texting me. We're over. I'm married. You're with JP.

> JP and I are done.

What the fuck?

I thunk my head back against the headrest.

Cheating on me with JP was unforgivable, and I've also come to realize that I was more hurt by JP's betrayal than by hers, but now I'm actually pissed off that she's doing the same thing to him. Only this time it appears she actually had the ovaries to tell him they were done before moving on to another guy, unlike with me.

> I'm sorry to hear that. But the fact remains . . . you and I are done. I'm married. Bye, Emma.

I tap a couple of buttons on the messaging app to block her number from being able to get through to me. There. That takes care of that.

I sure hope JP isn't crazy in love with her. But at least the awkwardness of family gatherings will be no more with Emma out of the picture.

Ha! Who am I kidding? Emma was the least of the reasons for family awkwardness!

I go pick up the pizza and booze. But when I get home and walk in the door, I'm greeted with loud music and laughter. I stand still for a moment, my hands full. What the hell is going on?

I set the food and beverages down, noting a bunch of empties already on the counter, and follow the noise to the patio. There's a fuckin' party going on out there, with a whole bunch of people.

I survey the group—Lacey. Taylor. Everly? For fuck's sake. Also Manny and Wyatt Bell, who's apparently back in town, and another guy I don't know.

"Hey! You're home!" Lacey jumps up to greet me with a smile as big and sunny as California, coming at me for a hug. I set my hands on her hips and murmur in her ear, "What's going on?"

"Oh! I invited Everly over for a drink, and Taylor was walking on the beach so I asked her too, and then the guys heard us out here so they invited themselves over, but it was okay because they brought beer." She laughs.

She invited Everly for a drink. Doesn't she know Everly is from the enemy side of the family? Although, I'm working for the enemy side of the family.

I glance over at my aunt, who's talking to Wyatt and wearing a look on her face as if she'd rather be eating cockroaches. I shake my head.

"Grab a beer, dude!" Manny calls to me. "In the kitchen."

"Yeah, okay." I turn back to the kitchen, Lacey following me.

"Oh, you brought pizza!"

"That was the plan. Although I didn't bring enough for a party." I thought it was going to be just the two of us.

"We can order more, no problem." She grabs a bottle of wine out of the fridge and refills her glass. "What kind of beer do you want?"

I sigh. "A cold one."

With a laugh, she hands me one from the fridge.

"I'll go change." I sure don't fit in, in my tailored dress pants and shirt, when everyone else is wearing shorts and T-shirts.

She gives me a cheerful smooch on the mouth and carries her glass and the bottle out to the patio.

I stand there for a minute. Weirdly, I'm disappointed that it won't be just the two of us. I'm also disgruntled. I hate last minute changes to my plans. I know this about myself, but it still bugs me. Lacey looked so happy—like she was having fun. She's young and vibrant and sociable—I'm a boring number cruncher who plans his spontaneity.

I also remember that her life hasn't been a lot of fun lately, after caring for her mother, being the grown-up for her piece of shit brother, working multiple jobs to pay the bills and bail him out. She deserves a little fun in her life.

So I swallow my aggravation as I trudge upstairs to change.

A Friday night with pizza, Netflix, and . . . okay, yeah, sex, sounded good to me. But maybe I need to make other plans with Lacey. Maybe she'd like to go out to a club or a concert. Even a movie or a nice restaurant for dinner. Like . . . a date. We kind of skipped over that part.

Back downstairs, I find Lacey in the kitchen just ending

a call on her phone. "I ordered more pizza," she says. "I hope that's okay."

"Sure. Gotta feed our guests."

I'm not exactly an experienced host. Back in Vegas, even when I was home, I was usually working. I pick up the beer I left on the counter and saunter out to the patio.

"Hey, Théo," Wyatt calls, standing. We move together for a bro shake. "Good to see you."

"You too."

"Should I call you boss?" he asks with a smirk.

"Yes. You absolutely should."

I don't know Wyatt well, but we were drafted in the same year and met then.

"This is my buddy Malcolm." He introduces me to the guy I haven't met.

I grab an empty chair next to Lacey. She's chatting away to Everly about the hat she started knitting after their trip to some yarn store the other day, but flashes me a smile. I had no idea Everly liked to knit. Apparently, they both also want to take a cake-decorating course.

"What are you up to for the rest of the summer?" I ask Wyatt.

"I'm working with Matt Heller," he says, mentioning a former player who now runs an elite conditioning facility for athletes. "So I'll be around. I may take one more trip back home before training camp."

"Matt has a great reputation."

"Yeah, I'm sure he's gonna kick my ass."

Conversation flows until our pizza arrives. I pay for it while Lacey carries it into the kitchen and pulls plates out of the cupboard. She put the pizza I brought into the oven to keep it warm, so she slides it out too, then calls to everyone to come help themselves.

She added a tossed salad to the order, which is good because the women all seem to want that. We all fill our plates and go back outside. The setting sun creates a magnificent view over the ocean and a mellow, relaxed feeling washes down through me.

It's an unfamiliar feeling. I've been told I'm wound a bit tight. I know I'm intense when it comes to my work, and I like structure and predictability. I'm not sure if I like feeling this way . . .

"There's no such thing as a shower or a grower. A guy's penis is either small and gets bigger when it's erect, or it's big and it gets bigger when it's erect. That shower versus grower thing is a myth."

My head whips around to see Wyatt smirking at Everly. What the hell are they talking about?

"Hmm." Everly taps her chin. "I'll have to conduct some research on that theory."

Wyatt's smirk slips.

"The penis is just a muscle," Manny adds. "When blood flows into it, it gets bigger. It's all about elasticity. And it's better to be a grower. Your junk is better protected when flaccid, but more impressive when erect."

Everly scoffs. "Come on. Every guy wants to be a shower. I have three brothers. You guys all get naked together. Are you telling me you don't sneak a glance at each other and compare yourselves?"

Lacey and Taylor are laughing their asses off at this conversation, and I shake my head, a smile tugging my lips.

"So size does matter?" Wyatt challenges Everly.

"Well." She again presses a finger to her chin. "What really matters is functionality."

"True," Lacey chimes in.

"I agree," Taylor says. "As a heterosexual woman, I do have an appreciation for the male organ and the pleasure it can bestow. But every woman has personal preferences when it comes to peen."

"Sure," Lacey agrees. "Long, short, thick, thin . . ."

"Circumcised or uncut," Taylor adds.

"Right." Everly nods. "But if anyone asks what kind of penis I prefer, my answer is 'a hard one.'"

Laughter breaks out, including me. Jesus.

Wyatt is looking at Everly like he wants to whip out his dick and show her how impressive he is, and Manny's hanging on Taylor's every word. And as I meet Lacey's dancing eyes, both of us clearly thinking about the size of my junk, which she seems quite happy with, I want to drag her upstairs and get naked.

Our impromptu party continues until midnight, when Taylor gets up to leave and Manny says he'll walk her home because it's dark.

"It's three doors down," she protests, but he insists and they're gone.

Wyatt and his buddy get up too, leaving only Everly.

"Wow, that guy's an asshole," Everly says.

I blink. "Who?"

"Wyatt." She shakes her head. "You should trade him."

"Jesus. Don't *you* start telling me who to get rid of. Your dad's bad enough."

Everly grins. "Is he giving you a hard time?"

"Yeah." I shake my head. "It's okay, I can handle him."

"Yeah, me too. Let me know if you need any help." She wrinkles her nose. "Did he hire you to be his yes-man?"

I choke. Because I had that thought myself. "If he did, he made a big mistake. I already told him that's not what I'm here for."

"Good for you. He respects people who stand up to him." She stands, yawning. "I'll pick you up at one," she tells Lacey.

I frown. "What for?"

"We're going for pedicures." Everly grins at me.

This is another thing I'm not sure I like—Lacey being friends with Everly. What if she lets it slip that the reason she's here is to prop up my bruised ego? And also to save her ass from mobsters. I don't know if I totally trust Everly, given who her mother is.

"My toes are a mess." Lacey straightens her legs to inspect her feet.

"Thanks for the wine and pizza." Everly crosses the patio. "Where did I leave my purse?"

Lacey and I follow her into the living room.

"It's here." Lacey grabs the designer bag and hands it to Everly. "It was fun, thanks for coming over."

"See you tomorrow."

And we're alone.

Lacey meanders into the kitchen and contemplates the mess. "This can wait until morning."

"I'll do it."

She sighs. "You just can't leave it, can you."

"Nope."

"I'll help."

"No, go to bed if you want."

"I want you to come to bed with me."

She meets my eyes. My blood sizzles.

"Okay then, let's be quick." I toss boxes into the trash and load the dishwasher in record time.

2 0

LACEY

"I got a job!"

Théo has barely walked in the door after work the next week when I spring my news on him. He stops. "Huh?"

I bounce on my toes, hands clasped together. "I got a job!"

He takes a couple more steps in and drops his keys on the small table. "Where?"

"At Jolie!"

He squints. "Jolie?"

"It's a big beauty store! We passed by it when Everly took me to the wool shop, and I had the idea to apply for a job. I've taken some cosmetology courses, and with my experience doing stage makeup, I thought it might be something I could do. I applied online and went for an interview today, and they hired me! I start Monday."

I do a twirl.

Théo grins. "Well, that's awesome."

"It's not that far from here, so I don't even need a car."

He frowns. "You should have a car."

"I can't afford a car." I wave my hand. "But now I'll be able to contribute to the rent here and maybe save up."

"You're not contributing to the rent here."

My bottom lip pushes out and my eyebrows pull together. "What? Why not?"

"You don't need to. I didn't expect to have a roommate. I can afford this place."

I nibble my bottom lip. We haven't talked about money, which I guess is okay since we're not "really" married, but . . . "You make a lot of money, don't you?"

His lips twitch. "Yeah."

"Like . . ." I swallow. "Millions?"

"Yeah."

"Shit, Théo! You should have gotten me to sign some kind of prenuptial agreement!"

"Yeah, I don't think there was much time for that between deciding to get married and actually doing it." His eyes gleam.

"But seriously!"

"Yeah." One corner of his mouth turns down. "I will. I haven't had time to call my lawyer."

"Okay, good." I nod emphatically.

"Anyway, you don't need to pay rent. I know you used some of your money to pay another month's rent on your apartment, which you probably couldn't afford." He fixes me with a firm stare.

"Yeah." I purse my lips. "Our furniture is there. And what if Chris needed a place to go?"

"Well, he could pay the rent himself. Like a goddamn adult."

I bit my lip. "Yeah, I guess."

"You haven't heard from him?"

"I did text him the other day just to ask how he's doing, and he said he's fine, but that was it. I guess he's still angry at me."

"He'll get over it."

"Will he?" I eye him. "Are *you* going to get over what your brother did?"

He frowns. "That's different."

"Not so much. You said you miss him. You were best friends. Maybe you should make an effort. Especially since he and Emma are done."

He'd told me about the text messages he'd exchanged with her and the news that she and JP had broken up.

His frown darkens. "No."

I shrug. I'm not going to push it. Right now, anyway. "So, let me take you out for dinner to celebrate!"

"I'll take *you* out." He pulls me closer and kisses my forehead. "Congratulations."

"Thank you." I smile up at him and then he kisses my mouth, a slow, lush kiss that melts me inside. Like all his kisses do.

I was so excited to share my news with him, eagerly waiting for him to get home, anticipating his happiness for me, and I love the feel of his arms around me, his mouth on mine . . . the support I feel from him making my small accomplishment seem so much bigger.

It's been a long time since I've felt this . . . this caring. This feeling of not being on my own. I was *fine* on my own. But this is . . . lovely.

I kiss him deeper, showing him my gratitude for him just

being there. It's not about the rent. It's about cheering each other on. Believing in each other. Backing each other up.

Oh hell. My feelings for Théo are starting to get . . . complicated.

I pull back and give him a shaky smile.

"Where would you like to go for dinner?" He smooths my hair off my face with a tender gesture that dissolves my bones.

"I don't know. Maybe that place we went for breakfast?"

"Phht. We can go somewhere nicer than that."

"It doesn't matter where we go. It's nice just to go out . . . with you."

Gah. I probably shouldn't have said that.

But he just smiles. "Yeah. How about seafood? I've heard there's a nice place on the marina."

"Sure. I love seafood."

We move apart and he pulls out his phone, swiping and tapping. "There. Seven o'clock."

"Ack! It's quarter after six! I better get ready."

"You look fine."

"I can't go wearing shorts! I'll change."

I still keep my clothes and most of my toiletries down here, although some of my things are migrating upstairs to Théo's bedroom and bathroom. We haven't really talked about what's going on between us, sleeping together and going out on dates together and living together . . . but this isn't real. It's temporary. And I can't start liking this feeling of togetherness too much.

THE RESTAURANT IS CHARMING, WITH LOTS OF WINDOWS AND a view of all the boats in the marina. The sun hangs low over the ocean which probably means a pretty sunset soon.

Once we've ordered—extravagant king crab for me and prime rib for Théo—over glasses of wine Théo tells me, "I had to fire someone today."

"Oh no." I lean forward studying his face. Judging from his tone and his expression, it wasn't a fun thing to do. I guess it never is. "Was it awful?"

"It wasn't a party." He grimaces, turning the stem of his wineglass between his fingers.

"You're the big boss."

"Yep. That's my job. It had to happen."

"Who was it?"

"The head coach of the team."

"Oh. That's . . . big."

"Yeah. Obviously, it's a pretty important position."

"For sure. Do you know who's going to replace him?"

"I've talked to a few people, but I honestly think the assistant coach we have is the best man for the job. Grandpa's not so sure."

"It's your decision though, right?"

"Yeah." He gives a short laugh. "In theory. Grandpa's not exactly giving me the total control he said he would."

"He's not letting you make decisions?"

"Well, in the end he is, but it's taking a lot more work than it should."

"Is he okay with you firing the coach?"

"Yes. But not for the same reason. He didn't think he was doing a good job. I wasn't so sure of that, but in the end, Joe didn't respect me or my plan. He didn't come right out and say it, but today it was pretty clear he thinks I'm a punk kid who knows nothing and shouldn't be doing this job. *Wouldn't* be doing this job if it weren't for the fact that the owner of the team is my grandfather."

"Well, fuck him."

He laughs, this time a genuine one of humor. "Exactly."

"What does he know?" I wrinkle my nose. "You were the assistant manager in Vegas. It's not like you have *no* experience."

"Yeah." He meets my eyes, and his are warm. "Thanks for the vote of confidence."

I nod firmly. "Also you have hockey in your blood, so you just know stuff."

He chuckles. "And you will probably be running the Jolie store in no time." He lifts his glass.

"Ha. As if. There *was* an opening for a store manager, but I'll start as a beauty advisor." I pause. "I can work my way up, but I don't know how long I'll be here."

I meet his eyes.

The moment goes static.

"Should we talk about that?" I ask quietly.

He slowly shakes his head. "You told Chris you'd go back when he showed he could deal with his shit."

"Right." I move my chin up and down, holding his gaze.

"He hasn't done that yet."

"No. But . . ." I swallow. "What if he never does?"

"I told you, Lace, you can stay as long as you want."

"No, I can't!" I close my eyes. "I mean, we can't just have this weird, open-ended relationship forever. Your mom wants a wedding. Someday you'll meet the woman you want to have that wedding with. The woman you want to spend the rest of your life with."

He reaches out and curls his fingers around mine on the table. "Lacey. I'm fine right now. I'm not interested in a forever relationship."

I feel that like a throat punch, but I try not to flinch.

"I'm focused on this job and proving myself," he continues. "I'm fine with the way things are now. I like you here. We have fun together."

"Sometimes I think you don't want to have fun."

He flashes a rueful smile. "I'm not used to having fun. But I kind of like it."

"I don't want to distract you from your goals."

For a moment, he doesn't respond to that, and fear scrapes inside me that I *am* distracting him. Then he says, "I won't let you."

That doesn't make me feel much better.

"Look, this is weird for me too. I like having plans and knowing what's going to happen. But I don't think either of us is in a position right now to make plans other than maybe for next week." His lips quirk up at the corners.

He's right.

"So," he continues. "I'm learning to live in the moment and just enjoy what we have right now."

I suck briefly on my bottom lip, then nod. "Okay. I can do that too. And . . ." I hold his gaze. "I *am* enjoying what we have right now."

He squeezes my hand. "Me too."

Okay.

He tells me more about firing Joe, the coach, and we take our time eating our delicious food and drinking the amazing wine he ordered and watching the sunset, and even though everything is sort of bizarre, I'm having the best time of my life.

"They didn't give me much training."

I'm having lunch with Everly and Taylor on a Saturday a few weeks later, talking about my new job at Jolie.

"Just threw me into things."

"Sink or swim," Taylor says. "You're doing fine, though."

"It's been hard." I sip my mojito. "But I think I'm figuring it all out. And I really do love helping people with makeup. The rep from Smashbox was in the other day, and she was really impressed with how I helped a customer."

"That's great."

"And how's the course going?" Taylor asks.

I signed up to take a course at Bella Academy, a prominent cosmetology school in Hollywood. "So far, so good. It was expensive, but hopefully I'll learn more."

"That's awesome, Lace."

I really am enjoying the course and my job, although customer service jobs have their frustrations. One day a group of teenage girls came in and started applying makeup straight from the testers without using applicators, contaminating them all. Then there was the woman who came in and licked all the lipsticks, and when I asked what she was doing told me that she didn't buy lipstick she didn't like the taste of. So gross!

It's nice being busy and feeling like a productive, contributing member of society. Much as I appreciate Théo and all he's done for me and his offer to forgo rent, I've learned that I can't rely on anyone else to look after me; I have to look out for myself.

Right now I'm having fun talking to girlfriends about it and listening to their stories about their jobs and Taylor's frustrations at living with her parents who think that even though she's twenty-four years old she should be coming home by eleven o'clock every night.

I wish I could talk to them about what's happening with me and Théo, but how do I tell them that I'm afraid I'm falling in love with my husband? I can't tell Everly, that's for sure; but we're getting to be friends, and this feels like a big barrier between us. I'm not the kind of person to keep secrets or not say what's on my mind, and this is hard.

"Have you seen or talked to JP?" I ask Everly.

"Um . . . yeah, actually. I saw him and Emma the other night when I was having dinner with some friends."

I frown. "You saw him and Emma?"

"Uh . . . yeah." She gives me a strange look. "Why do you act like that's a surprise?"

"When was it?"

"Thursday night. At Valentina. Why?"

I set my hands in my lap. "Emma texted Théo a few weeks ago and told him she and JP had broken up."

Everly's eyes expand. "What?"

"Yeah. That's weird, huh?"

"Why'd she say that? Was she trying to get Théo back?"

"Yes." I smile grimly. "He told me about it. He told her they were done and then he blocked her number."

Everly blinks. "Well. If they did break up, they're back together."

"Wow."

"I'm starting to think she might be a bitch."

I burst out laughing. "Yeah, I already decided that from the way she treated Théo."

Everly leans forward. "Did she cheat on him with JP? We always were curious how they got together so quickly."

"Ugh. I don't know if I should talk about it. But yes."

Everly scowls. "No wonder Théo's so pissed at JP. Dad was right. JP shouldn't be with her. What an asshole."

"I agree." I sigh. "But Théo's over Emma. I just wish he and JP could make up. He misses his brother."

"Maybe we could help that along."

"Uh . . . I don't know. I don't think I want to get involved."

"Come on. You're family now."

I hold up my hands. "Don't be dragging me into all your family drama."

Everly laughs. "There's enough of it."

"I know." I tip my head. "Théo's told me some of it. It's sad that you all grew up not liking each other."

"When we were kids, we all got along. It wasn't until we were older that we started to realize that Mark and Matthew hate my mom." She pushes out her lips and wrinkles her nose. "We figured that they thought she was trying to take their inheritances away from them."

"Maybe it was just that they were worried about their dad," I offer gently.

She rolls her eyes. "As if they need to worry about him. He knew what he was doing."

I prop my chin on my hand, elbow on the table. "So what was it like growing up with him? He must have been older when you were born."

"He was forty-eight. And in his fifties by the time Noah was born. But it didn't seem weird to me. He was a good dad, if somewhat embarrassing at times."

"Aren't all dads?" Taylor asks.

"I wish I knew." I sigh. "I never had a dad."

"Aw. I'm sorry."

"I would have taken an embarrassing dad who made dad jokes. Like, why do crabs never give to charity?"

I get blank looks.

"Because they're shellfish."

They sputter with laughter.

I smile wryly. "See? Embarrassing. Théo will make a good dad someday. His jokes are terrible." Shit. I don't want to think about Théo being a dad with someone else. I look back at Everly. "Théo said they think your mom married your dad for his money."

"I know they think that." Everly's voice hardens. "But it's not true. They love each other." Her eyes shadow though, with something that looks like . . . worry.

"I got that impression," I agree. I lift my hands. "Not that I know anything."

She smiles. "Sometimes the people outside the family see more than we do. I'm glad you think so."

Later, as Taylor drives me home, I decide to confide in

her. "Do you have time to come in for a glass of wine or a margarita? I, um, need to talk about something."

"Sure." She shoots me a curious look. "I'll drop the car off at home and be right back."

Théo's at his office, so we have the place to ourselves. I mix up margaritas and we take them out onto the patio. The beach is busy, with groups of people beneath colorful umbrellas, stretched out in the sun, walking on the sand.

"So what did you want to talk about?" Taylor sips her drink.

"It's sort of a long story, and you have to pledge to never tell anyone, especially Everly or any of the Wynns. Or Manny, or any of the players."

"Okay, so nobody. I get it." She slaps her hand to her heart. "I won't tell a soul."

I take a breath. "Okay. Théo and I aren't really married."

21

LACEY

Taylor gives me a blank look. "That's the big story? Jeez, Lace, lots of people shack up these days." Her forehead crinkles. "Is his family super old-fashioned or something?"

"No." I shake my head. "We're married. We did the quick Vegas thing, like I said. But it wasn't for real. We didn't even know each other. I needed to get out of Vegas because my brother's bookies were after me for, uh, the money he owed them." I tell her more about that night.

"Oh my God." Her eyes bug out.

"Yeah. And . . . Théo had his reasons for wanting to bring a girl home to meet the family. You heard why earlier…Emma cheating on him with JP. So we're faking the marriage for a while."

"For how long?" She's still gaping at me.

"We don't know." I twist a piece of hair. "I told Chris I'm not coming back until he gets his shit together. That might never happen." My voice quivers, because, damn, it's still hard to think of him throwing his life away because of a goddamn addiction. "But Théo could meet someone that he f-falls in love with and wants to really be m-married to." My throat squeezes.

Taylor's eyes soften. "You wouldn't like that."

I inhale a wobbly breath. "No." I meet her eyes. "I'm afraid I'm actually falling for him."

"Would that be so bad?" She tilts her head. "You two seem great together. You're . . . uh, you're sleeping together, right?"

"Yes." I close my eyes as a small heat wave washes over me. "And it's amazing."

"So, he likes you too."

"We get along great. Mostly. He's kind of a neat freak and a bit OCD about where his things are." I make a face. "He also works way too much. But we're learning about each other. I probably make him nuts because I hate doing dishes and leave my shit all over his bathroom. I mean, not literal shit." My eyes pop open in horror.

A laugh spills from her lips. "I knew what you meant. And that sounds like a normal marriage."

"I don't know what to do." I drop my gaze to the ice cubes floating in my pale green beverage. "I know how it feels when you rely on someone to be there, and then . . . they're not. My mom. I mean, she couldn't help it. But after she was gone and it was just Chris and me, I thought we were there for each other. Only it turned out . . . he wasn't. He let me down over and over again, and then in the worst way. I can't risk feeling like that about Théo. Like I need him. I have to look out for myself, because nobody else will."

"Oh, sweetie." Taylor's bottom lip pushes out in sympathy. "You have people who'll look out for you. Me."

"Aw, thank you. I'm just trying to be strong and independent."

"You *are* strong and independent. That doesn't mean you can't fall in love."

"But it's going to end. He told me outright he's not looking for a long-term relationship. He's focused on his career and trying to turn the team around. He has no time for love. Not to mention . . . he's been burnt too, so I don't blame him." I blink back tears. "I'm sorry. I didn't mean to get all emotional. I just wanted to tell someone . . . and I can't tell Everly. Théo's family all think our marriage is for real. Not that it matters . . . he's over Emma."

"Well, there you go."

"What?" I scrunch up my nose.

"He doesn't need you anymore. But he still wants you here."

I cock my head. "He's just being nice."

"Uh-huh. Okay. I'll admit, he's a decent guy. Byron likes him. Especially when Théo throws sticks into the ocean for him."

I smile.

"Do you want advice? Or did you just want to share?"

I laugh. "Thank you for asking. Unwanted advice is so annoying."

"Right?"

"Hit me with it."

"I think you should just go with it. I think you and Théo have a good thing. See what happens."

"Well, I don't want to go back to Vegas. Yet." *Or ever?* "So I guess I'm either stuck here with Théo—"

"Such a hardship." Her lips quirk.

"Or I move somewhere else. Hey, you and I could get an apartment together."

She stares at me, then shakes her head. "While I do love that idea, I think you should stay here."

"Okay. But keep it in mind."

She finishes her margarita and heads home, and Théo arrives a few minutes later. He's taking me out on a date tonight, for dinner and dancing at a hot club, which I'm pretty excited about.

But when he walks in, I take one look at him and my heart squeezes. He looks beat. Like, literally beaten up. His face is drawn, his shoulders are slumped, his shirt is wrinkled.

"What's wrong?" I rush over to him and set my hands on his shoulders.

"Nothing." He talks as if his teeth are permanently gritted.

"You look terrible." I stroke his face, then his hair, studying him. "Did you have a bad day?"

"It was . . . rough." He sighs and sets his hands on my hips. "I've been talking to a bunch of agents about contracts. Some we're making progress on, others not so much. Fuck, that Jack Burnside is an asshole." He shakes his head.

"Yeah." I have no idea who he's talking about but I assume he's an agent.

"Tough negotiator. We can't pay what his client wants. And dammit, we want to keep him."

"Oh no." Sympathy floods through me, along with a helpless feeling because I can't do anything to help with this. I hate seeing him so stressed. His body is tense; his jaw is tight. I can feel the rigidity of his shoulder muscles.

This isn't the first time he's come home stressed, but this seems the worst. The pressure on him is building as the off-season progresses.

"Yesterday I met with our scouting team," he says. "It's cool looking at the prospects that are coming up, but those are impactful decisions as well. The draft is happening in two weeks."

I know nothing about the draft. "Tell me about it over dinner. No . . . wait." I pause. "Let's not go out after all."

"But we planned it." His forehead creases. "You love dancing."

"I do, but we can go dancing another time. You need to decompress, and I know just the way."

His eyes darken and his eyebrows raise.

I laugh softly. "Okay, yes, sex is good stress relief. All those hormones. But let's order in dinner, have a glass of wine, and go in the hot tub. Then I'll give you a massage."

He gazes back at me. "Seriously?"

I nod. "I know you don't like last minute changes of plans, but I think this is a better way to spend the evening." I really want to do whatever I can to make him feel better.

His throat works and he still stares at me. The he nods briefly. "Okay."

"You go change. I'll order dinner."

He trudges upstairs and I grab my phone. He said the prime rib we had the other night at Del Rey was the best he'd ever had. I open up my Grubhub app and place the order. Then I uncork a bottle of Zinfandel and tip two generous pours into glasses. When Théo comes down, he's dressed in athletic shorts and one of his goofy T-shirts. This one reads, DON'T BE MEAN, BE ABOVE AVERAGE with a little line graph image. He already looks less tense.

I hand him his wine. "Dinner will be an hour. Do you want to go in the hot tub now, or after?"

"After." His lips quirk. "I might fall asleep before dinner if we do."

"Okay then, let's go out on the patio and watch the sunset and you can tell me all about your day, and I'll just listen because I have no clue. But I'm a good listener."

He moves toward me, cups my cheek with one hand, and kisses my forehead. "Yeah. You are."

My heart tilts in my chest, emotion flooding me. I so want to be here for this man.

We settle onto the loveseat out on the patio, our feet up on the wicker table, facing the ocean. As always, the faint, rhythmic rush of waves onto the shore, the soft breeze, the scent of salt and sand, and the endless stretch of water and sky soothes and calms. I know Théo feels it too.

"Tell me about the draft."

"Well, it sort of starts next weekend. I'm going to Buffalo for the combine to meet with players."

I hold up a hand, as if asking a question of the teacher. "Combine?"

He grins. "Yeah. All the eligible players who want to play in the NHL are there. They go through a bunch of fitness tests, and we get to sit down with them and talk to them, see who would be a good fit, physically and mentally."

"You meet with all of them?"

"No." He shakes his head. "Our scouts have been watching these guys and reporting back to us. They know what the kids' families are like, what their characters are, and we've narrowed down a list of guys we're interested in. We have lots of homework done before this, so this isn't the be all and end all. The fitness testing is valuable in terms of what skills and strengths the guys have. Also, I can talk to other GMs there. A lot of trade talks start at the combine."

"Huh."

"But it's like analytics. That can't be the only tool you use. Same with the combine. There's value in it, though. Then at the end of the month I go to Vancouver for the actual draft. Every team takes turns picking. We're in a good position this year because of our shitty record."

I huff out a laugh. "I guess that's good."

"Yeah. We have two first round picks, and the field is rich this year with talented kids."

"Is it your decision who to pick?"

"Yeah, but I do it in conjunction with the team, of course."

"Even the coach? Does he get a say?"

"Nah."

I laugh.

"No really, I don't want his input as much. He hasn't been watching these players for years like the scouts have."

"Years?" I'm boggled.

"Yeah, sure. They start watching kids in major junior hockey, maybe even sooner. They know these guys and have watched them grow and mature. The coach has no idea, other than maybe he saw them play in one game. So, Dave tells me what he thinks we need on the team, and we'll look to try to fill that, but he doesn't get a say in who that is."

"You have so much responsibility." I lay my hand on his thigh and squeeze.

"Fuck, tell me about it."

"But you wanted this."

"I did. I do."

"So, you have new guys to pick, but you also have these current players you need to sign."

"Yep." He leans his head back. "There are a few guys we'd really like to keep, but they're asking for ridiculous money, probably because they know we can't afford it and they really want out."

"They don't want to play for you anymore?" Outrage raises my voice.

He smiles. "Believe it or not, most players want to play for winning teams."

One corner of my mouth lifts. "Okay, yeah, I get that."

"I have to convince them that we can win. We *will* win, with the changes we're making."

No wonder he's so stressed.

Our food arrives and Théo's delighted with his dinner, devouring the prime rib and garlic mashed potatoes, and then we get naked and go in the hot tub with another glass of wine. We sink into the bubbling, swirling waters, the heat relaxing us. I *hope* it's relaxing Théo.

"That was so good." I let out a sigh and tip my head back to look up at the sky.

"It was. Thank you. I'll make it up to you by taking you dancing another time."

"Ah. Thank you. How long are you going to be away?"

"I fly to Buffalo on Sunday. I'll be gone a week."

"A whole week?" I push up out of the water.

"Yeah." He pauses. "Come with me."

"I . . . can't. I have a job. And school."

"Right. Damn."

"You'll be busy anyway."

"True."

Crap. I'm going to miss him "Feeling better?" I ask him.

"Come here."

I smile and set my wineglass down beside the tub then float over to Théo in the corner. He pulls me onto his lap, tilts his head, and kisses me.

I'm full. Full of love for him. I want this forever. I know I shouldn't. I know I can't have it. I just told Taylor earlier that I know Théo doesn't want forever.

But he wants right now. And so do I.

So I kiss him back with all the love I have for him right now, this moment, my arms twined around his neck, my aching center pressed against his hard-on. His hands tighten on me, his tongue slides into my mouth and out, again and again, in lush, sensual kisses that go on and on.

We move from the hot tub to the bedroom and even though we're both buzzing with arousal, I make him lay on the bed, facedown, and I bring my bottle of two-in-one massage lube with us.

Sitting astride his thighs, I squeeze lubricant into my palms and rub them together to warm it, then stroke them over his shoulders and down his back. I return to his shoulders because he's still tense there, his muscles like granite. I knead and press my thumbs into the flesh, finding the knots and working them until they release.

He groans. "That's fantastic."

"I hope so." I keep my voice hushed, my touches slow, working my way down his back, then back up to the shoulders again. I sweep my hands down his upper arms in a slow, firm motion, dig my thumbs into his upper back, and on the next move downward, I keep going all the way to his gorgeous ass.

Gorgeous. A sigh leaks from my lips as I massage his firm cheeks, which first tighten at my touch, then relax again. I shift lower for better access, slipping my fingers along the crease where his butt meets thigh, then lower still to his legs. I stroke up and down his thighs, to the knee and back, up the inside of his legs, eliciting a shudder, and he parts them for me. Oh Jesus.

I gaze at him, enthralled at the shadowy glimpse of his testicles between his muscled thighs. Slowly I slide my hands down those creases again, brushing over his perineum, fingertips caressing his balls. His body jerks and he sucks in a breath.

"Can I use that toy on you?" I ask quietly. He brought home a sexy little butt plug a week or so ago and convinced me to let him use it on me. And I loved it.

He tenses. "Is this a new form of stress relief?"

"Hey, it could work." I stroke him again.

"Okay," he chokes out.

I move over and find the toy in the bottom drawer of the nightstand and lube it up. Teeth sunk into my bottom lip, my pussy squeezing with arousal, I use more lube around his back entrance, gently petting around it . . . then over it. Then so, so slowly I insert the toy.

Another groan rumbles from him and he buries his face

in the bed. Slowly, I press the toy deeper, then deeper still, holding it in place as his body accepts it.

"Fuuuuck."

I release the plug, leaving it in place as I again use both hands to massage the grooves of ass and thigh, slipping my fingers down between his legs, up and down, using my thumbs to again press the base of the toy farther. He's making more guttural noises, his hips lifting.

I take a break, running my slick hands down over his thighs, the dark hair there flattened to his skin with the lube. He's shiny everywhere, his skin smooth over muscles. I admire him, stroke him, tease him until he cries hoarsely, "Jesus, I need to come."

"Mmm. Roll over."

He obeys instantly, his cock springing up against his belly, long, thick, heavy veins throbbing. I reach for him with slick hands and drag them from root to tip. He emits another jagged groan.

"Holy fuck, that feels good."

"I like it too . . . all slick like this." The lube adds sensation, my hands sliding easily, gripping him firmly. I slip a hand down to push the toy deeper again and in seconds he shouts as he comes, spurting over my hand and his stomach. I'm fascinated and turned on beyond belief, watching this erotic show.

He lays there, gasping, panting, one forearm over his eyes, his beautiful mouth open. I lean over and press a kiss to his chest, and he lifts his other hand to curve it around my head, holding my hair. "Jesus, baby, that was . . . holy hell."

"Did it feel good?" I kiss him again.

"Fuck yeah," he mumbles. "That was intense."

"You seem a lot more relaxed." I smile against his skin.

His lips curve up too. "Oh yeah."

"My work here is done."

He chuckles. "Best massage I ever had." He lets his arm fall to the bed and meets my eyes. "With a happy ending, even."

"Yep." I bend over and kiss his mouth, slow and lingering. I want to tell him I love him. I suck my bottom lip between my teeth and sit back on my heels. He's looking at me so warmly, so affectionately. My chest tightens and I can't speak.

Which is probably just as well.

22

THÉO

Fuck, I miss her.

This combine is what I love—hockey. All hockey, all the time. Watching players get tested, talking to players, scouts, other GMs. Also the media, constantly sniffing around for hints of any juicy news.

But I miss Lacey.

I call her every night before I go to bed. Text her every morning when I get up. Think about her all the fucking time.

I need to focus on business. This is important. I've been approached by a couple of GMs to feel me out about trades. I need to be smart and strategic, not lovesick and pining.

Since that night last weekend when I came home wound so tight, my neck, my shoulders, and my jaw all killing me, my head pounding, and she'd taken care of me . . . I'm bursting with weird feelings. I need her. I want her. I don't want to be apart from her, which this goddamn trip is forcing me to do. She gave up a night at a club that she'd been looking forward to, to make me feel better, and she's sneaking in behind the barriers I erected to keep my heart safe from betrayal.

Not only that, she destroyed me with the hottest hand job in the history of hand jobs, with that anal play I never thought I'd enjoy, and lube that had the top of my head nearly blowing off from the incredible sensation. That was a pretty intimate scene, something I've never done with anyone else.

Focus.

I've got my questions for this eighteen-year-old giant sitting in front of me, one of our highest picks, the questions developed by a sports psychologist. "Here's a picture of a train with two engines. Which way is it going?"

The kid's eyes flicker.

"Don't answer that," I say. "That's a fucking stupid question."

He laughs nervously.

I switch gears. "Last year you had a lot of personal success, but your team's finish was disappointing. How do you deal with that?"

I listen to his response, nodding. Okay, he did well.

The next guy I talk to isn't as big. He's likely still got growing to do, but I ask him, "How do you deal with going up against bigger players in the corners?"

The next guy we interview tells us his strength is his ability to play an all-around game. We pretty much agree with that. "I take pride in playing a strong defensive game, and I like to use my shot and my speed to my advantage."

Good, good.

Like I told Lacey, we've pretty much already decided before this who we want, but it's good to have a chance to talk to these kids and see how they perform on the testing.

Things wrap up Saturday. I'm supposed to have breakfast with the GM from Carolina Sunday morning, but I want to get the hell out of here and get home. So I quickly change the breakfast to a drink in the bar Saturday afternoon, change my flight, so I'll be home by ten o'clock after a painful five and a half hour flight. I manage to get some work done though, sitting in business class with a nice glass of scotch and unlimited snacks, thinking about my conversation with Tuttle from Carolina. They know we have cap issues and they have room. They're willing to take some players off our hands.

I mull over the options, entering numbers into my spreadsheets to see how the cap is impacted. Fuck. We may have no choice but to lose someone we don't want to.

I left my car at home so Lacey could use it while I was gone, and the car service is waiting for me outside the terminal at LAX. I jump into the Escalade. Should I call Lacey, or text her, to let her know I'm home?

Nah, I'll surprise her.

Except when I get there, she's not home.

I park my suitcase and gaze around the empty house dejectedly. Shit. Where is she?

I drop down onto the couch and text her. She doesn't answer right away, so I haul my luggage upstairs and change. Back downstairs with a beer in hand, I check my phone.

I'm out dancing with Everly and Taylor!

Great.

I blow out a breath and sink into the couch. I should have thought that she'd want to go out on a Saturday night. Especially since we didn't end up going out that night I came home so stressed.

She's already made friends since we moved here, one of them my aunt, for Chrissake. She's even made friends with my mom, going shopping, teaching her to knit. Everyone loves her. She needs a guy who's social and fun, not a nerdy workaholic like me.

I don't feel betrayed. Not exactly. Just . . . let down. Disappointed. I don't blame *her*. I should know better than to think I could have something—or someone—I want so badly.

I'm not going to kick her out or anything. I'm not an asshole. I just need to be more careful.

I don't tell her I came home early to see her; I don't want her to come home early herself. Not sure if she'd do that, but anyway . . . I drink my beer and turn on the TV to watch a recap of tonight's hockey game, the first game of the Stanley Cup final.

One day, I'll be there.

I just need to keep working my ass off and forget about a sexy, sweet woman with incredible hair and long legs and an enchanting smile . . .

"I DIDN'T KNOW YOU WERE COMING HOME EARLY!"

I was asleep when Lacey got home last night, and even

though I sort of heard and felt her get into bed, I pretended I didn't and went back to sleep.

This morning, she's yawning and making coffee and looking adorable as usual.

"It was a last-minute decision. Decided I wanted to get back so I could head into the office today and go through all my notes."

"But it's Sunday."

I grimace. "I know. But I have some phone calls to make to follow up on meetings I had this week. We need to make some trades and I need to figure things out."

"Oh. Okay."

"Did you have fun last night?"

"Yeah! It was a girls' night. Everly and Taylor brought a couple of other friends and it was fun. We went to Lux."

"Nice." I keep my expression pleasantly neutral. "That's good. Well, I'll see you later. I'm going to stop at Starbucks on my way to the office."

"Okay." Her smile holds a hint of disappointment. "See you later."

I feel like a giant turd as I drive to the arena. I've been away for a week and want to spend time with Lacey, and she's obviously disappointed that I'm disappearing, but it's better this way. I need to keep my distance. As much as I can, when we're living together, sharing a bed. Sharing all kinds of things.

Of course I can't stay away from her totally. I hate myself when she snuggles up to me in bed that night, but I've missed her so goddamn much and I want her with a blood-deep craving I can't ignore, and she feels so fucking good—all long silky hair and soft skin and lush curves. I pull her closer and find her mouth with mine in the dark and lose myself in her, in her taste, her scent, her arms around me.

"I missed you," she whispers in my ear as I move over her.

My chest constricts even as I push inside her body. "Yeah," I whisper roughly back.

Her hands move over me, pulling me closer, caressing my hot skin. Her body closes around me, tight, slick, inflaming me even more. I move against her, unable to resist, my need for her raging through me. I want to take her and take her and take her and never stop.

"You don't need to actually measure the water."

"But it says use ten cups of boiling water." Holding the measuring cup, I frown at Lacey. I've read the directions on the package of pasta.

"It doesn't matter how much water you use." She's starting to lose patience. "You drain the water off after it's cooked anyway."

"Well, that's true, but I think we should follow the directions."

She grips the edge of the counter, looking like she wants to scream. "It doesn't matter!"

"Well, it must matter somehow, why else would they put that in the directions?"

"Aaaah!" She lets out the scream I could see building.

Then she lets out a long huff. "Oh my God! It's a good thing I like you!"

I crack up. I can't help it. I like her too. So much. I wrap her up in a bear hug, squeezing her so tight, because I can't tell her how much I like her. Or . . . maybe even love her. I can't. "Okay, we'll do it your way." I kiss her forehead, pick up the pot, and run water into it straight from the tap. "There. Living on the edge, baby."

She laughs too. "Damn right."

We're making dinner then sitting down to watch the hockey game tonight—the final game of the Stanley Cup playoffs. The teams are tied at three games each, so whoever wins tonight wins the Cup.

We didn't plan on a bunch of people joining us, but somehow it happened. It always seems to happen, with Lacey here. Everyone is drawn to her. Pretty sure it's not me who's the attraction. Taylor arrives, followed shortly by Manny and Wyatt, and another neighbor couple, Rosa and Marshall. Lacey jumps into hostess action, setting out bowls of chips and dip, and platters of appetizers she magically conjures from our fridge and cupboards.

Once again, I have to go with the flow. I'm getting used to it. And I'm actually kind of having fun playing host to her hostess, acting as bartender, serving drinks to our guests.

"Thanks, man," Manny says as I hand him a beer. "How are things shaping up with the team?"

He knows I can't really tell him anything, especially since he's likely going to be one of the guys on the chopping block, so I say, "Making progress."

"Who've you got your eye on for the draft?"

"I could tell you but then I'd have to kill you."

Manny laughs. "Come on. Everyone knows Koskinen, Rintala, and Smith-Evans are gonna go top three. You have second pick, so one of them is likely gonna be a Condor."

I smile.

"Who are we cheering for?" Lacey asks as she settles onto the couch next to me with a beer in her hand.

I shake my head. "It's gotta be Pittsburgh, babe."

She nods. "Your team. Okay."

Most people there are cheering for the Sharks, so there's a bit of trash-talking going on.

"Morrison sucks," Manny says of a Pittsburgh center. "I've seen better hands on a digital clock."

"Are you kidding me?" I shake my head. "His numbers don't lie."

"He has to stop that puck, or they'll score!" Lacey cries at one point, talking about the Pittsburgh goalie.

I turn and give her a look. She immediately gets it and her cheeks turn pink.

"Sorry," she mumbles. "Captain Obvious, huh?"

I try to repress my smile. She's cute.

"Oh my God!" she says moments later, staring at the TV. "Can they *do* that? He just punched him in the face!"

"Not supposed to," I answer. "Guess the refs didn't see."

"Well, they should be watching better!"

Then she really makes me laugh.

"Oh, nice shot! Yay!" And she claps for a Sharks goal along with everyone else.

"Babe." I nudge her. "Wrong team."

"Oh. Right. But still . . . that *was* a nice shot."

Can't argue with that.

Everly shows up between periods. I have no idea how she knew there was a party going on. Maybe she didn't.

Lacey jumps up and dashes over to hug her. "Hi!"

"Hey." Everly gives her a hug in return.

They're best buds now, apparently. Weird.

Everly smiles at me. "Hi, Théo. Haven't seen you since you got back from Buffalo. How was it?"

"Productive."

"Good, good. Oh, hi," she says unenthusiastically to Wyatt, then turns her back on him and sits next to Rosa and Marshall. "What's the score?"

Wyatt's face pinches up.

Lacey brings out more food. I hand Everly a glass of wine and refill other drinks.

Pittsburgh scores early in the second period, tying it up. Lacey and I high-five each other. "Got it right this time," I murmur to her.

She knows I'm teasing and gives me a little elbow in the ribs. "I'm learning."

The Sharks take a terrible penalty for an illegal hit to the head, and in the power play, Pittsburgh scores again, taking the lead. This opens the flood gates, and they go on to score two more unanswered goals. But the game's not over. Late in the third, the Sharks put the pressure on and score twice. With seconds left in the game and their net empty, they're cycling like crazy in front of the Pittsburgh net, in total control of the puck in a last desperate attempt to tie it up. We're all on the edges of our seats watching, cheering, groaning, and shrieking with every shot attempt.

The horn sounds to end the game.

"Yeah!" I pump my fists in the air. I turn to Lacey and she raises her arms to smack my hands.

The Sharks fans are disappointed, but nobody here was that invested in the outcome. So our party continues as we watch the players shake hands, celebrate, and carry the Cup around the ice. Of course, I feel that pang of longing, that wish that someday I could hold that beauty in my hands.

I'm working on it.

Hockey season's over for everyone now; things are going to ramp up even more for me.

I'm back in Vegas.

It's weird coming back. Everything is so familiar.

Tonight are the NHL Awards. I'm not nominated for anything; nobody from the Condors is. But the Mustangs' goalie is nominated for the Vezina Trophy and one of the defensemen for the Norris, so I came back to support them and do some networking. There'll be parties, naturally, but I'm not big on those.

I have one other mission while I'm here.

I drive to the apartment building where Lacey used to live. Where she still pays the rent in case her brother comes back and needs a place to live. I take the stairs to the second floor, even though it's been nearly two months since that day we ran for our lives out of there. Of course the suitcase isn't there anymore.

I knock on the apartment door and wait. This is probably futile, but who knows.

The door opens and I'm greeted by a frowning young man with Lacey's eyes and nose. He's a few inches taller than her, but shorter than me, with dark gold hair and beard stubble. "Yeah?"

"Chris Olson?"

"Yeah." His frown deepens. "Who are you?"

"Théo Wynn. Lacey's husband."

His eyes bug out, then he frowns again. "Where's Lacey?"

"She's still in L.A. She couldn't come with me because she had work and school."

"Huh. Yeah. She told me she got a job and was taking a course."

"What about you?"

His forehead creases and his eyes narrow. "What about me?"

"What are you doing with your life? After stealing money from your sister to pay your gambling debts or possibly gamble more, and trying to pimp her out to your bookies to get them off your back . . . after letting her bail you out time after time . . . what are *you* doing?" I fix him with a harsh glare.

"Uh . . ." He seems at a loss. Then he shakes his head. "I'm trying. I am."

I push past him to enter the apartment.

"Sure, come on in," he says sarcastically.

"We don't need to have this conversation in the hall." I turn to face him. "You say you're trying. What exactly does that mean?"

He stares back at me for a moment. "I've gone to some

meetings," he finally says, a bit defensively. He rubs the back of his neck. "I know I have a problem."

I nod slowly. "Like they say . . . that's the first step."

23

LACEY

I'VE JUST GOTTEN HOME FROM MY THURSDAY MORNING class. I have a few hours before my shift at Jolie starts, and I'm opening the fridge to see what I can have for lunch when the doorbell rings. Théo's in Vegas for the NHL Awards that happened last night, and he's going to fly from there to Vancouver for the draft this weekend, so he won't be home until Monday. I scoot to the door to answer it, expecting Taylor and Byron inviting me to go for a walk on the beach, or maybe Manny wanting to hang out, and throw open the door with a smile.

I freeze in shock at seeing Théo's brother.

"Uh . . . JP. Hi."

"Hi."

"Théo's not here."

"I know. He's in Vegas."

"How'd you know that?"

"Everyone knows that. I saw him on TV last night."

I saw him on TV too, looking so handsome and professional in his suit and tie.

"Can I come in? I need to talk to you."

"Why me?" I stare at him as I move aside to let him enter the condo.

He walks in. "Because you know Théo. You know what's going on with him."

"Uh . . . yeah." I'm not sure what he's talking about. I move around him and lead the way to the living room, gesturing at the couch. "Have a seat. Can I get you anything? Coffee?"

"Nah. I'm good. This is a great place." He crosses to the big couch.

"It is." I sit in an armchair. "Okay, what's going on?"

"Did he tell you about . . . Emma and me? What happened?"

"You mean when you both betrayed him and stabbed him in the back?" I narrow my eyes at him. "Yes. He told me."

He winces. "I need to know something."

I chew on my bottom lip. "What?"

"What did Théo tell you about Emma? About how things ended?"

I think back. "He said he found her cheating on him with you. He said . . . you were staying with him last summer. Visiting Vegas for a while. He came home early and found you two on the couch . . ."

JP hangs his head, nodding. "Did he tell you that he'd already broken up with her before that happened?"

I frown. "No." I squint at him. "I don't think that makes it much better, frankly, if you're looking for forgiveness."

He shakes his head. "That's not what I'm looking for. I know I fucked up. Big-time."

"Yep." I nod firmly. "But in any case, no . . . they were still together when that happened." I pause. "Weren't they?"

"Emma told me they weren't. She told me she'd ended things with him, because she had feelings for me. We'd been hanging around for a couple of weeks, mostly with Théo, but sometimes just she and I would do things . . . chill at the pool, or go to a show when he was busy. There was an . . . attraction between us." He swipes a hand over his face and looks away. "I was at Théo's place when she showed up. She said she came to get some of her things she'd left there. I know I shouldn't have hooked up with her, regardless, but it was hard to resist when she was right there coming on to me, and she's really hot and she was telling me how great I was compared to Théo . . . who's always, *always* been better than me at everything."

My eyes fly open wide. I stare at him. Then I slowly stand and move over to the couch to sit next to him, my heart swelling with sympathy. I can imagine Théo *was* a hard older brother to live up to—not only athletically talented, but brilliant. And insanely gorgeous. But I say, "I'm sure that's not true."

"It's true. And I lost my mind." He shakes his head. "It's okay, this has all just proved that point. He *is* better than me." His tone is laced with bitterness.

I actually do feel sorry for him, even though he did a terrible thing and hurt Théo. "Backing up, though . . ." I say slowly. "Emma lied to you about ending things with Théo."

"Apparently. Théo didn't exactly want to have a conversation about it. He kicked us both out. We drove back to L.A. together. He wouldn't talk to me about it."

"Do you blame him?" I level an incredulous stare on him.

"No." He sighs. "I get it. But . . . I just found out that Emma recently told him the same thing . . . that we'd broken up."

"Ohhh." I nibble my bottom lip. "How did you find out about that?"

"Everly."

I suck in a long, slow breath and let it out. Well, I never told her that was a secret, and she *was* talking about trying to help JP and Théo get past this. I don't know if Everly told him she heard it from me, though. "I see."

"She wanted to get back with him."

I nod. "Yeah. He told me."

"Oh. Okay. Wow. That's . . . great."

"Why is that great?"

"Obviously you two have a strong relationship if he can be that honest with you."

"Oh. Yeah. Théo is an honest person."

"Yeah. He is. Of course he is."

Annoyance flares inside me. "You know, Théo hasn't exactly had things easy his whole life."

JP looks up at me. "You mean his injury."

"Well, yeah, that was a pretty big blow. Especially to a guy people didn't believe could play professional hockey."

"Everyone always knew he'd play in the NHL. He's a Wynn."

"They *didn't* always know that," I say quietly. "*He* didn't always know that. You know about the kids that made fun of him when he was young. But maybe not about the hockey coaches who didn't want him on their teams."

"What?" He frowns. "Didn't want him on their teams?"

I nod. "Yes. Your parents probably sheltered you from that."

"Shit." His eyebrows pull together. "I *did* know about the bullying. I stuck up for him when kids called him names and made fun of him. I was two years younger though, and some of those kids were big. Once I got in an actual fistfight." He grimaces. "I took a shit kicking."

"You did that for Théo?" I gaze at him in awe.

"Yeah. He's my brother."

I press a hand to my heart, my eyes brimming with tears. "You two really need to talk."

"You think?" He meets my eyes. "I had to find out . . . if it was true or not that Emma had ended things with him. Because then she lied to me . . . twice."

"Are you in love with her?" My heart beats faster, hoping he's not, because damn, this woman has really messed things up for two brothers who really love each other.

He closes his eyes and exhales sharply. "I don't know."

I set a hand on his shoulder. "I'm sorry. It hurts."

The door opens and Théo walks in.

He stops short at seeing us. His face goes stiff, his mouth a harsh line. "What the hell is going on here?"

I jump up. "Théo! You're not supposed to be here."

He scowls. "I can't fucking believe this." He glares at his brother. "What the fuck, JP?"

JP stands. "Théo."

"Why are you back?" I rush over to hug him, happy to see him but confused.

He shakes his head, his face rigid, his expression forbidding. He steps back from me.

I stop, my heart lurching. "What's wrong?"

"What's wrong?" He waves a hand at me, then JP. *"What's wrong?"* This comes out as a near bellow.

Oh. Oh no. He doesn't think . . . oh my God. "No, no, Théo." I grab his arm. "It's not what you think."

"Where have I heard that before?" he snaps. "Fuck this." He turns and heads back to the door.

"Wait! Théo, wait, seriously, this isn't anything."

"Get back here and talk to us," JP calls. "Bro, you're being a dumbass."

Théo stops, then turns his head and says over his shoulder, "Yeah, I sure as hell am."

Then he grabs his suitcase and slams out the door.

After a shocked beat, I run after Théo, my feet bare, out onto the sidewalk. The sand there is cool beneath my soles and I skid in it, nearly falling. I parked Théo's car on the street when I got home, and he's already there, tossing his case into the trunk and yanking open his door. "Théo! Stop!"

He shakes his head. "Got a flight to catch."

I watch him drive away, my mouth open, my eyes wide. What the hell?

I turn back to JP, who followed me to the door.

"Well, shit," he says. "Does he seriously think we were screwing around on him?"

"He can't possibly think that. If he does, he's an idiot." I well know he's not an idiot, but sometimes very smart people can be kind of clueless. I roll my eyes. "I'll call him and explain things."

"Okay. Shit." He presses his thumb and fingertips to his forehead. "What the hell is he doing showing up?"

"Uh, he lives here." Never mind I had the same reaction. "You can understand why he'd be freaked out."

"Yeah, but this is different."

"Don't worry, I'll tell him. I'll tell him that you're ready to . . . apologize to him." I study him. "You are, right?"

"Yeah," he mutters.

I nod. "Okay."

He nods glumly. "Sorry to cause problems. I just came here to . . . I don't know. I wanted to confirm I'm right about Emma and I was right to tell her I never want to see her again."

"You told her that?"

"Yeah."

"Well, good." I blow out a breath. "Okay, when Théo gets back from Vancouver, we'll all get together and sort things out. It'll be fine."

JP leaves and I sink down onto the couch. My heart hurts that Théo could actually think I would do something like that—cheat on him. Cheat on him with his own brother. I hate that he's hurting. But I'll explain things, and it'll be fine.

I go grab my phone out of my purse and call him, but it goes to voicemail. I leave a message. "Hey, it's me. You *are* being a dumbass. Call me back; we need to talk."

By the time I have to leave for work, he still hasn't called. Okay, he's probably on a plane and can't. I send him a text that he'll get when he lands.

> JP came to talk to me about Emma. He knows she's a bitch who lied to you both and they broke up and he's ready to apologize to u. U 2 need to talk.

I hit send.

Then I type more.

> And if u think I was cheating on u with ur brother, u really are a dumbass.

Send.

I still haven't gotten a reply by the time I'm done working at nine.

Now *I'm* getting pissed.

24

LACEY

"Whoa. What the hell?"

"What?"

I just opened the envelope that has my Vegas apartment as the return address and now hold in my hands a check for a thousand dollars.

I show it to Taylor. "From Chris."

"Holy shit."

"I know." I shake my head. "Where did he get this money? Oh jeez." My stomach cramps. "He must be still gambling."

She makes a face, looking anxious.

"Ugh. Where's my phone? I have to call him. Even though he probably won't answer." I tap his number in my contacts and it rings. To my surprise, he answers. "Hey, Lace."

"Chris." I hesitate. I'm so surprised he answered, and so happy to hear his voice my heart squeezes. "How are you?"

"Not bad. How are you?"

"Okay. I, uh, got your check today in the mail."

"Oh. Good." I hesitate. "Chris . . . where did you get the money?"

"Don't worry, I didn't steal it. Or win it. I earned it." He pauses. "I got a job."

"Uuuh . . . wow. That's great."

"Yeah. It's kind of a crap job, but the pay is pretty good. I'm working for a filter manufacturer, doing assembly work."

I don't even know what to say. "That's awesome, Chris."

"So I sent you that. I know it doesn't repay you for everything you did, but . . . it's a start."

"You don't have to repay me." I suck in a quick breath and let it out. I said that automatically, but maybe I shouldn't be so forgiving. It's hard though, especially when he's making an effort.

"I probably *can't* pay you back everything," he says. "But part of the program is trying to make amends."

"Program?" I meet Taylor's eyes which are curious but soft. I sit down at the dining table.

"I'm going to a gambling addiction program. It's like Alcoholics Anonymous."

"Oh. Chris." I close my eyes as tears sting them, my throat constricting. "I'm so glad."

"I'm sorry for all the shit I caused. And I'm really sorry for using you to try to appease those fucking criminals."

"Have you . . . dealt with them?"

"Um, yeah. I now have a large loan at the bank, but I'm out of debt. I had to get a job first before they'd give me a loan, and it'll take a while to repay it. Sometimes it feels like it'll take forever." He gives a harsh chuckle. "But I just need to focus on right now."

"Yeah." I want to offer to help, but I fight back the words. He needs to do this himself.

"You said you'd come back when I got my shit together. But . . . you're married now. Your dude seems like a straight-up guy."

I cock my head. "What? How do you know?"

"He came to see me the other day."

My lungs compress painfully and I can't breathe. "He did?"

"Yeah. He was tough, but it's okay. He's looking out for you. You totally deserve someone like that, Lace."

I blink rapidly, my eyes prickling again. "Well, it's not what it seems, actually." I don't really want to tell him the whole story right now.

I'm so hurt by Théo's silence and refusal to talk about what happened. I know he has to focus on business. The draft is a big thing and he has all kinds of meetings, plus he was sitting in a hockey arena last night for the first picks and again all day today. I watched it on TV, anxiously looking for any glimpse of him, then staring at the TV when he got up on the stage to make their picks, so proud of him and impressed and admiring. But he could take a minute just to message me back. I've told him the truth about what happened and if he doesn't believe me . . .

He doesn't believe me.

I guess that's pretty obvious from his silence.

Well, fuck him then.

My chest aches and pressure burns behind my eyes and

cheekbones. I draw air into my lungs, slowly, shakily, and expel it out. "I'm coming home," I whisper to Chris.

Taylor's eyes nearly pop out of her head. "What?" she mouths.

"What?" Chris says.

"I'm coming home." I say it louder. Stronger.

"What about your husband?"

"It's a long story. I'll tell you when I'm there. I'll text you when I know when I'll arrive."

"Okay," he says slowly. "Are you okay, Lace?"

"Sure! I'll s-see you soon." I end the call.

"What are you doing?" Taylor demands.

I sigh. "Théo's pissed at me and apparently not speaking to me."

"Uh . . . why? Did you leave the lid off the toothpaste again?"

"Ha ha. No." I tell her the story of what happened when he came home from Vegas. "He's such an idiot."

"Uh, yeah. How could he think that?"

"Déjà vu, I guess." I shake my head. "I've texted him and left voicemails for him and he's not answering. Clearly he doesn't believe me and I'm not staying with someone who doesn't trust me."

"No." Taylor shakes her head. "No, you're not leaving."

"I am." My voice is thready. "I can't stay here if Théo really thinks I would cheat on him with his brother."

"You need to talk to him."

"Tell *him* that." I'm already looking up flights. This money Chris sent me will come in handy. I can leave tomorrow morning and be back in Vegas by noon. Perfect. "He's the one who won't talk."

"At least wait till he gets home." She flattens her hands on the table and leans forward.

I shake my head, my heart heavy and hurt. "No. I can't do this anymore. I love him." My voice fractures. I close my eyes. A fist squeezes my throat while another one twists my guts up painfully. "I shouldn't have let myself fall for him, but I did. I knew I needed to look out for myself. Nobody else will. So that's what I'm doing." I lift my chin. "Chris seems to be turning things around. I don't need to hide here anymore. I can go home and go back to my regular life and . . ." My regular life wasn't all that great, to be honest. There's so much I'm going to miss from here . . . the ocean, the beach, the people. Especially Taylor and Everly. And Byron. "And start again."

"I'm going to miss you," Taylor whispers, her eyes shiny.

I reach across to grab her hands. "I'm going to miss you too."

THÉO

The moment when I announce our first draft pick up on the stage in the Rogers Arena in Vancouver is an emotional one —of course it brings back memories of that day not so long ago when it was *my* name being called, *me* getting up there on the stage and pulling on the Penguins jersey, me with my whole hockey life ahead of me.

It hasn't turned out how I envisioned it that day, but it's still been pretty damn fantastic. I love this sport. And I'm thrilled to be picking Edvin Rintala from Finland on behalf of the California Condors. This kid is amazing and has the potential to be a marquee player.

I'm having a helluva time focusing on business, but since that's all I have, I better fucking do it. Succeeding at this job, managing this team, turning it from a losing team into a winner and a moneymaker . . . that's all I have. All I am. The numbers guy. I have to be the *best* numbers guy . . . or I'm nothing.

I'm working on autopilot. In Vegas, the NHL and the NHLPA announced the salary cap for next season, which will be five million dollars higher than this season. That helps us some . . . but not enough. We need some depth players and we need them now. Luckily with all our preparation and with a good team here with me, we acquire some outstanding prospects *and* trade one of our players we knew we couldn't keep for another second-round pick, which results in getting a player the scouts all think will have excellent value down the road for us.

I ignore Lacey's messages. She keeps sending them.

I know she wasn't screwing around with my brother. That would be too improbable. What are the chances that would happen to me twice? Like, a thousand to one odds. I don't even know the statistical likelihood of that.

But it did totally freak me out, seeing them together. A hot wave of jealousy hit me, all the feelings I'd had when I walked in on JP and Emma that day roaring back, making me want to puke. I'd lost my shit and stormed out, and when I'd calmed down and thought about it logically, I believed what Lacey tells me in her endless messages. But . . . anytime I trust someone or believe in something, I get shit on. I'm not going there again.

I knew Lacey wasn't going to be around forever, but I was getting crazy, stupid ideas about love and keeping her here and having something good and beautiful and joyful in my life. Something other than the work that I used to distract myself from the fact that I didn't have much else going on in my life. I thought that was what I wanted. Then I started wanting more. But I know better than that.

I keep telling myself this all weekend. When I board the plane back to LAX on Monday morning, I can feel satisfied with a job well done.

Except I feel like I've been used as a target in the net for shooting practice, my entire body bruised and beat up.

Now I have to deal with things at home. I'm looking forward to that as much I'd look forward to blocking an Ovechkin slap shot. My gut cramps with dread the entire flight. I try to ease the pain with whiskey. The flirty flight attendant is happy to keep refilling my glass, but I need to ease up because I have to drive home from the airport.

I have no idea if Lacey works today; I know she doesn't have a class on Mondays. But the condo is empty when I walk in. I'm both disappointed and relieved. Much as I don't want to admit it, I want to see her again. I missed her. Again. Yet I'm relieved that I don't have to have the conversation I've been planning in my head. I even made notes on my laptop, for Chrissake, so I'd know what to say.

I haul my suitcase and garment bag with my suits upstairs and unpack. I carry my toiletry bag into the bathroom and set it on the vanity. I look around. The bathroom is unusually neat and tidy. Lately every time I walk in here, Lacey's girl stuff is all over the place—hair products, moisturizers, shower gel that smells like her . . . apples and flowers . . .

It's all gone.

I frown. My chest seizes up. I whip open the drawers of the vanity and doors of the medicine cabinet.

Her stuff is gone.

For a moment, I can't move. Can't think.

Then I pound downstairs and rocket into her bedroom. I skid to a halt. It's empty too.

There is nothing of Lacey left in this room. The closet is empty. The bathroom is bare as well.

My lungs deflate, leaving me winded. What. The. Fuck.

I stumble through the condo. Her flip-flops aren't sitting by the door onto the patio. Her magazines and knitting aren't cluttering up the coffee table.

She's gone.

Okay. Okay. Why am I freaking the fuck out when I was going to have a conversation where I gently suggested that we'd get a divorce and she'd move out. I could help her find an apartment, if she's not ready to go back to Vegas. I was dreading that conversation. I should feel thankful I don't have to do it. She made the decision on her own.

For some reason though, there's a burning in my gut, spreading up into my chest.

I need to ignore it.

It's pretty fucking hard to ignore. I rub my chest. Maybe I need to take a pill.

A thought bursts into my mind. What if . . . those douchehole bookies came here and got her?

No. They couldn't find her here.

Could they?

Now panic rushes through me, scalding my veins. *Calm down, dickhead. Calm down.*

I grab my phone and fire off a text to her.

> Where the hell are you? Are you okay?

It strikes me that she very well may not answer, given that I ignored her messages the last few days. But Lacey isn't a petty person. She doesn't play games. She says what she's thinking. And her reply comes quickly.

> U have a lot of nerve texting me and asking me that when u wouldn't answer MY texts. Asshole.

I want to hit the button that will call her number and talk to her, but Christ, she's right. I am an asshole.

> You're right. Where are you?

> I'm in Vegas, asshole. Home. I'm fine.

Vegas? Jesus! I pause, trying to gather my thoughts. I tap in another message.

> Just wanted to make sure you're safe.

> Thanks for your belated concern. I want a divorce.

Well. That's exactly what I was going to suggest. A burn

hits my chest again, and pressure builds inside me, all the way up into my head. My temples throb.

I can't move. I don't know how long I stand there staring at my phone, not even seeing it. It feels like the condo fades away around me, and I'm standing in shadows. I swallow past the hockey puck lodged in my throat and tap in another message.

Of course.

Then I add,

I'm sorry.

I watch my phone for a long time, but nothing more from Lacey comes.

25

THÉO

"G ET YOUR ASS OVER HERE."

My demand is met with silence. Then JP says, "New phone, who dis?"

I snort-laugh. "Ha ha. Look, we need to talk."

It's been a week since Lacey left, and I'm losing my fucking mind. I can't stop thinking about her. I need to talk to someone. The only one I can think of is JP. He's always been my best bud . . . until the last year. I also need to know what was going on with him and Lacey that day I came home early, even though I know it was innocent.

"Yeah, I guess we do." He sighs. "You come here."

"Jesus Christ. Not everything's a competition."

"Okay, let's meet halfway. Time Out Sports Bar on Sepulveda, in Manhattan Beach."

I shake my head. "Fine. I'm leaving now." I end the call and google the sports bar.

It takes me about half an hour to get there. I find JP already there, which means it wasn't halfway.

"You made me drive further," I say, dropping onto a stool at the high-top table against the wall where he's sitting.

"Nah. I just drive faster."

I roll my eyes. He doesn't have a drink, so he must have just gotten here. TVs above the bar are playing baseball and soccer games. A waitress in jeans and a black Time Out T-shirt approaches with a friendly smile to take our orders. We both request beer, JP an IPA, me a craft lager.

"What up, bro?" JP asks, carefully casual.

I'll just get right to it. "Why'd you come to my place that day when I wasn't there?"

"I wanted to talk to Lacey."

"Why?"

"Because I figured she's probably the person who knows you the best. Besides me." One corner of his mouth lifts wryly. "I wanted to know if what Emma said was true."

"What Emma said?" Now I'm confused.

JP's face tightens and he drops his gaze. "I know this doesn't make it any better at all, believe me, but she told me that she'd broken up with you, that day . . . you found us."

Thinking about that day for once doesn't make my stomach hurt. It's just something that happened in the past. "She didn't break up with me."

"That's what Lacey said. So Emma lied to me about that. And . . . apparently she told *you* that she and *I* had broken up."

"Yeah."

"She's a fuckin' piece of work."

"Yeah. Can't argue with that. She comes across so nice . . . fun. Sexy. But . . ."

JP sighs. "Yeah. Anyway. I broke up with her. I never

should have gone out with her." He snorts. "Grandpa was right about that."

I meet his eyes. "You never should have gone out with her because she's a piece of work? Or you never should have gone out with her because she's my ex? Or, actually, she was my *girlfriend* when it started."

He closes his eyes briefly, the corners of his mouth tightening. "Because she was your girlfriend. No matter if she's psycho or she's the nicest girl in the world."

I nod, my chest expanding. "Thank you," I say quietly.

"Can you forgive me?"

"Tell me why. Why'd you do that?"

The waitress arrives with our beers, and we stop talking for a moment. I pick mine up and take a healthy swig.

"I don't know. Honestly. She's hot. She came on to me. We hung out while you were working, and she flirted and made me feel good about myself . . . when she said she broke up with you and . . . well never mind exactly what she said. But for the first time in my life, I felt as if someone liked me better than you."

I gape at him. "What the hell are you talking about?"

He picks up his glass. "Do you know how hard it was being your little brother? I was never as smart as you. As good a skater. As good a goal scorer."

"Are you fucking kidding me? I had to work my ass off to get anywhere. You have more raw hockey talent than I ever did."

He lowers his glass and stares at me searchingly. "Seriously?"

"Hell, yeah." I can't believe he doubts that.

"Uh, wow." He shakes his head. "You really think that?"

"Yeah."

"I never . . . I guess there are things about each other we never realized. Even though we were best buddies."

"I guess so." My eyebrows pull down. I rub my mouth, then shove my glasses up on my nose. "I never realized you felt that way. You . . . stuck up for me." I remember the time he took on a big kid in grade seven who'd been tormenting me about my grades, accusing me of kissing up to the teacher and calling me a weirdo. JP had ended up with a black eye and a trip to the principal's office.

"Yeah."

"Those kids who bugged me all the time made me feel like something was wrong with me."

JP's face twists. "That's fucked up."

"Yeah." I sigh. "I loved it that you defended me, but I kind of hated it too."

"Huh?"

"I was glad you did it. Grateful. But I didn't want to have someone else defend me. I wanted to be able to stand up for myself."

His forehead creases. "Shit."

"I know, I know, your intentions were good. It was just a little . . . humiliating. Also, I felt guilty because you got in trouble that day."

He shrugs. "I was always getting in trouble."

I study his face, the practiced casual expression. "You knew I didn't want Mom and Dad to know what was going on. You didn't even try to defend yourself to them."

He makes a face. "I think they knew what was going on."

I nod slowly. "Yeah, they did. I know that now. Mom told Lacey about it." I roll my eyes. "Thanks, Mom."

JP laughs.

"I was obsessed with trying to figure out why those kids hated me. You know me . . . trying to analyze it." I grimace. "I tried to make sense of it . . . but how do you do that when you're a kid, and another kid is jealous or just plain mean?"

"Hell."

"After that, I tried to hide that I was smart. I stopped answering questions in class, stopped doing extra credit projects. I tried harder at hockey, tried to be tougher. I tried to be perfect. I figured that way they'd leave me alone."

JP closes his eyes briefly. "And I just tried to be badder, because I felt like I couldn't be as good as you." He opens his eyes and meets mine across the table. "I really hated that they were little pieces of shit to you."

One corner of my mouth lifts. "Thanks."

"And you shouldn't have had to change to fix things. We should have both come clean about what was happening and let Mom and Dad and the school deal with it."

"I survived. I know it made me a little obsessive and analytical. I know I have high expectations of myself. But I've done okay."

"You absolutely have. And I'm proud of you, and how you overcame adversity."

"Thanks." I suck in a slow breath throw my nose, my chest full. "When I took that puck in the eye . . . you were there for me. Every day."

"I thought it should have been me. You were the good

guy. I was the trouble maker. I should have been the one who lost an eye."

"Christ." I bow my head, focusing on breathing, my lungs burning with every inhalation. This isn't easy, talking about this shit. Hearing how JP really feels. Telling him how much he hurt me. It makes me feel so vulnerable. I hate that. It's hard to trust him after what happened, and yet… he's my brother. He fought for me and stuck by me when I was down. I have to be honest with him. "That's why . . . that's why it hurt so fucking much . . . what you did with Emma. I don't know if I can forgive you." I pause, then quickly add, "I don't care about Emma anymore; that's not it."

"Obviously. You're married to someone else. Who's awesome, by the way." At my harsh stare, he lifts his hands. "Just saying. Nothing happened between us. You have to know that."

"I do know that," I admit. "It hurt so much because it was you."

He nods, his face somber. His throat works and his voice is thick when he says, "I'm sorry."

Our eyes meet. I nod, accepting his apology. "Lacey's gone."

His jaw slackens. "Huh?"

"When I got back from Vancouver, she'd packed up and left."

He turns his head and gives me severe side-eye. "What did you do?"

"What do you mean, what did I do? I was pissed because I found you with my wife, all cozy."

"You just said you know nothing was going on. For Mr. Logic, you're not making a lot of sense, dude."

"Ugh." I shove my hand through my hair and look across the bar. "Okay, I *was* pissed. She kept texting me and leaving voicemails trying to tell me it was nothing, but I didn't answer her."

"Why not?"

"I was busy. I was at the draft!"

"Bullshit."

"The draft is important," I try again. I sound lame as hell.

JP leans forward. "Okay, you want to know what Emma said about you when she told me she broke up with you? I know she was lying about the breaking-up part, but the rest . . . I get the feeling it's true."

My forehead tightens. "What?"

"She said she was tired of taking second place to your job. You worked long hours. You canceled plans or wouldn't even make plans." One corner of his mouth lifts. "Why do you think she and I were hanging out together so much when I was there?"

I stare at him. I feel like I was just slammed into the boards and had the wind knocked out of me. My lungs strain and I can't breathe.

"You seriously went away and didn't answer Lacey's calls because you were *too busy*?" He shakes his head. "Then you deserve to lose her."

My heart bangs against my ribs and there's a hard pulse in the pit of my stomach. Oh my fucking God. He's right.

I've been trying so hard to overcome my past, that feeling of something being wrong with me . . . I worked so hard at hockey so I could succeed at that and be admired . . . be worthy. Then I lost that because there *was* something wrong with me, something *really* wrong with me because I couldn't see and I couldn't play hockey. I turned back to numbers. This time people admired me for being smart. They *wanted* me for my smarts. But I was so focused on that, trying to be the best, trying to prove that I deserved good things, that I didn't pay enough attention to the most important things...people I care about. Emma. JP. And now . . . Lacey.

I've lost her because I was too fucking busy to text her and tell her I knew she wasn't cheating on me. Or actually because I was too afraid that I *cared* about her cheating on me.

I cared.

Only . . . she was never really mine to lose.

"Fuck," I mutter. "Okay, here's the deal." I eye him, ready for him to die laughing at my lame attempt to preserve a little pride and self-esteem. "Lacey and I only got married so I could come home with a hot wife so everyone wouldn't feel sorry for me after my little brother stole my girlfriend."

He looks like I just told him I like to wear women's underwear. "What?"

I reluctantly explain the story. He nods, his facial expression changing from confusion to disgust at Lacey's brother's shenanigans, to understanding, then to confusion again.

"I was going to tell her we needed to end things anyway. I can't get involved with someone. Every time I get something I want in life, it gets fucked up. I don't want to do that again. But . . ." A stabbing burn heats my chest. "I miss her so goddamn much."

His eyes crinkle up and his mouth turns down at the corners. "Sorry, man. I really didn't mean to take away something you wanted. I really thought you and Emma were done, even though that doesn't make it right, what I did."

I nod. "Thanks."

"You're in love with Lacey."

"No, I'm not."

"Yeah, you are. You were almost crying, just now, talking about her."

"Fuck off, I was not!"

"Dude, it's okay to cry."

"Jesus!" I glare at him. Then I sag, my head dropping. "I'm fucked."

"How so, bro?"

I can tell he's keeping his tone deliberately casual, and I'm grateful, because he's right . . . I might cry.

"You're right," I mumble to the table. "I love her. I want her back."

"Say what?"

"You heard me."

He chuckles. "I did." He drinks his beer. "So tell her that."

"She wants a divorce."

"Hmmm. I don't believe that."

I lift my head and peer at him through burning eyes. "Why not?"

He lifts one shoulder. "Just the things she said when we

were talking. The way she talks about you. She's crazy about you."

"She hates me."

"You hurt her feelings, man."

I bury my face in my hands. "I did. She makes me lose my mind. I do crazy things around her. Things that aren't like me."

"Being horny makes you impulsive. That's why."

"That's ridiculous." I lift my head to frown at him.

He looks affronted. "No, it's not. The Japanese even have a word for it—Kenjataimu."

"Shut the fuck up."

"I'm serious. That's why you're supposed to jerk off before making important decisions."

"I've gone my whole life without knowing this."

He chuckles. "Come on, every guy knows that rubbing one out is good stress relief."

"True." But no . . . it's not just sex. "She makes me . . . I don't know. She makes me want more. She makes me want to make her happy . . . even if it means jumping into a pool with my clothes on."

"What?" His forehead creases.

"Never mind."

"Okay, what are you going to do now? About Lacey?"

I probably don't deserve her. All my life, I've felt like I don't deserve the things I want. But I can't think like that. She's too important. I can't let her go that easily, without at least trying. I square my shoulders. "I need a plan."

"Of course you do." He lifts his beer. "I expect nothing less from you. How can I help?"

26

LACEY

I'M STRETCHED OUT ON MY BED IN THE APARTMENT, STARING at my penguin. Just looking at it makes me want to cry, but I keep doing it. Basically, I'm torturing myself.

Théo gave me a replacement penguin. That makes my heart hurt.

He came to see Chris. Gave him a stern talking-to. Chris was actually impressed with Théo, although he admitted to being annoyed at first.

He left me heart-shaped rocks he found on the beach because he knows I like them.

I turn my face into the pillow, hot tears sliding down my cheeks again. I'm a mess.

I miss him so much.

I also miss his crazy, messed-up family and my new friends.

Chris works eight to four at the factory, but often works overtime because he's trying to make as much money as he

292

can. Plus, working more means less time for the temptation of gambling. He's also started taking anti-depressants. He went to see a doctor who thinks he has depression and that gambling was his way of self-medicating. It's only been a couple of weeks and apparently it takes a while for the medication to work, but I hope that helps. I'm proud of what he's done so far. He even paid the rent on the apartment for this month.

We had a long talk when I got back, both of us ending up crying. My disappearance, leaving him on his own to deal with things, was enough of a kick in the butt to scare him. He actually thanked me for it, and broke down over how badly he felt about how he'd treated me. I love him and I want to believe him, and so far he seems to be back on the right track with his life, but I'd be lying if I said I was completely confident about it. But now I know what I have to do if he relapses . . . I have to let him deal with it.

I've been hanging out mostly alone in the apartment. I got a job at Mary Jane's but I've only worked one shift so far, mostly learning about the different types of marijuana on the menu. Tonight I brought home some Blueberry Muffin to try. I roll off my bed and find the stash to light up a doob. It tastes like—duh—blueberry muffins, and is supposed to help with anxiety, chronic pain, and nausea.

I've never smoked marijuana even though I worked as a budtender. I just pretended I knew what I was talking about. But I'm miserable and this might be better than drinking a whole bottle of wine. Again.

I swipe another tear away, tired of feeling sorry for myself.

Soon I am pleasantly mellow, with no more tears. I spy my knitting bag and reach for it. I've also been knitting like crazy. I now have about a dozen cute knitted penises. Is that the right plural? Hmm. Penii? I don't think so. I giggle as I lay out all the cute pink sculptures, complete with testicles, on my bed. Now I'm branching out into something more functional—willie warmers.

I relax back into the pillows of my bed, my fingers moving with the needles and wool. This is really coming along.

A loud knock on the door doesn't even startle me, I'm so serene. Maybe Chris forgot his key? I slide off the bed again, carrying my knitting, to open the door for him.

It's not Chris.

It's Théo.

"Wow. That Blueberry Muffin is hallucinogenic."

His eyebrows snap together. "What?"

I reach out a hand and touch his chest. It's warm and solid. "Are you really here?"

"Yeah."

"You feel good." I caress his pecs.

"Uh. Thanks." He gives me a squinty look. "Are you drunk?"

"No!"

"Can I come in?"

"Sure." I let him in and close the door. "You're just in time. I'm knitting a willie warmer, and you can try it on."

"What the . . ." He sniffs the air. "Are you *high*?"

"Just a little." I smile. I hold up my knitting. "See? Isn't it cute?"

"Baked as a fuckin' cake," he mutters, shaking his head. "Now what the hell do I do?"

I eye him. "I don't know."

He sighs.

"This one looks like a rooster, see? But I can also make an elephant."

"What is that?"

"I told you. A willie warmer. Peter heater." I pause. "Cock sock?"

"Jesus."

"I don't think this is big enough for you, though."

He rubs his mouth. "This isn't going how I planned. But I should have known that, when it comes to you."

"You always have a plan, don't you?" I motion to the couch. "Have a seat. Would you like a drink? I'd offer you a toke but I only had one."

"Thank Christ for that. I'm good." He walks over to the couch and sits, setting a colorful gift bag on the floor.

I take a seat too. "So what's your plan?"

He sits. "Aren't you still mad at me?"

"Yeah." I resume my knitting. "Why are you here?"

He doesn't answer right away. Then he starts laughing and shaking his head.

I stop knitting and cock my head. "What's so funny?" A smile tugs at my lips.

He laughs harder, falling back into the couch cushions. "You. This. Us. Jesus, Lacey."

"Uhhhh . . ."

"Yeah, I had a plan. I came here to bring you home. After I grovel for a while. We're not getting a divorce."

"Oh." A bubbly sensation starts fizzing in my chest. I set

aside the willie warmer, my eyes fastened on his face. "Please proceed with the groveling."

He stops laughing, though his lips still twitch. He slides off the couch and moves in front of me on his knees. He takes my hands. "It wasn't supposed to be quite like this . . . you will remember this, won't you?"

"Of course. I'm not stoned."

"Just a little high."

"Actually, I think it's wearing off because I'm starting to freak out." My heart is racing so fast it's in my throat. My hands are trembling and I curl my fingers around his.

"Don't freak out. Okay, first . . . I'm sorry. I'm so, so sorry. I fucked everything up."

"Yeah."

He huffs another laugh and drops his head forward briefly. "I don't believe anything was going on between you and JP."

I meet his eyes, all humor disappearing. "Really?"

He holds my gaze steadily. "Really. Okay, I was upset when I walked in and found you two. I was shocked, and you can understand why."

"Yes." My tone is soft.

"But once I thought about it and analyzed the odds of something like that happening again—"

I can't stop the laugh that escapes my lips. "Oh my God."

"And the fact that I do trust you, Lacey . . . I knew there was nothing going on."

"Plus I kept telling you over and over in every text and voice message I left. All damn weekend."

"That too. And that's what I'm really sorry about. I

should have talked to you. But this is what freaked me out—the fact that I was so hurt and jealous when I saw you and JP together. I . . ." He stumbles a bit, and I can see this is hard for him. "That meant I really cared about you, and I didn't want to, because I knew you were leaving at some point. Our marriage wasn't real, and I kept telling myself that was fine, because I was too busy with my new job, trying to prove myself and build a winning team. I had no time for a real relationship."

I nod, my throat squeezing.

"But it *was* a real relationship . . . it *is*. I'm in love with you, Lacey."

I go very still. I stare at his face, his dear, familiar, beautiful face. His eyes are earnest, a little notch between his eyebrows, his mouth firm but with a hint of anxiety. "You are?"

He nods slowly. "I love you. I couldn't help it. Everyone loves you. But not like I do. I love your honesty. Your open heart. Your loyalty to people you care about. I love how you looked after your brother, even when I disapproved of it. I love your fifty billion hair products all over my bathroom."

"My hair is high maintenance."

"And I *really* love your hair."

I nod. I know this.

"I love how you've made friends with my family and the people who live around us. I love how parties just seem to spring up out of nowhere when you're around."

"Are you sure you love that?" I bite my lip. I know there are times he likes to chill, just the two of us.

"I do love it, as long as I get you to myself sometimes. I love that you laugh at my bad jokes. And

I love your massages. Actually, it's not the massages . . . it's the fact that you know when I'm stressed and you're willing to give up your fun to make me feel better."

"Because . . ." I choke up and have to swallow past a massive blockage in my throat, blinking my eyes. "Because I love you too."

"Ah." He lifts my hands and kisses them, keeping his eyes on me.

My heart swells up huge in my chest and I pull in a shaky breath, fighting tears. "I love you too. I love your bad jokes." A smile trembles on my lips. "I love your nitpicky OCD tendencies. I love that you went to see Chris and kicked his ass."

"I didn't have to kick his ass. He was already doing what he had to do."

"Still." My chin quivers. "You're so generous and smart and honest. I love you."

He closes his eyes and presses my hands to his lips. I think he might be about to cry.

"I love you," I say again softly.

He nods and opens his eyes, and they're shiny. "I also came here to give you this." He reaches behind him to grab the gift bag he brought and hands it to me.

Curious, I take it and reach inside. Wrapped in bright pink tissue is . . . Pete. My heart leaps and my jaw goes slack. "Oh my God! You got him back!"

"Yeah."

"How did you do that?" I clutch Pete to my thudding heart.

"I asked at the leasing office if anyone found your

suitcase. They did. The guy tried to return it, but nobody was home at your apartment."

I nod slowly.

"He kept it in the office for a while, and then he gave it to Goodwill."

My eyes widen. "You . . ."

"He didn't know which one it ended up at, so I spent today driving around to every fucking Goodwill store in Las Vegas." He shakes his head, but he's smiling.

Because I'm smiling too. Hugely.

"I finally found it in Paradise."

I laugh because it sounds funny. "I can't believe you did that."

"I can't believe I remembered what Pete looks like."

I hug Pete tightly. My heart expands hard against my breastbone, obstructing my breath. My eyes sting and I squeeze them closed. He did this for me.

"I didn't get anything else back," he says apologetically. "But this is what I was looking for."

I open my eyes and they fill with liquid. I rub a hand under my nose. "Thank you." My heart is bursting. *He did this for me.* "Thank you so much." My bottom lip trembles, and I sniffle and swipe my wet face.

"And then . . . there's this." He reaches into the pocket of his jeans, digs around, and pulls out . . . a ring.

My eyes go big as dinner plates.

The diamond in the ring is nearly that big. Okay, I'm exaggerating, but it's *huge*.

He lifts my left hand. "You're still wearing your wedding ring."

My cheeks heat. "Yes." I didn't want to take it off.

"I love that. Now you can have the diamond engagement ring to go with it." He takes my left hand and hesitates, peering up at me before sliding the ring on, waiting for my response.

"We're already married, you goof," I say huskily. I wiggle my fingers.

He slips the ring onto my ring finger. It's a plain, shiny gold, the same as the wedding band, with one solitaire diamond. It's gorgeous.

"You'll remember this, won't you? I don't want to tell our grandkids that I proposed while Grandma was lit."

I sob-laugh. "I'll definitely remember this." I slide off the chair to my knees too and throw my arms around him. "Although, the first time you proposed I think I *was* a little ham sandwiched."

He chokes on a laugh, and then our mouths meet in a long, heartfelt kiss. My heart is hammering, my body trembling. I'm floating and it's not because of the weed I smoked . . . I'm in love and Théo loves me back.

He lifts his head to change the angle of the kiss, going deeper, his tongue sliding against mine. His hands on my body are shaking too as he pulls me closer. Then he slides a hand up my back and into my hair, tangling in it, tilting my head so he can devour my mouth.

I love him.

I pour all my love into the kiss, my hands moving over him, and then kneeling on the rug isn't working for either of us anymore and he plants a foot into the floor, standing and lifting me with him. He picks me right up off the floor and carries me into my bedroom while I cling to his shoulders, going straight to the bed. Then he stops.

"What the . . .?"

He's staring at all the cute knitted peens spread over my bed.

"I made those."

He turns incredulous eyes on me.

I gaze back at him, trying for an innocent expression. "I missed you."

He cracks up laughing. "You missed one part of me a lot, apparently." We fall together on the bed, on top of the penises. I'm laughing too now, until he kisses me again, rolling me under him. His weight on me is blissfully heavy, his hands in my hair send shivers sliding down my spine, his mouth moving on mine arouses a flood of longing, a yearning between my thighs.

I'm breathless, dizzy, excited. "I need you," I murmur when he kisses my cheek then my jaw, my hands clutching his shoulders. I lift my hips urgently against his thick erection.

"Need you too, baby." He sucks gently on my neck. "We'll get there, don't worry." He brushes a kiss over my mouth. "Have more to tell you."

"Oh." My eyes are heavy. I stroke my fingers through his thick, silky hair. "What?"

He props himself on his elbows to look down at me. "I talked to JP."

"Oh! That's so good."

"Yeah. I told him too that I knew nothing was going on that day. But I wanted to know why he was there."

"Emma." She spits the word out. "He's done with her. Thank God."

"So I hear. We talked things out. We're good now.

Mostly. Just don't let me ever find you alone with him again."

I glare at him.

He laughs and teases the sides of my neck with his thumbs. "Kidding. Anyway, he told me something that kind of stabbed me right in the heart. I told him I didn't call you that weekend because I was so busy at the draft, but that was bullshit. I didn't call because I was scared. But he also told me Emma said she ended things with me because I was never there. Always working. She felt she came second."

"Ohhhh." I pull my bottom lip between my teeth and eye him. "I mean, she didn't end things with you, but . . . I can sort of understand that."

"Yeah." He screws up his face briefly. "My work is important to me. I work hard. I've been trying to prove myself again, like I did when I was a kid. But by making my work the most important thing in my life, I've lost other important things . . . and people. And the most important thing is . . . you. I don't want to ever make that mistake again." He meets my eyes. "Really. I promise to put you first . . . always."

My bottom lip quivers. "Thank you. But I know how important your career is to you. I want to support you in that."

He closes his eyes for a second. "Thank you."

"I think a relationship is give and take. There'll be times where your career is demanding and I'll support you on that. Time when your family needs your attention. And there'll be times when *my* family or…or…well, I don't feel like I have much of a career at the moment, but I'm working on it. And you'll support *me*." I pause and meet his eyes. "Right?"

"Right." His agreement is swift and heartfelt.

I lean up to kiss him. "But *you* are the most important thing to me. Always."

"And you are to me. Always."

And he rolls me under him and proceeds to show me how he really feels.

2 7

———

THÉO

"THERE'S NO WAY WE CAN STAY UNDER THE SALARY CAP AND keep Bertelson, Belmont, and Bell, with the money they're looking for."

I look around the table, taking in the frustration on the faces of my grandfather; Scott; Dave; our new assistant coach, Stanislav Pretrov; and Barry Betlach, our director of hockey operations. "I have a solution."

Barry shakes his head. "We have to lose one of them."

"No. We can do this. We can change how we do business in this cap era."

"How?"

"By carrying twenty-two players instead of twenty-three."

The room falls silent, every face pulling tight. Except Scott's, because he and I have already talked this through.

"What?" Grandpa finally says. "What the hell are you talking about?"

I expected this reaction, so it doesn't faze me. "Teams

304

typically carry either fourteen forwards and seven defensemen, or thirteen forwards and eight defensemen. But we could go with thirteen and seven."

They're shaking their heads already. Except Scott.

"Think about it. It's the perfect model."

"With eight healthy D-men, practices *are* slower," Dave says thoughtfully. "You don't get enough reps in."

"But you don't *know* you're going to have eight healthy D-men," Grandpa points out. "Guys are always getting injured."

"True. But we're in a good position because our farm team is nearby," I point out. "If someone gets hurt, we can get a guy from Pasadena here in an hour, if we need to."

"Yeah." Grandpa's still frowning.

"It does make calling a player up easy," Scott adds.

I can see they're coming around to the idea.

"So let's look at which defensemen we definitely want on the roster and who we can send down," I continue. "That'll save us money and give us room for our top three forwards."

The air in the room changes from flat to vibrant, and excitement sizzles over my skin. I love it when I solve problems in unique ways. We all turn to face the screen where I've got my charts projected and get to work.

WHEN I GET HOME LACEY'S WAITING FOR ME. I EXPECTED this.

"What the hell!" she cries on seeing me, rushing toward me.

"I know, I know. I'm sorry."

"Why didn't you tell me?" She lays her fists on my chest like she's going to pound on me.

I rest my hands on her hips. "I couldn't tell you. You know I couldn't."

She's nearly in tears. "Taylor's going to be so hurt."

"I know."

"This is awful!"

"I get it."

The news broke today that Manny's been traded to Nashville.

She leans her forehead against my chest and says nothing, but I can feel the emotion vibrating in her.

"It's a business," I say softly, running my hand down her hair. "I'm sorry. I had to do it for the team."

She gives a tiny nod and says in a small voice, "I know. It's still hard."

"Yeah. It is. I'm dealing with people. Their lives are impacted. It makes it hard."

"I know. And I admire you for being able to do what you do. I'm just . . . hurting for Taylor. She and Manny just got together."

"Maybe she'll go with him."

Lacey lifts her head and blinks. "Maybe?"

I shrug.

"But then I'll miss her too!" She sighs. "Well, I do have some good news."

"Oh yeah?"

"Yeah. Today I was at my class, and my instructor told me that Gina Peregrino approached her about someone to work with her on the set of her next movie."

"Who?"

"Gina Peregrino. She's a makeup artist in Hollywood. She's worked on a couple of big movies. Anyway, my instructor recommended me! I'm meeting with Gina tomorrow!"

"That's fantastic!" Pride expands in my chest.

"Yes! Milly Bobby Brown is going to be in this movie! I'm so excited!"

"This is something to celebrate."

"Yes! But maybe not tonight . . . I'm going to stand by in case Taylor needs me."

"Okay." That just makes me love her more . . . that she wants to be there for her friend instead of celebrating her own success. "I fucking love you, Lacey."

"I fucking love you too." She wraps her arms around me and squeezes. "Even if you did trade away my friend's boyfriend and break her heart."

"Shit."

Do you want to read an epilogue? Click here to add your name to my mailing list and get access to more of Théo and Lacey!
https://kellyjamieson.myflodesk.com/gbgtkrnyrl

And Wynn Hockey continues with...
In It to Win It

Read on for an excerpt from
In It to Win It
A Wynn Hockey Novel

J P

I SHOULD HAVE KNOWN A WYNN FAMILY WEDDING WASN'T going to go off without drama.

Didn't think it would be me in the middle of it, though.

Then again, it totally makes sense, because apparently, I can never be trusted to do the right thing.

Let's go back to last night…

My brother Théo is getting married, but this isn't a typical wedding (it's the Wynn family, need I say more) because Théo and Lacey are already married, after a quickie Vegas wedding a few months ago. My mom was so disappointed about not being at their wedding, she wanted another one, and shockingly Théo agreed.

So there haven't been bridal showers or bachelor and bachelorette parties. Tonight is the first time the wedding party and family are getting together for the rehearsal at Shores Hotel in Santa Monica, where the wedding will be held tomorrow.

I'm standing next to Théo where the ceremony will take

place. Right now the arch next to us is bare but tomorrow it'll be decked with flowers and bows and shit. We're outside on a raised terrace, the beach right behind us.

I'm the best man. Except I'm *not* the best man. A year ago I fucked up and screwed over Théo, my own brother. It's taking some time for our relationship to recover, but he says he's forgiven me.

I haven't forgiven myself.

And neither has the rest of our family.

I've had dirty looks, subtle shade, and outright hostility from my cousins, my aunt and uncles, and especially from my grandfather.

Which sucks, because Grandpa is my idol.

Bob Wynn, the King of Hockey. The man I looked up to my whole life. Until the last couple of years. He's made some…um, interesting decisions lately. To be honest, I'm not sure what's really going on, except I know my dad and my uncle Mark are pissed as hell at him, so much that they're actually suing him, claiming he stole money from them.

This makes family gatherings—like this wedding—a tad uncomfortable.

But never mind all that…my attention is on the hot bridesmaid.

Taylor Hart.

I keep looking at her over on the other side of Lacey, the bride. Taylor's so fucking hot—perfect oval face, long dark hair, dark eyes and a mouth that's perpetually curved into a smile. For the rehearsal, she's wearing a burgundy dress that wraps around her body and stops just above her knees, and suede heels that match the dress.

I catch her eye and grin, and she smiles back...a wide, bright smile that lights up her face. She has a great smile.

And a great rack.

She's not here with a date. She's not wearing a ring. Fuck yeah.

I can't wait for this formal stuff to be done so we can party. Everyone knows what's supposed to happen and when. I have to hand over the ring, Lacey's best friend has to take her bouquet, blah blah blah. Now let's have some fun.

There are about twenty of us who move to the private room after the rehearsal, and I see there are three round tables set up. Place cards identify who sits where, and since I'm one of the first ones in the room, I quickly find my own name...and Taylor's. She's at a different table, but I make the switch speedy quick so she's now sitting beside me instead of my aunt, Everly. Then I head to the bar at the end of the room. Of course there's champagne, so I grab two flutes and turn, searching for Taylor.

There she is, just entering the room. I make my way over to her and stop. "Champagne?" I hold out a glass to her.

Her lips quirk up at the corners as she reaches for the glass. "Why, thank you."

"You're most welcome." I gesture at the table. "Apparently we're sitting beside each other for dinner."

She bursts out laughing. "Oh my God. Did you change the place cards?"

"How did you know that?"

"I helped set up the tables." She sips her wine, eyes dancing.

"Damn." I rub my chin, smiling ruefully. "Busted. But can you blame me for wanting to sit beside a beautiful woman instead of my aunt?"

She shakes her head. "Your aunt *is* a beautiful woman."

My Aunt Everly is only a year older than me. It's weird, but my grandfather married for the second time later in life and had four more kids, Everly being one of them. She's also a bridesmaid, having become good friends with Lacey. "Well, yeah, she is. But she's my *aunt*. I can't flirt with her."

"You're going to flirt with *me*?"

"All night long." I meet her eyes and heat slides down my spine.

"Well, calling me beautiful is a good start."

"It's the truth."

"I don't know." She tilts her head and studies me. "You seem a little cocky. You probably say that to all the girls."

I grin. "Only the beautiful ones."

Everyone is taking their seats for dinner, so I pull out Taylor's chair for her.

"Thank you."

I take my seat next to her. "We can get to know each other better over dinner."

Her eyes meet mine and she purses her lips.

"Why are you looking at me like that? I'm a nice guy." I lay a hand on my chest.

She laughs. "That's not what I've heard."

"Oh no." I groan. "Théo's been talking about me."

"Well, yeah. But you also have a…reputation as a hockey player."

"You like hockey?"

She nods.

"You've seen me play."

"I was at the game last year when you hit Novotny and got suspended."

I press my lips together, my jaw tightening. I look down at my place setting. "That shouldn't have happened." I lift my head and meet her eyes. "I don't play to hurt guys. Really."

She nods slowly. "But that wasn't the first time you got suspended."

I suck in a long breath. "True. Sometimes my emotions get the best of me. I'm working on it. Trying to do better."

It's true. This year I have to show the team I'm worth keeping on the roster. Last year didn't go so well. In a lot of ways.

The others are now sitting at our table…six people. We make small talk, Lacey and Théo stop at the table to chit chat, and then servers start bringing out salads, so they take their own seats.

"How long have you known Lacey?" I ask as we dig into greens with blueberries, walnuts and feta cheese.

"Not long. Just since she moved here."

"You must have become friends pretty fast."

"Yes. We met when she helped me catch my dog. And my dog liked her, so I knew she was okay."

"What kind of dog do you have?"

"Golden retriever. His name is Byron."

"Nice. So that's your test of whether someone is worth hanging out with? If your dog likes them?"

She nods, her lips quirked. "Dogs are smart."

"Yeah. I like dogs. We had a standard poodle growing up. He was so smart it was scary."

"And you know, sometimes you meet someone and things just…click." Our eyes meet and hold again and the air buzzes around us. Yeah, I know that feeling. "When I met Lacey, right away I felt like I could talk to her about anything. She's so…alive. Just fun to be with, but yet she can be serious and she's smart, too."

I nod. I kind of feel like that about Taylor. This feels so easy…and yet so electrifying. "What do you do for a living?"

"I'm a speech language pathologist."

"Whoa."

She laughs. "What? What's wrong with that?"

"I'm not even sure what a speech language pathologist does."

A server removes our plates and we sit back for a moment. I pick up the wine glass someone has thoughtfully filled with a golden wine.

"I work primarily with kids," she says when the server has moved away. Her face softens. "I love kids. I help children who have speech delays or disorders, language delays, sometimes swallowing or feeding disorders."

I'm…blown away, I guess. This is not what I expected. "Do you work at a hospital?"

"No. A private clinic. I haven't worked there long. I just graduated last year. You have to have a master's degree to practice."

Jesus. "Where did you go to college?"

"For my graduate degree, Seattle. University of Washington. I got my undergrad degree here in California."

"Six years of university?"

"Yep."

"That's impressive." I could never do that.

"Thanks. I love it." She tilts her head. "You must love playing hockey."

"I do."

"What do you love about it?"

"Everything." I give her a lopsided smile. "I love the action, how fast it is, the skills you need. I love competing. I love winning."

"Don't we all."

I chuckle. "Yeah."

"Right. Obviously, with my family, if you didn't love hockey you'd be a complete misfit."

Now our meals are served…charred lemon chicken piccata served over pasta. It looks delicious.

"There's nobody in your family who doesn't like hockey?" Taylor picks up her fork. "I mean, I know Everly doesn't *play* hockey, but she watches the game and works with the hockey team, sort of."

"Yeah." I nod and tip my wine glass to my lips. "The only ones who aren't really involved in hockey are Chelsea —my grandpa's wife—"

"Yes, I know who she is." She nods and cuts a piece of chicken.

"And my mom. But my mom was a hockey mom, driving Théo and me to practices and games at ungodly hours, lugging our equipment around, cheering us on at every game. So that counts, I guess."

"And Chelsea married into a hockey family."

"Right."

"I have to admit I didn't grow up watching hockey, but I

got free tickets to a game once when I was about seventeen, and I loved it. It was so fast and fierce."

"Yeah." I like it that she enjoys hockey. "Do you play any sports?"

"I played volleyball in high school, and college."

"Hey, no kidding. That's awesome."

"I still like to get together with friends on the beach and play some ball."

Every nerve ending in my body goes on alert as I picture Taylor in a bikini, jumping up and down in the sand, setting and spiking the ball. "I'd love to do that."

"Well, sure. There are volleyball nets right near where I live. Which is right by Lacey and Théo. We should do that sometime."

Sparks crackle between us. I lean closer. "For sure. That would be fun."

"You know how to play volleyball?"

"Yeah." I shrug.

"You're probably good at it."

"Eh. Not as good as hockey."

"Volleyball's not as rough as hockey."

"I play a physical game," I admit.

"Do you get in a lot of fights?"

"No. Not a lot. Sometimes you gotta step up, but I don't go around instigating things." I'm not ashamed of my style of play, but I want her approval. "Okay, I know you like dogs and kids and volleyball. How about tattoos?"

She laughs. "Do I like them on other people? Or on myself?"

"Both."

"I have no tattoos. But I like them on other people. Do you have any?"

"Yeah. Just one, one my back." I pause, then lean closer to ask in a low voice, "What's your opinion on porn?"

She bursts out laughing again. "Wow, we're really getting to the good stuff."

"Just curious."

"Maybe we could talk about this later." She glances around at the others at the table.

"Absolutely." I don't hesitate because I'm perfectly willing to talk to Taylor about porn later...preferably up in my hotel room, where I'm staying for the weekend nuptials.

For a while we join in other conversation at our table, until we're served the tiny slice of chocolate cake served over raspberry sauce.

"Raspberries are my favorite fruit," Taylor says.

With my fork, I lift the berries garnishing my plate and transfer them to hers.

She shoots me a startled glance.

I smile. "Enjoy."

"Thank you." She gives her head a small shake and pushes the tines of her fork into one berry.

With dinner finished, Théo and Lacey stand at one end of the room to say a few words, thanking all of us, and then presenting their wedding party—me, Taylor, Karine, Everly, Andy and Leo with our gifts, gold bracelets for the bridesmaids and for the guys, a wooden box with whiskey stones and shot glass, and a bottle of Crown Royal.

"This is awesome," I say to Théo. "Thanks, bro."

Some people are moving out to the hotel bar for another

drink and since Taylor is one of them, I join them too. We're at a smaller table with a little more privacy. She orders a glass of sauvignon blanc and I go for a beer this time.

"I can't stay too late," she says. "Don't want to be posing for pictures tomorrow with big bags under my eyes."

I scoff. "You could never look bad." She really is one of those natural beauties, with high cheekbones, perfect skin and full lips.

"And you're full of it." She smiles though.

Damn, that smile. It makes me hard. "Now you can tell me what kind of porn you like to watch."

"Did I say I like to watch porn?"

I catch the teasing twinkle in her eye and grin. I pick up my drink.

"Okay, okay," she says. "Porn is fun sometimes. I'm kind of an 'everything in moderation' person. I don't like stuff that's demeaning to women, though. I like romantic porn. But I don't think it's good for anyone to watch too much of it. Real life sex is better."

"Oh hell yeah." I hold her gaze meaningfully. Heat Slides through my veins, my dick thickens arousal. "I bet real life sex with you is amazing."

"That's…" Her eyelashes flutter, but she's looking at my mouth. "Inappropriate."

"I often am," I admit. "But I'm not taking it back."

I want to kiss her so damn bad. I've always had a little problem with impulse control, and it's all I can do to stop myself from leaning in even closer and kissing her. But there are others around us, friends and family, so I restrain myself, giving myself a mental pat on the back.

"Have you ever made a sex tape?" I ask.

Her eyes widen. "Uh…no. That's not really smart."

"Sadly, that's true. You have to trust the person you're with."

"Not only that! What about that actress who had her sex tapes stolen from the cloud? Hackers can get into anything."

"Right."

"And maybe you trust the person at the time, but then you discover he's a pill-popping addict with a gambling problem who hits on your friends, and you dump his ass and next thing you know he's sending the video to all his buddies on Snapchat."

"Whoa." I frown. "You're not speaking from experience, I hope."

"No." She gives an impish smile. "But it could happen."

"I guess. I would never do that."

"So you say."

"You don't trust me?"

She leans forward, her smile sultry. "I don't trust anyone to make a sex tape with, but I'd trust you for…other things."

"Oh. I'm good at…other things." Lightning-hot desire jolts straight to my groin.

Her eyes darken and her lips part. "Too bad I'll never know."

"Ouch." I sit back, pouting.

She laughs lightly.

I shake my head. "Cut off at the knees by a gorgeous woman."

"Thank you. You're pretty gorgeous yourself." She pats my shoulder.

Her hand lingers on my shoulder as our eyes connect again. Excitement sparkles through my veins. "You're just busting my balls. You want to come up to my room with me."

Her breath hitches.

Leaning closer, I murmur near her ear, "No video, I promise. But I can guarantee you several orgasms."

"Th-that's a bold promise."

"Confident. Also I'm dying to taste you…and make you feel good…"

"Oh god." She gulps some wine.

I sit back and try to look casual, but when I meet her eyes, sexual urgency sizzles around us. I finish my beer. As I set it on the table, I lean in close to her ear. "I'm going up to my room. Four fourteen. I'd love for you to join me. Your call."

I say good-night to the others there, who I'll see tomorrow for the wedding, and stroll out of the bar, across the lobby and into the elevator.

My skin is prickling and my veins are buzzing as I enter my suite. I flick on a light, the door closing behind me, drop my gift from Théo onto the desk, and stroll over to the window. I have an ocean view room, and I can see the lights of the Santa Monica Pier, the Ferris wheel glowing against the night sky.

I don't know if Taylor will come to my room or not. I'm going to be disappointed as hell if she doesn't, because there's some crazy chemistry between us. There's always tomorrow, though. A sexy bridesmaid always makes a wedding a little more fun.

I kick off my shoes, sprawl onto the couch in the living

room and pick up the remote for the giant TV. Tomorrow, Théo and the other guys will join me here to get ready for the wedding and have some pictures taken. I've got drinks and snacks for the pre-game.

I flick through various channels and end up watching a sports news show even though hockey season hasn't started yet.

Soon.

After a while, I glumly turn off the TV. She's not coming.

I stand and as I move toward the bathroom, I hear a soft knock on the door.

My heart kicks against my ribs. I casually stroll to the door, though, and use the peephole.

Taylor.

I drop my forehead against the door, every nerve ending lighting up. Then I yank open the door.

She eyes me, her mouth soft and uncertain, her eyes big and luminous. "Hi."

"Hi." I step aside so she can come in. "I thought you weren't coming."

She walks past me, carrying her purse and gift bag. "You promised me I would."

A surprised laugh erupts inside me. "So I did."

In It to Win It

Welcome to the Wynn family! I'm in love with this big crazy hockey family, and I hope you will be too!

Théo Wynn has embarked on a mission to turn the California Condors into a winning team. Rebuilding a team is a long-term project, so we don't know how this is going to work out for him—yet! Each of the Wynn Hockey books can be read as a standalone, with the romantic relationship ending in a Happily Ever After, but if you want to know how things turn out with the Condors . . . and how things turn out with the family feud . . . and how things turn out with some of the other story lines . . . I hope you'll keep reading the rest of the books. All the characters will make repeat appearances in future stories so you can see how our couples and the family and the teams are doing!

ABOUT THE AUTHOR

Kelly Jamieson is a best-selling author of over sixty romance novels and novellas. Her writing has been described as "emotionally complex," "sweet and satisfying," and "blisteringly sexy." She likes coffee (black), wine (mostly white), shoes (especially high heels) and hockey!

Kelly appreciates your help in spreading the word about her books, including sharing with friends! Please leave a review on your favorite book site! You can also join her Facebook group, Kelly Jamieson's Sweet Heat Reader Lounge, to hang out with her, and for exclusive giveaways and sneak peeks of future books.

Visit her website at www.kellyjamieson.com or contact her at info@kellyjamieson.com

WINDY CITY KINK

SWEET OBSESSION

ALL MESSED UP

PLAYING DIRTY

BREW CREW

LIMITED TIME OFFER

NO OBLIGATION REQUIRED

ACES HOCKEY

MAJOR MISCONDUCT

OFF LIMITS

ICING

TOP SHELF

BACK CHECK

SLAP SHOT

PLAYING HURT

BIG STICK

GAME ON

LAST SHOT

BODY SHOT

HOT SHOT

LONG SHOT

BAYARD HOCKEY

SHUT OUT

CROSS CHECK

WYNN HOCKEY

PLAY TO WIN

IN IT TO WIN IT

WIN BIG

FOR THE WIN

GAME CHANGER

BEARS HOCKEY

MUST LOVE DOGS…AND HOCKEY

YOU HAD ME AT HOCKEY

TALK HOCKEY TO ME

THE O ZONE

GOOD HANDS

SCORING BIG

MERRY PUCKING CHRISTMAS

LIGHT 'EM UP

STORM HOCKEY

CROSSING THE LINE

STANDALONES

THREE OF HEARTS

LOVING MADDIE FROM A TO Z

DANCING IN THE RAIN

LOVE ME

LOVE ME MORE

2 HOT 2 HANDLE

FRIENDS WITH BENEFITS

LOST AND FOUND

ONE WICKED NIGHT

SWEET DEAL

HOW SWEET IT IS

HOT RIDE

CRAZY EVER AFTER

ALL I WANT FOR CHRISTMAS

SEXPRESSO NIGHT

IRISH SEX FAIRY

CONFERENCE CALL

RIGGER

YOU REALLY GOT ME

SCREWED

FIRECRACKER

BIG WITCH ENERGY

HATE ME UNDER THE MISTLETOE